Taken, Not Spurred

Also by Ruth Cardello

The Legacy Collection

Maid for the Billionaire
For Love or Legacy
Bedding the Billionaire
Saving the Sheikh
Rise of the Billionaire
Breaching the Billionaire: Alethea's Redemption

The Andrade Series

Come Away with Me

LONE STAR BURN

RUTH CARDELLO

This is a work of fiction. Names, characters, organizations, places, events, and incidents are either products of the author's imagination or are used fictitiously.

Published by Montlake Romance, Seattle

www.apub.com

ISBN-13: 9781477825129
ISBN-10: 1477825126

Cover design by Kerrie Robertson

Library of Congress Control Number: 2014907478

Printed in the United States of America

This book is dedicated to my husband. Thank you, hon, for supporting my writing from day one. You're the reason I believe in happily-ever-afters.

Chapter One

No real adventure ever started by waiting patiently on a doorstep.

Still, Sarah Dery hesitated before reaching for the handle on the screen door of her friend's immense white farmhouse. The shelter of the wraparound porch did little to alleviate the heat of the midday Texas sun, but was that a good enough excuse to enter? *What if no one is home?* Since there was no cell phone service, there wasn't much else she could do unless she was willing to wait in her SUV.

Wiping one suddenly cold hand across a jean-clad leg, Sarah straightened her shoulders and opened the door decisively. She hadn't survived the three-day drive from Rhode Island only to pass out from heat exhaustion on the porch because Lucy was late.

"Hello?" she called out. "Anyone home?" No answer.

The interior of the house was similar to the mammoth horse barn she'd searched a few minutes ago: well maintained but lacking any personal touches. She was surprised that her friend lived like this, but perhaps when you worked all day on a ranch, decorating wasn't a priority.

Sarah assessed the living room. It looked and smelled clean—the best compliment she could give it. The few pieces of wooden furniture, decorated with outdated, plain blue cushions, had probably never given a person a moment of comfort. She returned to the foyer and appreciated the beauty of the room's woodwork, even as she noted that the walls lacked photos and artwork.

The house reminded her of the mansions in her hometown, built by wealthy factory owners who had long since left the area, along with their businesses. Although this house showed no obvious signs of disrepair, it felt cold. Empty. *Can a house be sad?*

She wandered through the downstairs rooms and marveled at the absence of electronics—no television, not even a radio. Lucy had hinted that her life in Texas wasn't happy, but this was Sarah's first glimpse of how truly barren her life down here was.

No wonder she invited me.

Although she hadn't seen her old roommate since college, they'd kept in touch via email and the occasional uneventful video chat. Until Lucy had asked, "How's your writing going?"

What writing?

"I've been busy," Sarah had said lamely.

"Didn't you say that you'd taken the job at your parents' company so you'd have time to write?"

Yes.

Apparently, time was not the issue.

Can you be a writer if you don't write? Like a musician who never picks up an instrument? Who are you when the person you are in your heart doesn't match the life you're living?

I always wanted to be a writer—tell stories that would sweep readers away on a journey of laughter, tears, and growth. I dreamed of discovering myself through the characters I crafted.

So why can't I write?

What's stopping me?

God, I need this trip.

Lucy said she was desperate for companionship, and the invitation to spend a summer on a working Texas cattle ranch had been too tempting to pass up. Taking a deep breath, Sarah announced to the empty house, "I'll admit, so far this isn't living up to how exciting I thought Texas would be, but it'll work out." *Maybe I watched too much* Dallas, *but I'm not ready to give up on my fantasy just yet.*

She could almost hear her brother's telltale sigh, which was often followed by a lengthy lecture. Charles Dery was a successful Wall Street investor and a self-appointed dictator when it came to his little sister. Moving to New York rather than staying and working for their family's construction company hadn't stopped him from getting involved as soon as she'd announced she was taking a leave of absence from her office job at Dery and Son—a company that should have been named *Dery and Reluctantly Employed Daughter.*

"Mom and Dad called me," her brother had said. "They're upset. There is no way you're quitting your job to travel cross-country alone."

"Yes, I am, Charlie."

"Why the hell are you doing this?" he'd stormed.

"I need this," Sarah had fired back, knowing that a deeper conversation wasn't possible between them. *I need this.*

Before it's too late.

Maybe it already is.

Twenty-five.

What is it about a milestone birthday that makes a person reassess her life? She'd graduated from the University of Rhode Island with a bachelor's degree in English, but she could easily have gotten a degree in basket weaving for all she'd done with it since.

Lucy's question had haunted her, especially during her last birthday party when the forest of candles on her cake had hit Sarah like a flaming dose of reality. *How did I lose myself?*

She wished there had been one grand event she could blame, but the truth was discontent had arrived much less dramatically than that—more like a flower wilting in the sun until the life she thought she was meant for was nothing more than a pile of dried-out, brittle regret.

Charlie said I should think of how this is affecting others and not be so selfish. Easy for him to say from New York.

I tried to be the one who stayed behind to make everything okay, but the price was too high. Be good. Follow the rules. Avoid all unpleasant topics. I can't do it anymore. I can't be the perfect daughter in the perfect family. I'm an adventurer. A pioneer. Texans hadn't stayed where the Mayflower dropped their parents. They'd boldly left for parts unknown.

Like I did.

Life in Rhode Island wasn't awful. Her office position at her parents' company paid enough for her to live in her own apartment and afford Scooter, the horse she rode four nights a week at an exclusive equestrian facility.

I didn't have anything to complain about.

Or anything to look forward to.

Until Lucy called.

"Hello . . . anybody here?" The silence was eerie, but this wasn't the movies—nothing extraordinary was going to happen.

Sarah grimaced. Nothing ever did.

Lucy had probably just run to the store for some last-minute supplies. *Isn't that how it always works? You step away for a few minutes and your company arrives.*

A bead of sweat trickled down Sarah's neck. The light cotton shirt she had chosen so carefully that morning was now plastered against her back. Sarah plucked at it while renewing her resolve.

She'd adjust to the heat. Comfort didn't matter. This was about finding herself, finding her voice.

She returned to the living room, plopped on the unforgiving couch, and flung out her arms in victory. *I did it!* The drive may have taken her three days, giving her trailered horse time to rest along the way, but even that part of the journey had been amazing. Each bed-and-breakfast she'd stayed at on her way down had intensified her anticipation. Each time she'd told the other guests where she was going, she'd felt even more alive.

This is what life is about: seeing new places, meeting new people, grabbing life by the balls and squeezing until it coughs up a story worth telling.

I should write that down.

She whipped out the purple spiral notebook she'd purchased specifically for this trip and stopped halfway through recording her thoughts, hesitating before writing a word she normally avoided: *balls.*

I'm twenty-five, not five. Writers are not afraid of words. On the very first page of her notebook, she wrote:

Balls. Balls. Balls.

And smiled with pride. With renewed enthusiasm, she wrote:

Big balls. Hairy balls. Bald balls?

Chewing on the end of her pen thoughtfully, Sarah decided to designate a section of her notebook to research topics. She drew a margin on the right side of the paper. In her finest penmanship she wrote:

Do some men shave their balls?

I should write: What woman my age doesn't know that? But this is not about passing judgment. Positive energy brings positive results. Accepting yourself is the first step toward improvement.

God, I've been reading too many self-help books.

It's time to stop thinking about why I'm not living the life I want and just live it.

Which was why she'd chosen to bring a notebook instead of her laptop. *Real change sometimes requires a clean sweep.* No more wasting time searching the Internet hoping a topic would end her writer's block. No more reading countless articles on how to write. *Just a pen, a notebook, and Texas. If I don't write something this summer, I deserve to work for my parents for the rest of my life.*

Time to color outside the lines.

No more settling for good enough.

Like Doug.

Her recent breakup with the man she'd dated chastely in high school, then slept with through college, had been as unexciting as any of the sex they'd ever had. Not that they'd had sex at all in months. Which should have mattered, but it hadn't. *Because I didn't love him. Just like every other choice I've made up until now, he was safe, the type of man everyone expected me to be with.* Smart, successful, and someone who fit into her parents' social circle. He'd never said a single thing anyone objected to. *Tapioca in a suit. Bland in and out of bed.*

Why was I with him for so long?

The wrong-size shoe doesn't fit just because you want it to.

She slammed her notebook shut and hugged it to her chest. She took another look around the room, then whispered, "The only one who can give me the life I want is me. Right now. Right here."

Returning to her more immediate concerns, Sarah looked down at the damp cotton material of her shirt. Who knew how long Lucy would be gone? *What if she comes home and she's not alone? I can't meet people looking like this.*

Coming to a quick decision, Sarah rushed back to her SUV and hauled her luggage into the foyer. She rummaged for a change of clothes and, taking just her small bag with her, headed off in search of a place where she could freshen up.

The bleached-white downstairs bathroom was as Spartan as the rest of the house, but it revealed a beautiful . . . no, a *heaven-sent* shower. She closed her eyes for a moment and imagined washing off the dirt and sweat under the cool spray.

Would it be so wrong?

Tony considered taking the shotgun from the back of his truck when he saw the vehicle parked in his driveway, but quickly decided to toss this intruder off his land with his bare hands. *Hell, it might even make my day.*

A Rhode Island license plate? Someone had traveled a long way for a good old-fashioned Texas beating.

'Course, there was a slim chance that his ranch manager, David, had invited a buyer to pick up his horse directly from the ranch. *No, David's smarter than that.*

Tony opened the door of his truck with more force than was necessary and took stock of the scene in his driveway. No one he knew would have driven this flashy gray two-horse trailer or matching silver Lexus SUV—both of which looked spanking new.

Upon closer inspection, the trailer looked more like a delivery truck than a pickup. The rear-loading ramp was still down. Clearly, someone had unloaded a horse and led it into the barn.

He checked the barn's interior first. Nothing out of place. The stalls were secure. He scanned the paddocks. All his horses were accounted for.

What the hell? Whoever had driven that trailer had had the gall to put their small horse in one of his paddocks, smack-dab in the middle of his prized quarter horses.

A delicately boned bay horse, Paso Fino by breed. Tony's eyes narrowed. Pampered, by the looks of it. Definitely not used to working. The sparkling painted black hooves and pink halter stopped him in his tracks.

The intruder is a woman. Cursing, Tony strode toward the house, the pace of his footsteps picking up speed as his anger grew.

He considered each of his past female companions, although none were recent. He chose partners with care—experienced women who understood that he had nothing more than a few hours of mutual pleasuring to offer them. He didn't promise them anything, and they were too smart to think they could come to his ranch uninvited and receive anything but a cold escort back to the road. The only people who were welcome on his ranch were the ones who worked there, and even they knew to stay out of his way.

The pink-and-green checkered luggage that greeted him as he entered the house brought a rush of heat up his neck. He heard the downstairs shower running and a female voice mixed with the sound of the spray. Almost positive he must be hallucinating from the heat of the day, he walked toward the bathroom. With a bang he opened the door, stepped inside, and stopped dead when he saw the outline of a small woman dancing behind the fogged glass.

She must not have heard him, because she kept singing—some pop song, he figured. Not a tune he knew. The tone he chose was one that had caused many grown men to cower over the years. "What the hell are you doing in my shower?"

The water cut off and a hand shot out, grabbed a towel, and snatched it back behind the glass door. A second later, a wet blonde head poked out. "Hi, I'm Sarah," she stated, as if that explained everything. "I didn't think you'd mind if I took a quick shower while waiting for you. Sorry if I surprised you."

Her face wore a warm, sheepish smile even while water dripped down from her hair across her forehead. He caught a glimpse of a bare arm as her hand came out to wipe the water away. His gut tightened in response.

Gorgeous.

Long, wet eyelashes framed two unguarded brown eyes. Small dimples made her classically beautiful features less intimidating.

Here was a woman who seemed unaware that a man could have the air sucked right out of his lungs and be rendered speechless by just one look at her.

The crotch of his jeans became uncomfortably tight as his body came alive with the desire to strip and join her in the shower. He could see the outline of her towel-clad body and the expanse of exposed legs behind the lightly fogged glass. In her rush to cover herself, she hadn't taken the time to dry off. He imagined sinking to his knees and burying his face in her damp pussy. Would it taste as sweet and fresh as her lips looked? Would she throw her head back and to the side when he lifted her naked against the shower wall and suckled the full breasts he could now only see the rounded tops of? Would her smiling mouth round in a gasp of pleasure as he drove his cock into her for the first time?

He wasn't an impulsive man when it came to women, but the throbbing need that swept through him made him want to be.

Easy, cowboy. A man can't be blamed for where his thoughts go when he finds a beautiful, naked woman in his shower, but thinking and acting are two different things. She could be anyone, with God only knows what sort of intentions. Something that appears too good to be true almost always is. "I don't know what made you think—"

Securing the towel chastely around herself, she stepped out of the shower. With shocking audacity, she smiled and put her hand out to shake his. "I admit I wasn't sure if it was okay to take a shower before you came home, but I figured since I'm staying here for the summer you wouldn't mind."

Oh, hell no. "You're what?"

Her extended hand wavered, then fell to her side. She took a quick step back, eyes darting past him to a pile of clothes she had stacked on the counter near the sink. "I thought you knew."

He towered over her, more out of habit than a desire to intimidate her. Members of the press had become more creative recently in their attempts to interview him, but would they go this far? Her pale, creamy skin and pink manicured toenails warned him she'd be trouble. But damned if he didn't care. "I'm listening."

She looked down at her state of undress, then back at him. Her eyes were as wide and expressive as a young filly's. "I'm not dressed," she said.

He hoped his swollen dick wasn't as obvious as it was painful. "I noticed."

Emotion deepened her already dark brown eyes. A line of exasperation creased her brow. "I'm sorry you didn't know I was coming. I'm sorry I made myself at home while you were out." She stopped and her voice softened. "The truth is, I've driven a long way to get here and I'm just too tired to fight about it. I'd like to get dressed. Did Lucy come home with you?" She began to slide around him, inching toward her clothing.

He settled back on his heels a bit. "Lucy?"

"Your sister."

"I don't have a sister." This pretty little woman was about as loony as they come, but a man couldn't be blamed for overlooking that when she stood there with her skin still pink from the heat of the shower.

She stumbled back a bit at that. "Y-you don't?" Eyes big with surprise, she chewed her bottom lip nervously. "But this is the Double C Ranch."

"Yes, ma'am, it is."

"And you're Lucy's brother, Steven Albright."

"No, ma'am, I'm not. My name's Tony, Tony Carlton."

He waited for a reaction to his name, then received one he hadn't expected. His little shower beauty rubbed her forehead with the back of one hand. He watched her and worried for his sanity as he once again became mesmerized by her movements. He should care who Steven was, but instead all he could think about was how he wanted to redirect that hand to rubbing something else, something that was craving her touch in a bad way.

"I don't understand. Isn't this the Double C Ranch in Mavis?"

He removed his hat and wiped the wet sheen from his forehead. The residual steam from the shower added to an overall temperature spike caused by prolonged exposure to a scene worthy of mention in a men's magazine. "Fort Mavis."

Her mouth dropped open and her eyes rounded with real shock. Not too much amused him, but her look of horror tickled what was left of his funny bone. "We're almost a day's drive west of Mavis," he added.

She went pale, and then a deep red flush started at her neck and ran straight over her face. "You feeling okay, ma'am?" he asked, and went to her side right quick. He was not about to explain to Doc how a near-naked city woman cracked her fool head in his bathroom. Desire took second seat to concern.

He was relieved when she sat on the closed toilet seat. Her adorable shoulders slumped and she covered her eyes in a childlike attempt to disappear. "So," the little beauty groaned, "I'm in the wrong town."

"Yes, ma'am, it sure sounds that way." He knew he should step out of the bathroom and let her get dressed. The mystery was solved. She wasn't a reporter or a thief. No, she was just . . . blonde. The thought had the corners of his mouth itching to smile.

Regaining some of her composure, she brought her delicate hands down, stood, squared her shoulders, and met his eyes—knocking all coherent thought clear out of his head. "I knew I shouldn't have trusted that gas station attendant. I was just so happy that he'd heard of the place." Her color was back to normal, but her voice was a bit strained. "Does Texas have a lot of ranches named Double C?"

"Appears we have at least two," he said, and this time he could not restrain the lusty grin that spread across his face. She was as adorable as she was sexy, a disconcerting combination. Had she turned up the heat and come on to him, he would have lost interest—well, after sampling whatever she'd offered.

Apparently a man could only go so long without sex before he lost his damn mind, because it appeared that she wasn't the least bit interested in him. Truth be told, as the enormity of the situation sunk in, she wasn't paying much attention to him at all.

"I can't believe I did this . . ." A look of self-disgust crossed her delicate features. "Oh my God. My brother will never let me live this down. Only I would drive all this way to the wrong ranch."

She paused and her eyes widened. *"The wrong ranch."* Repeating the words slowly with new emphasis. She retightened the top of her towel with hands that shook a little. "I should get dressed."

Even though the towel concealed more than shorts and a tank top would have, picturing what lay under it was torturing him. He'd managed to clear his head of images of her writhing with pleasure beneath him, but they were clamoring to return. It was time to make a hasty exit while he still had a mind to. Mustering a nod, he stepped outside and closed the door behind him.

Too soon she was with him again. No makeup. No shoes. Just wearing a simple flowered sleeveless blouse and a pair of tan shorts, whose midthigh length was likely considered modest. And the sight of her still drove him damn near crazy. He wanted to run a hand up one of her legs, to test if they were, in truth, as soft as they appeared.

She rushed by him and disappeared into the living room. He followed, aroused but trying to remain irritated by the presence of this stranger in his home.

Gorgeous or not, she has to go.

"I really am sorry about this," she burst out with her rapid-fire Northern accent. "You probably think I'm crazy. I guess I am." She paced back and forth in front of him, a barefoot beauty. "I knew I should have bought a map." She waved her cell phone in the air.

"It worked the rest of the way down here, but not when it really mattered."

Leaning against the doorjamb, he felt the stirring of something even more worrisome than lust. A tickle of adrenaline licked through his veins as his high-energy intruder came to a stop in front of him. It had been years since anything had made his heart race and his breath catch in his throat. Something about this woman pulled at a part of him he'd long considered dead.

Oblivious to how close he was to hauling her to him and tasting those tempting, pursed lips, Sarah said, "I'll get my stuff and be out of here before I cause any trouble."

"Trouble?" *Dammit, now why didn't I simply agree?*

She turned away, bent, and gave him a delightful view of her never-ending legs as her shorts rose up. She didn't seem to notice, just kept rummaging through her luggage. "With your girlfriend or wife or whatever."

"No trouble," he drawled. Crazy must be catching, because he was having difficulty reconciling what he knew he should say with the damn fool things coming out of his mouth.

"There they are," she exclaimed happily, and pulled out the most impractical pair of boots he'd ever seen: knee-high, polished leather, with ridiculously spindly heels and some sort of strap across the top. She held them up next to one leg. "I bought these special for this trip. Do you like them?"

He didn't answer. His thoughts weren't the type that should be shared with a woman he'd just met. *Like them?* No man would ever ask her to take them off. Those were the kind of boots that stayed on all night.

She sat on the couch as she pulled them on. Her big brown eyes studied him intensely. He'd bought horses with less of a perusal than she was giving him. He wished he had taken the time to shave that morning. His plaid shirt was covered with dust and sweat from the time he'd spent working in the hot afternoon. The old jeans he'd thrown on without a second thought that morning were smudged with grass stains. Not much to look at.

"Could I bother you for one more thing?" Her voice was huskier than before. "May I use your phone?" She held up her cell phone. "This thing is useless here and my friends must be worried by now. They expected me hours ago."

He nodded, not trusting himself to answer. The way she continued to look him over . . . slowly . . . from head to foot had him fumbling for sanity. He pointed to the land phone on the small table in the corner of the room and wordlessly watched her walk to it.

Damn.

"There's still no answer." She waved the handset helplessly in the direction of her distant friends. "I guess I should just head over there and wait till they get home."

"Are you sure you can find the place?" he asked without missing a beat, surprising himself.

As she replaced the handset, Sarah's eyes narrowed at him even as her dimples revealed her good humor at his teasing. "A cowboy *and* a comedian?"

Tony shrugged. "Can't say I've ever been accused of being funny before." He'd never had much to laugh about and didn't see any merit in acting the clown, since the world was full of those who took to idiocy naturally.

Her expression softened. "Well, you should try it more often. It suits you."

The compliment jolted him like a brush with electric fencing. Tony retreated a step and almost tripped when the back of his boot met her suitcase.

She advanced and reached to steady him but he stepped back again, evading her touch.

The sound of the front door opening had never been so welcome. *Women make men stupid. Plain and simple.* Wasn't that what his father had always said? He didn't need more proof than practically falling on his ass because a woman half his size had complimented him.

The shuffle of boots across the wooden floor announced that someone was joining them. *Melanie.* Her presence wasn't a surprise. As his housekeeper, she used his kitchen on a daily basis to prepare meals for him. Normally, however, she was better at minding her own business.

Yep, she was fixing to break the one rule he'd laid down the day he'd hired her and, for a reason he wasn't comfortable exploring, he wasn't prepared to correct her in front of Sarah.

Melanie came to a stop at the doorway. "You have company? Do you need anything?" She looked over as she spoke, and for a moment the two women simply stared at each other.

A man would have been hard-pressed to say if these two women could get along. Life hadn't been kind to Melanie, and she'd spent almost as much time hiding on his secluded ranch as he had. Although she was likely only a few years older than Sarah, they couldn't have been more different. If the two were cats, Sarah would be the fluffy, white, pampered city type that would probably run at the first sign of a rodent. Melanie would be a brown, bad-tempered barn cat: useful to have but better kept outside.

Not that she ever showed her temper around him; no one did and stayed.

He was still debating how to get both of them out of his house when Sarah stepped forward with the huge, welcoming smile he'd seen on her face when she'd thought he was her friend's brother.

She took Melanie's hand in hers and shook energetically. "Hi, my name's Sarah."

Melanie pulled her hand free. Did he imagine the hiss? *Careful, Sarah. Feral cats aren't real good when cornered.* He figured he could intervene before things got ugly, but most creatures got along better if you let them sort it out for themselves.

Sarah's smile didn't dim as she waited for the other woman to speak.

"Melanie," his dark-haired housekeeper said curtly.

In the high-speed way she spoke, Sarah said, "I can only imagine what you must be thinking, but this is much more ridiculous and innocent than it looks." She took her phone out of her back pocket and waved it between them. "I mean, who knew it wouldn't work out here, right?" She looked over her shoulder at Tony and said, "Your husband was just letting me use your phone." Then she flushed a delightful shade of pink. "Okay, your shower, too, but he didn't let me use that. I mean, I did use it, but that was before I knew you would both be here. Which, you should be, because it's your house. So why wouldn't you be here? I'm the one who shouldn't be here. And I'm actually just leaving."

Melanie, who'd simply stared at Sarah during this overflowing river of speech, raised her eyebrows and stated succinctly, "I'm not his wife."

"Whew," Sarah said with a laugh, then stopped and looked at both of them again. "I didn't mean that the way it sounded. If you're his girlfriend or whatever, I'm cool with that. It was just that—whoa, explaining this to a wife would be so much worse. Not that anything happened." Sarah closed her eyes briefly as if the thought pained her, then continued earnestly, "Unless you count that he saw me naked, and that totally wasn't his fault."

Melanie said blandly, "I work here."

"Oh, I thought . . ."

"No," Melanie and Tony said in unison.

Another blush spread across Sarah's cheeks. The quick look she gave Tony sent his heart racing and his thoughts scattering.

"Sarah isn't staying," he said gruffly. "As soon as she locates her friends, she's leaving."

Sarah deflated a bit at his harsh declaration. "Yes, in fact, they should be there now. I should head out."

I'll probably regret this. "Melanie, make a second plate for dinner. Sarah and I will eat in the dining room."

Hard to say which woman he'd shocked more. Sarah looked back and forth between them as if seeking reassurance. "I *am* hungry. If you're sure it's not too much trouble?"

Melanie didn't say a word, but she didn't have to. In fact, he preferred she didn't. He wasn't ready to explain to anyone, not even himself, why he was reluctant to see Sarah leave.

It was more than how his body responded to the sight of hers. He wanted . . .

He wasn't sure what exactly.

Was it because she had no idea who he was? She was neither intimidated by his reputation nor excited by the idea of being with a man many considered dangerous. No, she looked at him like there wasn't a reason in the world why they couldn't be friends . . . or more.

Tony had been alone so long that he'd begun to believe he preferred it that way. In the beginning it had been easier, and over time it had become comfortable. Tonight he didn't want to be a man with a past he regretted. He didn't want to be angry. He wanted to have an uncomplicated dinner with a beautiful woman. Knowing she was leaving after their meal made it much easier to allow himself the possibility of enjoying it.

Melanie had just finished setting two places at one end of the dining room table when he and Sarah entered the room. No one would have guessed this was the first time anyone had sat there in the five years he'd owned the place. He preferred the solitude of the small kitchen table. He wasn't about to mention it, though—women would falsely read meaning into something like that.

Chapter Two

Standing in the doorway of the dining room, Sarah wished life had a "Pause" button. She wanted to slow time and savor each moment. Another woman might have been afraid, but the joy of the unexpected was the reason Sarah often chose riding the trails instead of sticking to the ring at the barn she boarded her horse at. Outside of the riding ring, she was free, and anything was possible.

This wasn't how my trip was supposed to go, but look at me, standing next to a real cowboy—one with a shy smile and a slow Southern drawl. He belongs in a book. She figured he was in his late twenties or early thirties, but the rugged lines of his face spoke of years of hard work, and his callused hands held a powerful promise she'd never imagined in the manicured, smooth texture of the city men she was used to.

He even smells like the outdoors.

How strange would I look if I took out my notebook and jotted down all the things I don't want to forget about him? I'd start with those muscles. Those heavenly muscles. Unlike the hulking men who strutted like peacocks at her local gym, this man had the understated, quiet strength that Sarah found a million times sexier. *He earned those delicious biceps and that rock-hard body in a way that wouldn't have diminished the size of his . . .*

In the middle of an appreciative sigh, Sarah realized her gaze had followed her thoughts in a less-than-subtle ogling of his lower assets. She looked up quickly, her face heating with a blush when she met his eyes. *Quick. Say something.* "I like your . . . uh . . . jeans."

Who the hell says that?

"Pardon the dust." He brushed his hand down one thigh, a move that sent responding flickers of heat through Sarah. There it was again, that almost smile. "I usually shower when I get home, but it was already occupied."

You could have joined me, Sarah thought, surprised at herself. *Oh my God, I'm smiling like some street lunatic. Don't look guilty; look away or he'll know what you were thinking.* She met his eyes and the heat that flew between them made her start considering all sorts of impulsive things—many of which included the removal of some or all of their clothing.

Sarah gulped.

Okay, this is not a good idea. I don't know this man.

But I'd like to.

Oh, how I'd like to.

Stop that! she chastised her raging libido. *This summer is about breaking free, living, finding my writer's voice—not about having a one-night stand just because my sense of direction sucks.*

She sought sanity by turning her attention to the table. The very long, very sturdy table. *What would it be like to push the plates aside and . . .*

A huge smile spread across her face as images of them entwined passionately elicited another thought. *I have a naughty side.*

Me.

Who knew? All I needed was the right inspiration!

Tony moved to stand behind one of the chairs and pulled it out for her to sit. When she did, he pushed it in with more force than she'd expected and she gasped. He took the seat across from her but looked far from happy about it, making her wonder if their attraction was indeed mutual.

Sarah had never considered herself a beauty, nor was she used to men glowering at her like she was an . . . *uninvited guest? I'm such an idiot. He's feeding me out of pity. This isn't a date. No amount of leering at him will change that.* Sarah groaned, pushed her seat back, and stood. "I should go."

"Sit," he said in an authoritative voice she was sure moved most people to obedience.

At first glance, she'd thought his eyes were hazel, but in the dim dining room lighting they were a deeper green. The air thickened with tension. Heart pounding in her chest, Sarah stood immobile, like prey frozen in a field.

What would it be like to be with a real man? One who wouldn't fumble with a bra strap or ask you so many times if you really wanted to do it, you began to ask yourself the same question. No, Tony would take what he wanted.

She shivered with pleasure at the thought.

Taken.

Now that would be something to write about.

"Sit," he ordered again, more softly, and Sarah did so only because her knees gave out beneath her. *He could ask me for almost anything in that tone and I wouldn't refuse.*

I should leave now.

He could be dangerous.

Or he could be the best mistake I've ever made.

The sound of Melanie organizing plates in the adjoining room shook Sarah free of her hormonal stupor. She said the first thing that came to her mind. "I saw your horses. They're beautiful. How many do you have?" She wasn't sure he was going to answer her at first. If the harsh set of Tony's jaw was anything to go by, he was enjoying their time together much less than she was.

"Depends on the season," he answered vaguely.

"And they're all quarter horses?" *Is it wrong to ask questions just so I can hear his knee-weakening drawl again?*

"Most of 'em."

Melanie placed two glasses of lemonade between them.

Sarah thanked her and took a long sip, half closing her eyes as she enjoyed its refreshing coolness. When she opened them, she noticed Tony gazing at her intently, looking even less happy, if that was possible.

She grew nervous, and when she was nervous she tended to ramble. "Did you see Scooter outside?" she asked, but continued without waiting for his answer. "I put him in a paddock because it was too hot to leave him in the trailer. I hope that was okay. I thought I was at Lucy's place when I did it."

"Are you married?" His voice broke through her monologue like a bolt of lightning.

"No," she said quickly, her mouth working faster than her brain. "I'm single. Totally single." She grabbed a napkin and practically shoved it in her mouth to stop the flow of words. *Could I be more obvious?*

Think.

Think of something cool to say.

Nothing came to mind.

Melanie returned with generous platters of steak and vegetables, explaining she would be back in the morning to clean up. The click of the outside door announced her departure and echoed through the quiet house. They ate in silence for what seemed like an eternity.

"I don't usually do this," Sarah blurted out. "Not that we're doing anything more than eating. And of course I do that on a regular basis. Eat, I mean. I just don't . . ."

"Do more than dinner?" he asked, his expression unreadable as he laid his fork down beside his plate.

She nodded. "Yes, that part. I don't want you to think because you saw me in a towel . . ."

The corners of his eyes crinkled with mirth.

Oh, God, he's laughing. My fantasy cowboy is laughing at me.

Embarrassed, she threw her napkin at him. "It's not funny."

A slow smile spread across his face. "It is, actually."

Sarah crossed her arms with a bit of a huff. "It had to be said or things could get awkward."

"You mean more than *this*?" His grin was unrepentant.

Imagining the evening through his eyes, Sarah groaned. He was probably hoping she would talk less, eat more, and get out of there quickly. "I do appreciate you not calling the police when you found me here."

"The sheriff would have loved that. Best break-in story ever."

"I didn't break in—" she started to say, but stopped when all the emotions of the day rushed in and, combined with her sudden fatigue, brought an embarrassing sheen of tears to her eyes.

All humor left Tony's face. He looked at the door quickly as if that would somehow conjure up his housekeeper. "Don't cry . . ."

"I'm not crying," Sarah denied hotly, and sniffed. *Great, I bet my nose is turning red.* A man like Tony probably dated sophisticated women: women who would know exactly how to flirt with him. They'd entice rather than entertain him.

What do I do when I'm given an evening alone with the sexiest man I've ever met? Sarah sniffed again and looked around for a tissue. *Nothing worth documenting unless I decide to write an article about how to make an idiot of myself in ten easy steps.*

He stood abruptly; his chair teetered and almost toppled behind him. "You should try calling your friends again."

Party's over.

Get out.

Sarah stood, too, and followed him back to the living room and the phone.

Hey, Texas, so far you're not that good for my ego.

"Thanks, but it's probably best if I just load Scooter and go. Sounds like I have a night of driving ahead of me."

Tony stopped and turned so abruptly that she walked straight into him. Everything she'd admired earlier was acutely more amazing pressed up against her. He steadied her with a hand on either arm and eased her back, but not before she'd experienced her first bout of gut-clenching lust that tempted her to launch herself back into his arms.

Although that would make a good story to tell my friends.

I thought you said he didn't call the sheriff when you broke into his house, so how did you end up arrested?

Oh, that happened when I mauled him even after he kept asking me to leave. You would have, too. He was gorgeous.

His hands dropped away, and for a moment Sarah forgot why she'd followed him. *You know, besides wanting to stare up at him speechlessly and drool for one last time before I left.*

"I can't let you go . . ." he said.

Thank God.

". . . until you contact someone. No telling where you'd end up on your own."

Okay, that last part killed the mood a bit.

Now I remember why I want to write. Reality sucks. Watch out, Mr. Cowboy. When I put you in a book, you're going to be kissing my feet and begging me to stay. Sarah raised her chin with renewed pride and said, "I'll call them one more time, but I'm leaving even if they don't answer. Where I end up is none of your concern."

Now I sound like a heroine in a romance novel.

Take that, Mr. Sexy Cowboy.

Tony looped his thumbs through his belt and said, "In Texas, if you find someone in your shower, you're responsible for their welfare for at least twenty-four hours."

Sarah opened her mouth to argue the point, then cocked her head to the side and asked, "Did you just make another joke?"

The corners of his eyes crinkled ever so slightly. *Note to self: dry humor in an otherwise stern character is intriguing—would even be sexy if I wasn't the butt of his joke.*

She defended her arrival. "I wouldn't be here if all the damn ranches in Texas didn't have the same name."

A hint of a smile curled one side of his mouth. "Yes, ma'am."

"Just give me the phone," Sarah said, and stepped past him.

He caught her arms midstep, spun her, and held her just in front of him. The hot look in his eyes sent another rush of desire through Sarah. *He wants me.* Her mouth went dry and she flicked her tongue over her bottom lip.

The move caught his eye, but instead of crushing her to him with the kiss she anticipated, he eased her back from him again and said, "My number is near the phone if you want your friends to call you back here."

With that, he turned on his heel and left.

Fanning her face, Sarah picked up the nondescript black phone and reluctantly dialed her friend's number.

Lucy is probably frantic by now.

The phone rang once. Then twice.

Or not.

A machine picked up after the fifth ring. "Hi, Lucy. It's Sarah. I had a little trouble finding your place, so I am at—I'm at a friend's house. Anyway, when you get this message please call me." She left Tony's number and hung up the phone.

He wanted me.

I know he did.

Or I'm desperate enough to see only what I want to see . . . like a cattle ranch where there are only horses.

Chapter Three

The cooler evening air helped clear Tony's head as he leaned against the gate of Scooter's paddock. *That woman has to go.* He wasn't celibate, but the women he'd been with had no illusions about why they were together. He didn't have to make excuses or pretend to want to stay with them until morning.

None of them had ever looked up at him with the open innocence of his little blonde intruder. He'd bet money on two things: she was a virgin and she wanted him. Her interest had been obvious, but in an entirely different way than the bold women he was used to.

A woman like Sarah would think sex came with a commitment. She'd be hurt when I asked her to leave. Exploring that tight little body of hers wouldn't be worth the aggravation that would likely follow. He went instantly, painfully hard as he remembered how she'd looked, mostly naked, in his shower. During his celebrity years, he'd encountered many beautiful women. Women who were taller than Sarah, thinner, more polished. He didn't remember any of them taking his breath away or scattering his thoughts with a simple smile. Dinner had made the situation worse rather than better and triggered an uncomfortable realization: *One night wouldn't be enough.*

He sensed Sarah's approach even before he heard her soft footsteps, but he didn't turn to look at her. Her image was already too vivid in his mind, and all he would see was a woman who had to leave. *Now rather than later.*

She stepped onto the bottom wooden panel of the paddock fence next to him and leaned forward to call her horse, which met her caressing hand eagerly.

Lucky horse.

"I put my luggage back in my SUV. All that's left is to load Scooter and I'll be on my way."

Don't ask. It's better not to know. "Did you finally reach your friends?" *And don't look.* He did and lost himself for a moment in those large brown eyes of hers.

"No, but they know I'm coming. I'm sure it'll be fine. I'll find a gas station on the way and buy a map." The forced optimism in her voice didn't fool him.

Don't get involved. "No."

A wrinkle of confusion creased her flawless forehead. "I'm sorry?"

"You're not leaving tonight."

Delicious pink lips pursed in displeasure. "I don't remember asking if I could." She seemed to consider her own statement and said, "If you're worried about me, I can call you when I get there so you'll know that I made it okay."

A reasonable solution. So why was everything in him rejecting the idea? "I'll call Melanie and have her prepare the guest room for you."

With a hand on one hip, his little blonde angel said, "I'm perfectly capable of finding Lucy's place. I made it here on my own." When he opened his mouth to reply, she cut him off and said, "By here, I mean Texas." She raised one hand between them to silence him. "Don't say it. I appreciate your offer of a room, but I can't stay here."

Walk away. She's not your problem. Nod, shake her hand, and head back into the house. The impatience he felt toward himself echoed in his curt tone as he said, "You're tired. Your horse is tired. It's almost a day's trip. It doesn't make sense to leave tonight."

Arms resting on the fence, Sarah chewed her bottom lip and studied her horse. "Is there a hotel nearby? I'd have to leave Scooter here for the night, but I could pay you."

"I don't want your money, and town is an hour away." God help him, he didn't want to be paid—he wanted her.

He leaned down, close enough so that when she turned her head he could almost taste her lips beneath his. The soft scent of her filled him with a desire to lay her down and claim her right then and there. She licked her bottom lip. The tip of her tongue left a wet trail that he eagerly wanted to follow.

She whispered. "I don't know you."

We can remedy that.

She was innocently wanton. Did she have any idea what her pose was doing to him? With one high-heeled foot hitched up on the lower plank, and leaning forward as she was, she was offering a temptation any man would have trouble resisting.

Didn't I just decide she was off limits? Nothing has changed. The best thing I can do is agree and let her go. Even if, more than anything, I want her to stay. Tony straightened and took a step back; his next words were a concession to the inner battle he was losing. "I want you to stay."

She looked over her shoulder at him, the crease returned to her forehead. "Do you always get what you want?"

He turned away, adjusted his hat, and rested his forearms on the top of the fence a foot away from hers. In a tired voice he said, "Never."

Oh, now that's just not fair.

I already want to throw all decorum to the wind and jump him—do you have to make me like him, too?

All that manly talk and now a hint of save-me sadness? Where do I sign up for this ride?

I should write that down.

Save-me sadness.

Which doesn't mean I can stay here tonight.

I can't because . . .

Wait, I don't have a boyfriend, a job, or, apparently, even reliable friends. If I leave now, it's a slap in the face of fate. Opportunities like this don't just happen. They're a gift.

Sarah used her peripheral vision to give the man next to her another once-over.

And what a gift.

So what if the last ten women who accepted his offer to stay are buried in the back field? Note to self: check back field for mounds. This is what I asked for, dreamed of, came out here determined not to leave without: an adventure.

Schooling her features, she hoped she didn't appear psychotically excited by her decision. "One night." She held her breath and waited for his response to her surrender. Their eyes met and held for a moment, charging the space between them. She leaned toward him, her eyes half closed in anticipation of his kiss.

"You should go answer that," Tony said abruptly.

Sarah's eyes shot open. Still in a bit of a daze, she asked, "Answer what?"

"The phone," Tony said, a glint of humor lighting his eyes. "I don't get many calls. It's probably your friend."

"Oh," she said. *Damn.* "Thanks." She tried but failed to sound happy about it.

If that's Lucy now, she has the world's worst timing.

Thanks for nothing, Lucy.

You never really get the apology you imagine you're owed.

Sarah listened to Lucy's long explanation about why she'd been away from home and had turned her cell phone off: last-minute errands; her brother needed her help with something. The whole story sounded a bit contrived, and Lucy's contriteness was sadly lacking. *You don't let a friend drive for three days, then play hide-and-seek with them on the day they arrive.*

Lucy said, "Things have just been crazy here these last few days. I should have called you and told you now isn't a good time to come, but I didn't know how to say it."

Well, this is awkward.

She continued, "Of course, I can't wait to see you. You could probably stay through the weekend, but after that, I don't know. My brother changed his mind about having someone here for the summer."

Because why not drive cross-country with your horse for a weekend?

Sarah opened her mouth to tell her friend just what she thought of her when a thought struck her. *Things happen for a reason, and a woman could find herself stranded in worse places.* "I'm settled in here for the night, Lucy. I'm fine."

Lucy said, "I didn't realize you had other friends in the area."

"I didn't know it myself until today."

"Then this all worked out for the best, I guess. How long do you think you'll stay there?" Lucy asked, her relief obvious.

Until Mr. Sexy Cowboy has me physically removed from his property or I wake up, realize how insane this all is, and leave while I still have some dignity.

"I'm not sure," Sarah said vaguely.

"Hopefully, we can get together before you leave."

Still irritated with Lucy, Sarah thought, *A few hours ago, I would have jumped at the chance to see you, but I've kind of moved on.* "Sure."

After replacing the handset in its cradle, Sarah smiled all the way to her SUV. Something inside her clicked into place and she felt inspired. She dug through her oversized purse for her notebook. She'd gone from having nothing to write about to not knowing how to start recording everything she didn't want to forget about this trip. A story was already forming in her mind, tickling her imagination. *A contemporary romance—a sexy one.* She jotted in her notebook: *Strong heroine who is willing to take risks. She yearns for something or someone she can't have.*

Yearns. Sarah underlined the word twice. *That's a good place to start.*

"Was that your friend on the phone?" Tony asked from beside her. Sarah let out a yelp of surprise and dropped her notebook at his feet. He reached for it, but she snatched it up from the ground, closing it quickly and clasping it to her chest while hoping he hadn't seen the first page.

Because nothing says "I'm normal" like a question regarding men's grooming practices on their genitalia.

"Yes," Sarah said, the word catching in her throat.

Tony scowled down at her and nodded at her notebook. "You jotting down the directions before you forget them?"

Looks like this conversation is going to happen at the corner of Awkward and Embarrassing. "Not exactly." She cleared her throat. "My friend changed her mind about wanting me to visit."

Those green eyes bored into hers. He drawled, "Doesn't sound like much of a friend."

"You think?" Sarah snapped sarcastically, letting her nerves momentarily get the best of her. *Calm down. None of this is his fault.* "Sorry. I guess I'm just tired. It's been a long day."

In the quiet that followed, Sarah tried telepathy. *See, this is where you could use an incredibly sexy bedroom voice to tell me not to worry since you have more than enough room for me. Lean in again, and I'll know having me here will be torture for you because you aren't sure if you'll be able to keep your hands off me while I'm sleeping right down the hall.*

His expression remained unreadable.

Screw telepathy. Sarah snapped again, "You could at least tell me that I'm welcome to stay here tonight."

"I said that earlier," he said matter-of-factly. He opened the rear door of her SUV, pulled out her suitcases, and started walking to the house. When she didn't follow, he stopped, half turned, and gruffly said, "Come on."

Sarah fought the urge to stomp her foot in frustration. *Oh yes, the fictitious you will be tormented with desire for me.* She sighed and followed him onto the porch. When he stopped at the door and held it open with his back, allowing her to pass through, she narrowed her eyes at him and imagined how the retelling of this night would go when she met with her friends back home.

Were you worried about staying at a stranger's house your first night in Texas?

Surprisingly, no.

Not concerned that he might try to take advantage of you?

Sarah gurgled on a laugh as she followed him up the staircase and down a narrow hallway. *Are you kidding? I was betting he'd lock his bedroom door.*

Tony turned and frowned as if her amusement annoyed him. He opened the door to the small guest room and placed her luggage beside the white wrought-iron twin bed topped with a surprisingly delicate flowered quilt.

"You need anything?" he asked in a tone that implied he'd prefer that she didn't.

If you only knew.

Or maybe you do and you're not interested.

She blushed. "All set." He was stepping out the door when she spontaneously said, "Tony . . ."

With a hand on the doorknob, he turned and raised one eyebrow in question.

Stay.

Nothing in his expression indicated that he would be the slightest bit tempted to, so instead she said, "Thank you."

He nodded and closed the door behind him.

Sarah tossed her notebook on the oak nightstand beside the bed and flopped onto a mattress that felt as cold and unwelcoming as the man who had led her to it.

Just because Texas wasn't living up to her fantasy, the trip wasn't a complete wash. *I didn't come here to meet a man. Honestly, I didn't really come to see Lucy, either. I came to find my story.*

She rolled onto her stomach and reached for her notebook. Pen met paper with an enthusiasm she'd feared she'd never experience. First she recorded what she didn't want to forget about the trip, then she tried to capture as much as possible of the story she'd been outlining in her head all day. Two hours later, she flipped back to the first page, reread everything she'd written, and then wrote her painful realizations at the end:

- I'll need more than my personal experience if this book is going to have sex scenes.
- Is that really how it was? No wonder we broke up. Why did it take me this long to realize how bad it was?

- Twenty-five and I've never orgasmed.

What is my problem?

Maybe I was born with a hyperactive imagination but subpar bits and pieces.

Looking around the room and feeling a bit guilty, Sarah stepped out of her shoes, pants, and underwear, then slid beneath the flowered quilt. She ran her hand down her stomach and over her short pubic hair.

Everyone does it.

Some even suggest it as a way to improve your sex life. If you know what pleases you, then you can guide your partner and all that crap.

She had to admit that it felt good to touch herself. She rubbed back and forth a few times, stopping occasionally when she was convinced she heard a sound at the door. She rubbed harder. She rubbed faster. She flipped onto her stomach and rubbed herself against her hand.

Ow, hand cramp. Great. She gave up with a pathetic sigh of resignation and buried her face in her pillow in disgust. *Oh, God, I have problems.*

Rolling onto her side, she reached for her notebook again and wrote a sarcastic note in the margin:

First attempt at masturbation—fail. Change book title to *Ultimate Celibacy: When Even You Don't Want You.*

Sarah added a few more lines, then threw the notebook back onto the nightstand. *I thought we had a deal, Texas. You are seriously disappointing me.*

Down the hall, clad only in cotton boxers, Tony lay on top of his bedding with his hands clasped behind his head, staring blankly at the ceiling. *I should have thrown her out the moment I met her. No one is as innocent as she pretends to be. The whole story about confusing my horse ranch with a cattle ranch sounded far-fetched from the beginning, but I wanted to believe the implausible could be true.*

He should have told her to leave when he caught her with the damning evidence of her notebook. He'd spent too many years avoiding interviews and banning reporters from his property to change now just because she had a body a man wanted to bury himself in. He closed his eyes as if that would diminish how vividly he could remember her long, lean thighs and those deliciously high boots. Whoever she worked for had chosen poorly if they thought that a pair of perfectly shaped breasts and a tight ass would be enough for her to gain an exclusive interview.

So why is she still here?

The reason was standing erect and proud, straining beneath the thin cotton of his shorts. His cock didn't care if his blonde angel was capable of deception. Was she sleeping? Was she lying there imagining, as he was, what would happen if he crossed the hall and knocked on her door?

I should let her believe she's conned me and test exactly how far she's willing to go to get her story. Hell, if she's good enough, I might even give her a quote to take with her when I throw her cute little ass off my property tomorrow.

No use hoping it doesn't come to that.

Tony rolled onto his side and punched the pillow before settling his head on it. Even after seeing the notebook, there was a part of him that didn't want to believe he'd been wrong about her. Those brown eyes were so deceptively open and trusting. The memory of them warmed his heart in a way that confused him.

There's a slim chance she's not a reporter.

Why the hell else would she have been taking notes by her car?

What was it about Sarah that made him want to prove her innocence?

He didn't like puzzles when it came to people. In fact, it had been a long time since he'd cared enough to question anyone's motivation for anything. Over the past five years, he'd lost interest in most everything. There'd been a time when he'd found a thrill in unlocking the potential of a horse, but even that had waned.

Slowly dying.

Until today.

He slid a hand beneath the elastic of his shorts, took his pulsing cock into his hand, and closed his eyes. His callused palm was a poor substitute for the hot, wet mouth he wanted around him. Not just any mouth—the one that had pouted at him when he'd told Sarah she couldn't leave. He imagined her opening the door to his bedroom and finding him jacking off.

A smile would spread across her face. She would slowly strip and saunter to the side of his bed, naked and aroused. Tony kept an even pump going while he pictured how she would look. He'd seen enough of her in the shower to be able to picture her all too clearly in his mind. He knew how round and firm her breasts were and how delightfully dark her nipples looked against her otherwise fair skin.

She'd boldly prowl to the bed, placing a foot on either side of his torso, giving him the perfect view of her wet and eager pussy. One of her hands would cup a breast and circle her nipple until it was standing straight with arousal. Her other hand would caress her clit with slow, rhythmic precision until she could no longer contain her moans. Then she'd slip her middle finger inside herself while continuing to rub the heel of her hand against her pink folds.

He jerked in his own hand and tore his boxers off, then relaxed onto his back as he pictured her throwing her head back, her long blonde mane loose and wild down her back, begging for him to bury his hands in it. She'd nibble that lush bottom lip of hers and shudder above him as she brought herself to orgasm. Her juices would run down her hand and she'd turn her hungry mouth to him. She'd swivel, sinking to her knees so her still-swollen folds were easily within his tongue's reach, and she'd take him deeply into her mouth.

The taste of her and the sensation of her lips around him would almost be his undoing, but he'd hold out as long as he could. He'd savor her and tease her swollen nub with licks and gentle sucks until he felt her ready to come again. Only then would he climax in her mouth while she did in his.

Tony shuddered as he came in his own hand.

Probably wouldn't hurt to find out what's in that notebook before I throw her out.

Just to be fair 'n' all.

Chapter Four

Early in the morning, Tony's subconscious turned on him as it had countless times before. He tensed, even in his sleep, preparing to meet an old adversary he'd never conquered.

Don't do this to yourself. Wake up.

But he was already lost to it.

He was cantering a white mare bareback down a long dirt road. They covered the miles with no sound of hoofbeats to break up the oppressive silence. No breeze. Sweat beaded on Tony's forehead. Torn between loving and hating the memory, all he could do was hold on. The violet-blue sky pressed down, as familiar to him as the decrepit ranch he was riding to.

As she always did, the mare headed for the crumbling farmhouse at the top of the hill. No amount of reining her in would turn the mare from her course. Try as he did, each time he took this ride he was incapable of leaping off. No, the horse always took him back to the one place he hated.

In the blink of an eye, he was standing in an old round pen with the mare. His father, as weathered and worn as his surroundings, leaned against the pen's rusty metal railings. "You still wastin' yer time with that nag? The meat man ain't gonna care none if she's muscled up."

"You can't sell her. She's mine, Dad. You said I could have her." His voice was a mixture of the child he'd been and the man he'd become.

"Don't go gettin' yourself attached, Tony. We need the money and that horse is goin' at the next auction." There was no cruel intention in his voice, just the cold sting of truth.

"You told me if I got her to stop bucking, I could keep her. She's as gentle as they come now."

Emotion had never had much effect on the older man, who had been taught several tough life lessons early. "If she is, maybe someone'll outbid the meat man."

The hand Tony buried in the horse's mane belonged to the twelve-year-old he'd once been. "I won't let you do it, Dad. Not this horse. Not to the auction. She's mine. I love her." A memory that should have faded with time was as sharp and painful in his dream as the day it had happened, and the desperation in his young voice as he pleaded with his father was equally real.

With a disgusted shake of his head, his father said, "There ain't no room for love in reality, Son. You'd best learn that now. Love just makes a man miserable. That horse goes to auction in two weeks. Train her real good, and maybe she'll find herself a home."

The weathered, neglected pen disappeared. Miles and miles of white fencing surrounded Tony. Tall green grass waved in the light breeze under a bright, cloudless sky. He heard the distant sound of a thundering gray stallion bearing down on him. The horse grew in size as it approached, morphing into a snorting beast intent on stomping the life out of him. The more he fought it, the more it knocked him down until he retreated from it. But it followed, as it always did, cornering him until he hated himself more than he feared any pain the horse could inflict.

An image of Sarah appeared and stood beside him, replacing the beast. Sweet, trusting Sarah. He reached for her, but she stepped back in horror, staring at his hands. They were covered and dripping with blood. He desperately tried to clean them on his shirt, but the blood remained. He wanted to reassure her, but even while screaming, he had no voice.

Sarah faded away and Tony sank to his knees in the tall grass. Despite the blood, he covered his face in his hands and did in his dream what he had never done when he was awake. He cried.

Long after he'd awoken, the dream lingered far too vividly. Tony cursed each bale of hay he threw down from the barn loft. Sweat plastered his shirt to his back, but the punishing heat of the day was a welcome discomfort.

He groaned when David changed direction upon spotting him. Only a year or two older than Tony, David successfully organized sales and handled the business side of things. He had quickly built up a reputation of integrity that trumped any amount of advertising another breeder might buy. He was also the best damn ranch manager in the area, possibly in all Texas, but he had a flaw: he was too fucking happy.

Wiping the sweat from his forehead with the sleeve of his shirt, Tony headed down the ladder in resignation. David was as unavoidable as weeds in a pasture. He was the one person on the ranch Tony couldn't avoid talking to. *But I don't have to like it.*

"I'm surprised you're here so early this morning," David said too cheerfully. "I thought you'd be . . ."

"I'd be what?" Tony bit out, stacking the leftover hay against the wall.

David paused a moment, pushed his Stetson back thoughtfully, and chose his next words carefully. "I heard you have company. I figured you might take today off."

"Do I pay you to think about who I do or don't have in my house?" Tony's body filled with fury. More, he knew, than the conversation called for.

"No," David said slowly.

"Then why the hell are we having this conversation?" Tony snarled, his fists curling at his sides.

Another man would have turned tail and run at the charged tone, but David simply shook his head in a patient way that only irritated Tony more. "Snow Prince won another reining futurity," he said as Tony piled the last bale on top. "I heard there was a huge purse. Word has it, he's worth almost a million now and climbing. His owner would like to come meet you. He can't say enough good about you. The papers are begging for interviews, too."

"I don't care about Prince's new owner and you know I don't give interviews," Tony said with disgust.

David opened the door to his small barn office nearby and stood just outside it. "If you don't want to be in the magazines, stop training horses. You've made enough money."

I would, but it's all I have left. That and one confusing houseguest. "What do you know about that idiot reporter you found snooping around here last week? Was he working with anyone?" He'd almost forgotten about that man, but Sarah had somehow brought him back, just as she had his nightmares.

"As far as I know, no one." It wasn't often that David looked embarrassed, but his face reddened at the mention of the hired hand who had turned out to be an undercover reporter.

"What about the rest of the hands? You might want to let them go and start fresh. One or another of them is always trying to talk to me."

"You know we can't run this place alone." David crossed his arms. "I'm not firing everyone midseason just because they admire you."

"Fine, I'll do it myself."

David scratched his jaw thoughtfully. "What put a burr under your saddle this morning?"

"You know my rule."

With a sad shake of his head, David said, "Some of these young men have worked here for years. They're loyal to you. It's your ranch, Tony. Fire the whole lot of them if you want, but I'm not cleaning the stalls. You let 'em go, and you find the next ones. That'll mean going to town, screening them, sorting through the ones with real skills versus the ones who think they can acquire some simply by watching you. By all means, go ahead." David shrugged. "I'll take the vacation I'm due to give you some time to figure out what a colossal mistake it was. Then if you ask me real nice, I'll try to find some qualified help before we lose a whole season."

Tony narrowed his eyes. "I can let you go just as easily."

David nodded. "Do it. I've made good money. It may be time for me to invest in something of my own." Lifting and adjusting his hat, David said dryly, "I'd miss your sorry, self-destructive ass, though." Tony caught a shadow of a smile on David's face and hated the twinkle of amusement in his eyes as David said, "Go on back to the house. I bet your mood will get a whole lot better if you stop hiding down here and go see your little blonde."

Tony opened his mouth, then shut it with a snap and a glare. Without a word, he turned on his heel and strode out of the barn.

I hate it when he's right.

The early morning light that filtered through the curtainless windows woke Sarah up. She squinted into the brightness, then grabbed a pillow to cover her head. It took her a moment to remember where she was, but when she did she sat straight up in the twin bed, dropping the pillow to the floor.

Yesterday was not a dream. I really did get lost, made a complete idiot of myself over the first cowboy I met, got ditched by a woman I thought was my friend, and slept in the home of a complete stranger. Sarah sat immobile on the bed, letting it all soak in.

Today can only go up from there.

She swung her legs to the floor, stood, and stretched. A light breeze from the window flitted across body parts she didn't normally air out. Sarah looked down quickly, past the T-shirt that rested just below her hips, and remembered she'd removed her underwear last night.

Probably not a good idea to stand in front of the window bare-assed. She scrunched down and made her way to the luggage she hadn't bothered to open the night before. Rummaging quickly produced clean underwear and a fresh pair of jeans.

A shower would be nice. What's the rule regarding the number of showers you're allowed when you break into a person's house? I'm guessing it's one.

Then again, some rules are meant to be broken, especially if it's for the common good.

After a quick shower, she slid on the snug-fitting jeans, tennis shoes, and a simple pink blouse, then sought the room's mirror. A dab of concealer, a quick sweep of her hair into a ponytail, and she felt brave enough to face the new day.

She told herself she wasn't disappointed when she discovered the only other person in the house was Melanie, washing dishes at the large sink in the kitchen. Sarah paused before entering and said, "Good morning."

"Tony skipped breakfast, and you're up late. You'll have to make yourself something if you're hungry." Dressed in worn cowboy boots, faded jeans, and an old gray T-shirt, Melanie looked as rough around the edges as she sounded.

If there was one thing Sarah prided herself on, it was her ability to make friends. She liked people and, in return, most people liked her. She supposed she shouldn't care how Melanie felt about her, since she was planning to leave after breakfast and it wasn't likely they'd ever cross paths again. Still, there was something about Melanie that drew Sarah to her side.

"Would you like help with the dishes?" Sarah asked.

The housekeeper stopped and turned the water off. She gave Sarah what could only be described as an insulting, dismissive once-over. "You don't need to be kissing up to me. I just work here."

But you wish things were different? I know how you feel.

"My mother would call you essential support staff."

Melanie turned away and snapped, "There's coffee by the stove."

Dismissed.

Sarah poured herself a cup of black coffee and turned to rest her hip against the counter as she sipped it. Almost instantly she spit the tepid bitter liquid back into the cup. *Whatever that is, it's not coffee.* If Melanie heard, she didn't seem to care. "Thank you for making dinner last night."

"It's my job," Melanie said without turning around.

"Well, it was nice," Sarah said warmly, deciding to ride out the arctic chill from the other woman. "And it may be the only home-cooked meal I have in Texas before I drive home to Rhode Island today."

Just the thought of that long drive was enough to seriously dampen Sarah's mood. She might as well start calling the bed-and-breakfasts she'd stayed at on the way down and hope they had rooms open for the return.

Melanie looked at her over her shoulder. "You really leaving?"

Sarah put the coffee cup down on the counter beside her and sighed. "That's the way it looks."

After wiping her hands on a towel beside the sink, Melanie turned around and faced her. "I figured you'd be staying longer."

A flush of embarrassment warmed Sarah's neck and cheeks. *Not when I'm taken in like a dog in a storm.* She smiled with self-deprecating humor. *Tony's probably in town stapling my picture on telephone poles with the caption: Found—stray woman. Please call to claim.*

"He doesn't usually bring women here," Melanie said.

Sarah let out a short rueful laugh. "I sort of brought myself. He was just too nice to throw me out."

Melanie raised both eyebrows as she said, "Really? 'Nice' isn't how most people describe Tony." Then she frowned. "I guess it's not a surprise he'd make an exception for someone like you."

Oh boy. I'm not awake enough for this. Tired, Sarah rubbed a hand over her forehead and joked, "If you're looking for a fight, you should make better coffee. I don't function until after my second cup."

Melanie folded her arms across her chest and studied her for a long moment before saying, "My coffee is fine. That's yesterday's pot."

And round one goes to the angry housekeeper.

If this is Southern charm, give me a Northern cold shoulder any day.

"I'm leaving today, so there's no need to try to poison me."

"We'll see."

Sarah wasn't sure if Melanie was referring to her leaving or the desire to poison her, but she wasn't going to ask. "Okay, well, I probably won't see you before I leave, so thanks again for dinner."

Melanie turned away without saying another word and returned to washing the dishes.

Sarah inched her way out of the kitchen.

My novel won't have a housekeeper.

She stepped onto the porch, and the heat of the day met her with a slap.

And it won't be ten thousand degrees by nine in the morning.

But it will have him. Freshly shaven, dressed in a light-blue plaid shirt and jeans that fit him snugly in all the right places, Tony walked up the driveway to the bottom of the porch steps. For a split second he looked like he might smile, but then he frowned instead as he looked her over.

Well, a happier version of him, anyway.

What? Was he hoping I had my luggage with me?

"Good morning," she said awkwardly, hooking her thumbs in the pockets of her jeans, attempting some Southern casualness.

"Morning," he said with a neutral nod of his head.

If I threw myself at him, would he catch me or let me face-plant in the dirt? Tough call. "I'm sorry I slept in. I must have been exhausted from the trip."

"Melanie make you breakfast?"

"I wasn't very hungry," Sarah hedged. She didn't need to stir up trouble for a housekeeper whose life, it seemed, had already been plenty harsh. "I thought I'd come out and check on Scooter, then make some calls. Do you mind if I use your phone again?"

He looked back at her wordlessly, and Sarah amused herself with fanciful thoughts. *At which point can I ask him to pose for a photo? You know, for research purposes only. Not to pin next to my bed like some lovelorn teenager.*

"You still planning on staying in Texas?"

His question brought back the sting of reality, and Sarah shook her head sadly. "I wish. Lucy implied this isn't a good time to visit after all. Honestly, I'd rather turn around and go home than stay where I'm not wanted."

Tony narrowed his eyes and said, "Long drive back."

"No kidding." Deciding to make the best of it, Sarah shrugged and said, "It won't be that bad if I can get rooms in the places I stayed at on the way down. At least it won't be a straight drive home."

"You must be disappointed."

"That's an understatement."

He lifted and settled his hat on his head, pondering something as he did. "Your horse could use a rest before traveling again."

Sarah shook her head. *Did I hear that right?* Her pulse sped up. "What are you suggesting?"

"No reason why you can't stay another night while you figure it out."

"Are you sure?"

"Just don't do anything that would get a person asked to leave."

I have no idea what that means, but not heading home right away is tempting. Okay, quick review of pros and cons. Con: I don't know this man, and he might expect me to pay for room and board with sexual favors. Sarah inhaled a shaky breath, closed her eyes, and admitted to herself: *That particular circumstance could also qualify as a pro.* She opened her eyes again and found Tony glaring at her. *Much more likely con: I make a complete idiot out of myself over a man who is simply inviting me to stay here because he feels bad for me. On the other hand, one pro that cannot be denied is that I won't have to end this adventure before it has a chance to even begin. I won't have to go home and explain to my parents and my brother that they were right and that the trip was a total waste of time. I could stay right here and at least outline the story that is coming to life in my head.*

Con: Melanie.

"It won't be an issue for anyone?" Sarah asked.

"I said it wouldn't." *And that's all that matters,* his tone implied.

Straightening her shoulders, Sarah gave herself a pep talk. *I'm not going to let a grumpy housekeeper ruin the fact that I'm in freakin' Texas on a horse ranch with a gorgeous man who is asking me to stay.* "Okay, I'll do you—I mean . . . *it*. I mean, I'll do it and stay here with you. On the ranch. In the spare room. Like last night." A flush of embarrassment heated her cheeks.

The corners of his eyes crinkled ever so slightly. *He's laughing at me again.*

Hands on her hips, Sarah said, "It's not nice to laugh at people."

His expression darkened and his tone held both a warning and a tinge of regret. "I'm not a nice man."

She stepped off the porch to stand in front of him. He was a good foot or so taller than she was, so she had to tip her head back a bit to see his face. Standing so close, she searched his face and was moved by a pain she sensed within him. *In those freakin' save-me sad eyes.*

Like hurt animals, injured people could be dangerous. She'd seen her parents' marriage take a dark turn after the death of her youngest brother. Something that should have brought people together—loss—had turned those in her happy family temporarily against each other in a way they had never fully healed from. There had been a time when she and others in her family had been close, but that was a different life, when they were all different people.

Something awful had happened to the man who stood before her. She'd bet her life on it. And whatever it was, he hadn't healed from it, either. Beyond any attraction she joked about in her mind, this connection to him touched her heart, overshadowing any self-consciousness she felt or second thoughts she had about her decision.

Sarah reached out, took Tony's hand in hers, and gave it a reassuring squeeze. She smiled up at him sympathetically and said, "I don't believe that."

He looked down at their hands and met her eyes with that guarded expression she was getting accustomed to. Just when she thought he was about to pull away, his hand shifted and his fingers laced with hers.

They stood there, saying nothing, the intensity of their connection building until everything around them disappeared.

As much as you want to, don't trust her.

No one is that fucking sweet, that innocent. Just because her hand is as soft as velvet doesn't mean she's incapable of deception. A woman could rehearse those wide-eyed expressions. Which scenario is more likely? That a beautiful, loving woman got lost and ended up in my shower purely by accident and then conveniently had a reason to stay? Or that she planned this entire scenario and is either a reporter or on the payroll of one?

Optimism is best reserved for fools.

So why hold her hand? Why invite her to stay another day? He couldn't justify either action any more than he could stop his heart from thudding wildly in his chest when she touched him. He wished it were a simple itch that a night of sex would cure, but in his almost thirty years he'd never felt anything close to this.

"You probably want to check on your horse," he said, needing to break free of whatever web of fascination she was spinning around him.

Her hand shifted as if she was preparing to pull away. His hold on hers tightened instinctively and she smiled. *Damn. I don't know if I care if she's a liar. A night with her would be worth whatever she finds here to write about.*

Idiot.

He let go of her hand with determination. It did matter. He'd protected his privacy for far too long to piss it away because some damn—though undeniably *beautiful*—woman thought she could play him. "Well, you know where he is. David will show you around the barn if you need anything. His office is in the main aisle, to the left."

The momentary confusion on her face was almost comically kissable. Her chin lifted in defiance and she said, “Thank you.” But in a tone that didn’t sound at all grateful.

A stronger man wouldn’t have stood and enjoyed watching her cute, jean-clad ass strut angrily down the driveway to the barn. Tony barely blinked.

“A woman like that would never be happy here,” Melanie said from behind the screen door of the porch.

I know.

“Is she leaving today?” she asked.

Tony shook his head but didn’t turn away from watching Sarah. She stopped at the entrance, looked over her shoulder at him briefly, then disappeared into the barn.

“Don’t suppose you’d welcome my opinion?”

With a brief shake of his head, Tony turned, strode up the steps, stepped around Melanie, who was holding the door open for him, and headed up the main staircase. It was time he found out what his little blonde visitor was hiding.

Chapter Five

Unlike the night before, the barn was alive with activity the second night. Two young men who were mucking stalls stopped and rested their picks for a moment when they saw Sarah. Another man paused from brushing down a horse in the aisle behind them. They all appeared to be in their late teens or early twenties. Hard to tell much more at the distance she was from them, but Sarah smiled and waved. Just because she wanted to strangle their boss didn't mean she couldn't be friendly.

None returned her wave, and all quickly returned to their work.

"Don't be offended," a deep male voice said behind Sarah. "They don't want to do anything that would risk their jobs here."

Sarah turned and her eyes widened as she looked over the man attached to the sultry voice. *Is every man in Texas hot?* The blond-haired beefcake took off his hat and held out a hand for her to shake. She had thought that suits were sexy, but jeans and plaid were blowing that theory away. His blue eyes smiled down at her. Sarah appreciated his beauty as one would appreciate a painting or a sculpture, but her heart didn't race when his hand closed around hers. She felt grateful for his warm welcome, but nothing more.

I guess I go for the broody type.

"You'd fire them for saying hello?"

"I wouldn't," he said, but his tone implied that others might. "David Harmon, ranch manager." He released her hand and replaced his hat on his head.

"I guessed as much. Sarah Dery. Tony told me your office was in here." Sarah stuffed her hands in the back pockets of her jeans. "I thought I'd come out and see my horse."

David walked with her through the barn to the shelter and paddock where Scooter was. "He settled right in. Most do." He rested a forearm on the top of one wooden rail and tipped his hat back. "You planning a long visit?"

Who's planning any part of this? I'm flying by the seat of my pants, hoping none of you turn out to be serial killers. Sarah looked over her shoulder at the entrance to see if Tony had followed her. Of course, he hadn't. "Not sure yet."

David followed her gaze before meeting her eyes and said, "He's not as bad as people say."

Okay, that's somewhat reassuring and a bit cryptic. I wish I'd brought my notebook with me. I could use that line.

"What do they say?"

David looked surprised. "You don't know?"

Sarah shrugged. "Should I?"

He scratched his square chin as he considered her question. "I doubt it would help."

Not only do Texans speak slowly, they also apparently talk in code.

They both turned their attention to the horse before them. Sarah decided to find her answers through less direct questions. "David, how long have you worked here?"

"Nearly five years."

"That's a long time. You must know Tony pretty well."

"I understand him."

That's more than I can say, so here goes. "He said I could stay until I cement my plans for my drive back to Rhode Island. Do you think I should?"

David didn't answer at first. Then he said quietly, "Sometimes the only way you can determine a good choice from a bad one is by how much you like the person you see in the mirror the next day."

Not really sure that helps.

She let his words echo through her again. *Do I like who I am? Not my nose. Not my expensive highlights. Me. Just me.*

Like *might be too strong of a word.*

I thought I would be more.

Matter more.

Which led to a life-guiding question.

Who do I want to see in the mirror tomorrow?

Someone who made her way no matter the obstacles, here or somewhere else in Texas. Success requires perseverance. Mountain climbers don't let a little rain stop them. Men went to the moon with less technology than I have in my phone.

I can do this.

I can find my story.

Tony stood next to the small nightstand where Sarah had left her spiral notebook. Would she have left it out if she had something to hide? Typically, he would never consider reading the private writings of anyone—mostly because doing so required a certain amount of interest on his part, which he hadn't felt about anything in a long time.

But he believed that notebook held the answers he needed.

Is Sarah taking notes on how I run the ranch? Is she working for a news rag? Why is she here?

He flipped the purple cover open and his jaw went slack with surprise as he read the first page.

Day One

This is what life is about: seeing new places, meeting new people, grabbing life by the . . . and squeezing until it coughs up a story worth telling.

Writers do not fear words.

Balls.

Balls.

Balls.

Big balls.

Hairy balls.

Bald balls?

A question was written in the side margin: *Do some men shave their balls?*

Tony stopped, shook his head, and reread the first entry. A grin spread across his face as he did. He picked up the notebook and flipped to the second page.

House:

Shouldn't use Tony's in the book. Porch is nice, but inside is too barren. Too cold. No one would believe that someone doesn't at least have a television. Don't want people to think hero is boring or out of touch. Visit neighboring homes for inspiration.

Tony stopped. He'd been right that she was taking notes on his place, but not in the way that he'd thought. He wasn't sure he liked what she thought his home said about him. *Boring? Out of touch?*

He read the next entry.

Characters:

Need a better name than Tony Carlton. Something more Texan. Something bold. Holt Johnson? Might want him to be a cattle rancher instead of a horse trainer. Something about rustling cattle is sexier. Maybe it's the rope.

Tony's mouth went dry at the images that last sentence sent racing through his mind. He shook his head and tried to focus on the words on the page instead of how Sarah would look, naked and tied to the headboard of his bed.

Physical description. Hazel/green eyes like Tony's. Eyes that change color in different lighting and with his mood. Tall, built like Tony, with broad shoulders and that perfect butt that looks great in jeans.

Pleasure whipped through Tony, his grin widening as he read that last part for a second time. *She likes my ass. But what does she mean my name is not Texan enough? She'd rather call her hero Holt Penis? That's Texan?*

He continued reading.

Tony is attractive, but . . .

Tony stopped at that word. *But what?*

He scanned the next few lines with less pleasure.

He'd be sexier if he smiled more. No woman wants to sleep with a man who always looks like he smells a rotten egg.

Miffed, Tony thought, *Is that right? Hasn't stopped you from following me around and giving me those take-me-now looks.*

He flipped the page of the notebook and kept reading.

Ridden Hard
By
Breshall Haas

Tony thought: *Who the hell is Breshall Haas? Her pen name? If that title is anything to go by, she'll need one.*

Still, he had to admit that he liked the idea of innocent Sarah having a naughty side. She was writing a dirty book—his little blonde angel. He shifted as his jeans suddenly became uncomfortably tight in the crotch. Short of Sarah coming in and ripping the notebook from his hands, nothing would have stopped him from reading further.

First draft

It's not stalking if you know he wants you.

I park at the end of Holt's driveway and curse the heavy rain that makes it impossible for me to see if his car is there. I consider coming back later, but wild acts of abandon cannot be postponed because of poor weather.

Still, it's a shame that the time I put into styling my long red locks was wasted along with the money I'd spent on the Jimmy Choo crystal-beaded pumps that likely wouldn't survive a muddy sprint to his porch. I regret not boldly driving to his doorway, but my plan depends on him not being home.

I have wanted Holt since the first time I met him.

And now, finally, I'm going to have him.

An arrow pointed to the margin where Sarah had written: *Outside of romances, is that kind of desire for a man plausible?* Tony's breath caught in his throat as a revelation rocked him to the core. *She doesn't know. She is as innocent as she looks.*

He kept reading, even as his cock countered with a pulsing argument for putting the notebook down, carrying Sarah back to his bed, and showing her what she's been missing.

His car isn't in the driveway.

No one answers my first knock or my second.

I shiver with anticipation as I open the door and let myself in.

The clock on the wall ticks away in an otherwise silent hall. Five o'clock. If Holt follows his normal schedule, he'll be here very soon.

I strip off my wet coat, careful to hang it in the closet, where it won't be seen. I wipe the evidence of my arrival off the hall floor and walk to where I know he'll head as soon as he gets home.

I fold my dress and tuck my underwear safely inside of it on the counter in the bathroom. I place my muddied shoes neatly beneath the counter and turn on the shower. My wet hair is cold on my bare back, and I welcome the warm steam that begins to fill the room.

As I step beneath the hot spray, I lose myself for a moment in the sheer pleasure of it.

I jump at the sound of the bathroom door being swung open, quickly followed by the swish of the shower curtain being pulled back.

"What the hell are you doing in my shower?" Holt demands angrily.

"Waiting for you," I say huskily. "I'm a dirty girl."

Tony burst out laughing at the line as he pictured Sarah saying it. A memory of finding her in the shower replaced his humor with gut-tightening lust as he remembered what she'd looked like in just a towel. His mind flooded with images of what he would have done if she'd greeted him that way yesterday.

He wasn't sure he wanted to read the scene she'd written with the improved version of him. He was already painfully aroused.

Holt's eyes burn with passion for me. He says, "Then let me clean you off."

Joining me in the shower, he soaps me down, careful to remove my nervous smell. He rinses the soap away before slowly drying me with a fluffy white towel.

His penis is erect.

I brace myself against the wall of the shower and prepare myself for when he enters me. I know how good it will feel in a few minutes.

Another arrow pointed to a comment in the margins: *Condom?*

Sarah had skipped a couple of lines on the page and then had added to the last paragraph.

I brace myself against the wall of the shower and prepare myself for when he enters me. I know how good it will feel in a few minutes. He pulls a foil wrapper out of his . . .

Notes in the margin read: *Ass? Mouth? Where the hell do people keep condoms when they shower together?*

Tony would have laughed again if he hadn't been so engrossed in her story.

I feel him shudder as he orgasms. The kiss he gives me before he withdraws and rinses himself off is every bit as tender as I had imagined it would be.

Tony read the last part again with a confusing mix of emotions. Why would an innocent like Sarah fantasize about bad sex? Then he read the notes in the margin and anger replaced confusion. The notes revealed:

- I'll need more than my personal experience if this book is going to have sex scenes.
- Is that really how it was? No wonder we broke up. Why did it take me this long to realize how bad it was? What is my problem? Maybe I was born with a hyperactive imagination but subpar bits and pieces.
- Possible spin-off article: "In Search of the Elusive Orgasm." Or: "When to Stop the Blame Game and Take Matters into Your Own Hands."

Her humor didn't distract Tony from the importance of her entry. Sarah wasn't a virgin. Just as she had used Tony's physical characteristics to describe her hero, she was using her past experiences to write the sexual content. He reread her story with this new information and found his fury growing with each word.

He'd enjoy slamming his fist into the face of whoever Sarah had been sleeping with. *Anyone who is that bad in bed should come with a fucking label. What an ass. Sarah deserves better. Way better.*

Angry yet still aroused, Tony read on, and his blood pressure soared to new heights—for an entirely new reason.

First attempt at masturbation—fail.

Tony slammed the notebook closed and returned it to the nightstand.

There is a reason God didn't give men the ability to read a woman's mind.

Too much knowledge is a dangerous thing.

He closed the door behind him. As he walked down the stairs, he saw his house through Sarah's eyes. It was empty. He'd never noticed that before. He'd lived there for five years, and not one picture or painting graced the walls.

It's a house, not a home.

As cold as Sarah described it.

He stopped at the hallway mirror Melanie had hung before he'd forbidden her to leave her mark anywhere in his domain. He looked older than he should have, with deep lines etched from fatigue and sun. He forced a smile to his lips and hated how out of place it seemed on his face.

"What are you doing?" Melanie asked from the door of the kitchen.

"Nothing," Tony muttered, then strode out the front door, angry with her for catching him and with himself for not being able to stamp out the feelings Sarah's notebook had stirred within him.

Just losing my mind.

Chapter Six

Tony was already working with a dark sorrel gelding in one of the ranch's large round pens by the time Sarah walked out of the barn with David. The horse was loose and walking in circles around him.

Sarah paused, and David stopped beside her. "It looks like he's just exercising that horse in circles, but it is more than that, isn't it?" she asked. David pushed his hat back a little from his forehead and rubbed his chin, also studying the scene before them instead of answering her. Tony stopped the horse with a shift of his body. He turned the horse on his haunches with a slight flick of his hand. The closer Sarah looked, the more communication she could see between the man and the horse. "He's talking to him with his body, isn't he?" she asked without realizing she had spoken aloud.

David nodded. "You could say that. Watch him here."

Tony raised his arm above his head and the horse began to lope around him. He lowered his arm and the horse slowed to a jog.

"Amazing," she whispered to herself.

"See how the horse never takes his eyes off Tony? Some call it joining up. Some call it becoming the alpha."

"What does Tony call it?"

Rubbing his chin again, David answered in a slow Texan drawl, "He doesn't talk about what he does."

How sad.

"Will it bother him if we go closer so I can see better?"

A quick flash of a smile came and went on David's face as if he might be enjoying a private joke. "Only one way to find out."

They crossed the distance to the pen and stopped just a few feet shy of it. Tony turned briefly at the sound. Their eyes met in a clash of unexpected heat. The look he gave her burned with promises she couldn't begin to interpret, so intense that she turned to see if it was meant for someone behind her.

Nope. Just me.

And David.

That look had better be meant for me and not him.

Sarah suppressed a nervous giggle.

Or it'll seriously kill my cowboy fantasy.

When Tony turned back to the horse, his expression was angry. His movements were suddenly rigid and the horse turned fully toward him in confusion. He made some small hand motions, then used his voice to urge the horse on, but the horse began to back away as Tony's temper soured. He raised his arm and issued a verbal command, which stopped the horse but didn't seem to improve Tony's mood. He lowered his arm and Sarah heard the echo of his swears.

She looked up at David, who was sporting a huge grin. Despite the growing heat of the day, Sarah's hands turned cold from nerves and she tucked them into the front pockets of her jeans. "I should probably go."

Adjusting his hat to shade his eyes more, David said, "No, ma'am, looks to me like you should accept his invitation and stay for a while." With a nod of farewell, David left her standing there questioning his conclusion.

Really? What exactly gives you that idea?

Tony whipped off his hat and slapped it angrily against one leg as his eyes raked over her again, burning with a desire that sent an answering heat cascading through her.

Oh, that.

Horse forgotten, Tony never broke her gaze as he bent to exit between the metal rails of the pen. He held it until he was standing over her. Sarah looked up at him from beneath her lashes, not bold enough to meet the heat in his eyes head-on. She didn't trust it to be real. Didn't trust herself not to quash it somehow. Better to simply savor the idea of it before reality dashed it away.

His tone didn't match the warmth of his gaze when he ground out, "I know why you're here."

Here? Like right here, mooning over you while you try to get some work done? Sarah licked her bottom lip nervously and kept her eyes fixed on his chin. "Because my friends are unreliable and I have no sense of direction?" she asked helpfully.

He shook his head slowly, both of his hands going to her hips and pulling her closer, close enough for her stomach to brush lightly against the physical evidence of his desire. "Look at me," he commanded softly.

She did and shivered at the intensity of emotion in his eyes. Whatever was between them was sinfully primal and everything she'd wished for but never experienced.

One of his hands came up and cupped her cheek, his thumb tracing her lips with a tenderness that was in direct contrast to the harsh set of his jaw. "I thought you were a reporter."

His words made no sense. Sarah shook her head silently, giving herself over to the wonder of his touch, the feel of his arousal pushing against her. She opened her mouth to defend her reason for being there, but fell silent when his thumb took advantage of her open lips and softly caressed them more fully. Unable to control herself, she snuck a lick at the tip, and they both froze from the shock of the connection.

"I'm glad you're not, because I want to taste every inch of you. I want you to beg to take my cock in your mouth and taste me. I can teach you everything you want to learn." His husky declaration was voiced as his mouth descended toward hers.

Yes. Yes. Yes.

Wait. Wait. Wait.

How does he know what I want to learn?

Taking a fast, shaky breath, Sarah asked, "Did you read my notebook?"

His lips replaced his hand on her jaw, lightly caressing their way to her ear. "Oh yes."

Sarah wanted to tell him that he'd violated her privacy when his tongue flicked at the spot just behind her ear, and she moaned in pleasure instead. His other hand shifted from her hip to cup her ass and lift her more fully against him. Her nipples hardened and pushed at the material that separated them from the rock-hard chest rubbing against her.

I'll tell him later.

Once again he was whispering in her ear. "I want to teach you to come until you can't think, until you can't move, until nothing else matters but having me deep inside you again."

Okay.

Adrenaline and desire swirled within Sarah. It's one thing to fantasize about having that experience with a man you hardly know, and it's another to receive the offer. *And oh . . . what an offer.*

His lips hovered over hers, his green eyes dark with conflict. He growled, “No promises. No expectations. You leave when you want.”

“This is crazy,” she said in a hoarse whisper.

“No, this is what you came for,” he said, and his mouth closed over hers. His tongue pushed through her lips without invitation and swept hers into a heated dance. His hands pulled her tighter against him, shifting her ever so slightly back and forth against his evident arousal. Then he nipped the shell of her ear and growled seductively, “I could fuck you right here, in full view of everyone, and not care what any of them thought. That’s what you do to me. What do I do to you?”

Feeling a bit like a fish gasping for air, Sarah opened and closed her mouth a few times as she sought the words to express this overwhelming rush of sensation. He smiled briefly down at her and claimed her lips in a kiss that erased the desire to speak. He trailed hot kisses across her jaw, down her neck, and back to the sensitive skin behind her ear. He murmured against her cheek, “My little blonde angel, don’t worry, you’ll figure it out. I’ll even show you what you could be doing with those shy hands of yours.”

Realizing they were still buried in her pockets, Sarah felt instantly self-conscious and went rigid with embarrassment. *I have to be the least sexy . . .*

He eased her back a step, but held her as she swayed a bit and shook her head. “If you want to go, I’ll help you find a room in town. Your horse can remain here until you’re ready. He’ll be safe here and you can visit him as much as you like. But if you stay tonight, you won’t sleep in the guest room.” A slow sexy smile stretched his lips. “You likely won’t sleep at all.” His hand slipped beneath her hair and cupped the back of her head, tipping it ever so slightly upward, raising her kiss-swollen mouth toward him again. “Your choice.”

A faint voice of reason attempted to be heard. *He could be dangerous. He showed no remorse about reading my private writings. What else would he do without remorse?*

I should leave.

And spend the rest of my life wondering what it would have been like?

She looked into those guarded cowboy eyes and weighed common sense against temptation.

Say yes.

He'd never been a man who had to ask, but he feared he might beg if she refused his offer. Nature had been kind to him in some ways. Female companionship had always been readily available to him. At the height of his career he'd made the "World's Sexiest" lists in gossip magazines and had enjoyed the benefits of that title for a time. So many women, their names and faces blurred and faded in the years since.

When that life had come to a crashing halt, there had still been offers, but none of them had ever shaken him the way Sarah did with one look. He'd meant every word he'd said to her.

I want her.

Now.

I want to push her to her knees and feel those soft lips on my cock. Right here. Right now. That hot little tongue needs to circle me, inviting me to fuck her mouth. And I will. I'll bury my hands in her long blonde curls and hold her head there while I go deeper and deeper. I'll show her just how to suck while I thrust and she'll open her mouth wider for me. When I come, I want to feel her eagerly swallowing as she cups my balls, begging for more.

I want to lift her up, taste myself on her lips, and fuck her mouth with my tongue while my hands rip away that pretty little blouse and those jeans that are molded to every sweet curve. I want to sink my fingers into her—into that tight little angel pussy. I'll show her what her clit was made for and love her wetness on my hand. I'll take those tits in my mouth and tease them until all she can do is cry for more. When she's begging for it, I'll lay her down and taste that honey. Because that's how she'd be—sweet and fresh on my tongue. I won't stop licking and sucking until she comes in my mouth.

Again and again.

Then I'll raise myself up, sink just my tip into her, feel those wet lower lips welcome me as her mouth had . . .

It was then he realized she was talking, had been for some time. He shifted uncomfortably and attempted to focus on what she was saying.

"Do you know what I mean?" she asked impatiently.

He shook his head and smiled. *Not one damn bit.* Then he waited. One thing he knew about women was if they made a point they thought needed saying, they'd say it again.

She put both hands on those adorable hips, hips his lips were itching to kiss. "This isn't funny."

"No, ma'am," he said with mock solemnness.

"You can't proposition me and then just stand there smiling like it's a joke."

"Do I look like I'm joking?" he asked. The heat of her gaze dropped to his bulging jeans, making his boner jerk and strain for freedom. "I'll admit I'm finding it hard to concentrate on anything but getting you up to my room and showing you just how serious I am."

"Oh," she said, and was silent for a blissful moment before she continued, "I was going over the pros and cons involved . . ." Her words trailed off as her eyes riveted on the front of his jeans.

He pulled her against him again, closing his eyes for a second as a wave of pleasure swept through him. "Give yourself to me, Sarah, just for one day. Let me show you how good it can be." He brushed his lips softly over hers.

When she hesitated, he gave in to a desire he couldn't contain and lost himself in kissing her. He couldn't get enough. He reached down, lifted her up, and settled her legs around his waist, turning so her back rested against one side of the pen as his hands ran over every inch of her.

A glimmer of sanity stopped him before he tore off her clothes. *Not here. Not like this.*

He eased her back to the ground and rested his forehead against hers as they shared a shaky breath.

Take your time.

Savor this.

Because nothing good lasts.

She took his face in both of her hands and searched his eyes for a long moment. A shy smile lit her face. "Okay."

He buried a shaking hand in her hair and lay her head against his chest, not caring that she could likely hear the wild beating of his heart.

She said yes.

Over her head he saw David leaning against the side of the barn watching them. With a circular motion of one hand, his manager directed Tony's attention to the area around him. In every doorway and every open space, there seemed to be a slack-jawed ranch hand doing just what David was: watching them.

I'll fucking kill them.

As if his thought had boomed through the ranch, there was an instant flurry of action while all but David rushed back to their work. David shrugged and with a flip of his thumb suggested Tony move the action somewhere more private.

He's right.

This is not the place for what I want to do. But he knew of a nice, secluded area nearby. "Would you like to saddle up and go for a ride?"

Eyes wide, Sarah asked, "What do you mean?"

What else could he mean? "Get your horse and let's go somewhere private."

"Now?"

He smiled. "Do you have better plans?" It was hard to look down into those trusting eyes of hers and not feel a bit guilty. By his standards, she was still an innocent. Whatever life Sarah had lived up in Rhode Island, it hadn't taught her to protect herself. A better man would walk away and let her learn about her sexuality with someone who intended to marry her.

He leaned down and kissed her lips hungrily.

Luckily, I gave up on being a good man a long time ago.

Chapter Seven

Sitting deep in his saddle, Tony adjusted his hat to shade his eyes and began to question the wisdom of his idea. The palomino beneath him had been chosen at random. All the gentled horses were pretty much the same to him. They went through the same program, and he had high expectations for their behavior and responsiveness.

Sarah was not sitting as calmly. Her horse was excited and refusing to stand still for her. He tossed his head and danced sideways in the other direction. Snort. Stomp.

"You sure you want to ride him without a bit?" Tony inquired calmly.

"I don't like bits," she replied. "Once we get going, he'll be fine. He's just excited to be somewhere new."

Tony held his tongue. He wasn't interested in giving her riding lessons, at least not this kind. He told his horse to move off and Sarah came up to ride at his side, then passed him. She pulled back on the reins a bit and her horse tossed his head in protest. Those little hooves flew beneath him even though his forward speed did not increase.

She leaned forward and whispered something to the horse, which instantly dropped down to a walk so the horses were side by side. She looked up, caught Tony watching her, and the most beautiful blush spread across her cheeks. "I told him that if he doesn't settle down, I am going to get his bit out of my trailer. Sometimes all I have to do is say it."

"You think he understands that?"

"It worked, didn't it?" She patted the Paso Fino's neck. "We understand each other. Scooter likes to stomp around and pretend he's a tough guy, but underneath all that he's a marshmallow and he loves me. We don't need a bit." A hint of his opinion must have shown in his expression, because she pursed her lips angrily and said, "You don't agree?"

He explained rather than defended his opinion. "You're attributing human emotions to an animal."

"You don't think a horse can love someone?" she challenged with a toss of her head.

Her question knocked on a door he'd slammed shut and wasn't about to reopen now. Instead, he fell back on his father's wisdom. "They'll bond with anyone who cares for them, but don't fool yourself into thinking you couldn't be easily replaced by anyone else with hay and a brush."

Those large brown eyes studied him for a few quiet moments. When she spoke, her tone was surprisingly kind. "You're wrong, and I feel sorry for you. There are many things I don't know, but I do know Scooter. And I think it's sad that you train so many and you don't know yours."

"Believe that if it makes you feel better," he said, stung by the criticism and, worse, the pity. An instant later he regretted not holding his tongue. He hadn't invited her out here to argue over ridiculous topics.

Horses were animals.

Plain and simple.

Like most men they were driven by two basic needs: food and sex. Women needed to believe that both species were more complicated than that, but that didn't change the facts.

She turned away from him and they rode in silence along the fence and onto a dirt road that led to one of his open pastures. The land sloped a bit, affording a view of a huge open space that ended in a lightly wooded area. With a flash of a smile, Sarah said, "I'll race you to the tree line." And off she went in a flat-out gallop, her hair coming loose and flying in the wind behind her as she leaned forward and urged her horse on.

It took Tony only a second or two to follow suit. He flicked his reins back, cracking his gelding on the rump, and they were off after her. He had the advantage of riding a larger horse with a longer stride, but she had covered quite a distance during his moments of indecision. He kicked in his heels and felt a rush of adrenaline. Unused to leather snapping on his flank or the surge of energy from the man riding him, his horse gave an excited buck before lowering his head and giving chase.

A sense of freedom washed through him as he and his horse flew across the open field. He vaguely remembered a time, long ago, when he'd ridden for the sheer pleasure of it. Back then it hadn't been about working them or training them. It had been simply this. This exhilaration.

When did I stop feeling this—feeling anything?

They were closing the distance and would have overtaken Sarah when she came to a sudden stop at the first tree.

"I win," she proclaimed with a huge grin, circling her Paso Fino in triumph like she'd just won the nationals.

Adrenaline still pumping, Tony brought his horse to a sliding halt beside them. He hopped down, letting the reins drop with the confidence of a man who had trained all his horses to ground tie. He reached up and, without a word, lifted Sarah out of her saddle and slid her down the front of him, holding her against him, stopping only when her toes reached the top of his boots. She tilted her head to look at him.

He bent his head to taste her sweet lips. She wrapped her arms around his neck and met him halfway. He led and she followed, opening her lips eagerly for him. She was every bit as hot and sweet as he remembered, so he took instead of asked.

He couldn't get enough of her. He ran his hands over every part he could reach, and his mouth explored all her bare skin until he needed more of her—all of her.

He reached down and unsnapped her jeans, continuing his sensual assault as he did.

She arched against him, momentarily pressing his hands between them as he slid her zipper down. When he began to ease her jeans over her hips, she froze.

"Trust me," he whispered, and began to kiss her neck as he undressed her. He hooked his thumbs beneath the elastic of her cotton panties so he could remove them at the same time as her jeans. Shifting his weight, he held her to him even as he pulled the jeans the rest of the way off, easing her sneakers off at the same time. Her blouse hung just to the curve of her ass. *That delicious ass.* He ran a hand over the soft bareness of it and pressed her wet pussy against the crotch of his straining jeans. Her head fell back in abandon, exposing more of her neck to his attentive mouth.

Nature offered him a delightful option. The tree just behind them had two low thick branches just the right height for what he had in mind. He carried her to it and lifted her onto the lower branch. "Open your legs for me," he commanded softly, and threw his hat to the ground behind him.

She sat there at first, her legs still together, on a branch about the height of his shoulder. She held on to the branch just above her head and looked down at him nervously. "I've never . . ."

He eased her legs apart, positioning her calves over his shoulders and savoring the view for a moment. She was perfection—wet, quivering perfection—and he couldn't wait to sink his tongue into her. "Then let me show you."

He waited until she nodded slightly and closed her eyes, then gave in and held her ass in place with both hands while he parted her lower lips with his tongue. She shook at his first intimate lap and he felt a resounding echo of pleasure course through him.

This was not a task to rush.

He explored her with his tongue, seeking out and finding her excited nub. Once there he brought one hand around and used two fingers to open her more to him. He lightly blew on her and loved how she moaned in response. One of her hands was braced on the higher branch; the other was clenched on her thigh.

He took her hand in his and laid it over her blonde mound. "You are so beautiful. Feel how beautiful you are." He pushed her middle finger between her wet lips and guided it to her clit. "Feel how much you like this."

Holding on to the branch above her with one arm, she closed her eyes and moved her hand up and down in small jerky movements. He said, "Look at me." She opened her eyes and he could tell that she wasn't yet relaxed enough to fully enjoy herself. "Did you like my tongue on you?"

Shyly, she nodded.

"Then touch where you want me to lick. Rub what you want me to suck. Pump that finger inside yourself if that's what you'd like to feel me do to you next, but don't close your eyes. I want to see you fuck yourself. I want to share it with you."

Beneath his hand, she began to move hers again. This time she started as he had, by circling her clit. Then she rubbed it.

Awkwardness fell away and was replaced by a rhythm that had them both breathing heavily as her eyes burned with the intensity of her pleasure.

He knew exactly when she dipped her middle finger inside herself, and the act sent a sledgehammer of desire through his gut. He shifted the position of his hand so his finger could enter her as well. She gasped and her eyes widened, but she didn't protest.

In unison, they pumped in and out, and he loved the wild look that entered her eyes when they did. He said, "Now taste your finger."

She shook her head.

He stopped moving and took her hand in his. Her finger was wet with her juices. He licked it, never looking away from her shocked eyes. "You will and you'll enjoy it, but I can wait." He kissed both of her thighs and then sank his face back into her beautiful pussy and caressed her as deeply as his long tongue would allow. He rolled his tongue and used the thumb of one hand to stimulate her while he continued. He went deeper and deeper, withdrawing now and then to blow on her excited nub until she was writhing on the branch in ecstasy.

She tensed against him, then began to cry out, "Oh, God. Oh, God." He held her securely as she started to shake and maintained his intimate invasion until she was shuddering beneath his hands and came in his mouth. Then he lapped at her swollen lips slowly, knowing how to gently soothe her.

When he stopped and looked up at her again, she smiled even as she blushed. "Now that's what I call a prize for winning our race."

He was beginning to understand that she used her humor as a shield. He didn't ease up and let her. Instead, he nipped her thigh and growled, "I can't wait to fuck you in my bed tonight."

She gulped visibly. "I thought we'd . . . uh . . . I guess I just assumed that you'd want to do it right now instead."

He shook his head. There was an intense pleasure in knowing that he'd been the first to bring her the ultimate pleasure, and that he'd guided her toward doing it for herself, but this was only the beginning of what he wanted to teach her. He helped her down from the tree, noting the red marks on her ass from the rough bark. Turning her around to inspect her, he said, "You should have said something if it was hurting you."

She peered around to her backside, then smiled sheepishly. "I didn't notice. It's fine."

He held up her underwear for her to step back into, loving how she braced herself with a hand on his shoulder as she did. "I'll kiss it better tonight." Next he held up her jeans and enjoyed refastening what he'd undone earlier.

Mine.

She stood there as he dressed her, in a flushed daze that tempted him to change his mind and take his own pleasure right then and there. He leaned down and stole one last kiss from those delightful rounded lips before setting her back from him. Her brown eyes widened with a mix of excitement and alarm. His pleasure could wait until there was no sign of the latter. Some men believed in pushing past resistance. That had never been his style. She would come to him boldly before the night was over.

With a nervous lick of her bottom lip, she asked, "What do we do now?"

He reached down and retrieved his hat from the ground, brushing it off on one thigh while noting the absence of one of their horses. "Looks like we chase down your damn fool horse."

Sarah spun away from him to search the field. When she didn't see him immediately, her whole demeanor changed. "Oh my God, he's gone." When she looked up at him, he was temporarily paralyzed by the real distress in her eyes. "I should have tied him to something. I wasn't thinking. This is my fault. He has to be okay." She gripped Tony's arm, tears instantly cascading down her cheeks.

His heart leapt into his throat. "We have to find him. You don't understand. I can't lose him," she said desperately.

Her reaction was extreme, so extreme that Tony wondered if it was about more than just her missing horse—perhaps a past loss she felt responsible for. He understood the second option far too well to be comfortable with it.

If she's broken, I'm not the man for her.

He wasn't the rehabilitation type—not with horses, and certainly not with people.

Her past is none of my business. Even if I want to help her, I can't. I don't get involved—not anymore.

Yet he couldn't look away from those pleading brown eyes.

He called to his horse, which instantly trotted over. He swung himself up into the saddle and reached a hand to Sarah, pulling her up behind him. She wrapped her arms around his waist, burying her damp face in his back. Had he been able to speak he would have told her that most likely her horse had headed back to the barn.

Find her damn horse and tell her to go.

Sex is only going to make this worse.

"Do you see him?" she asked urgently, her arms tightening around him.

He shook his head. He would have said something to comfort her, but her fear seared through years of numbness and unspoken words choked in his throat. Her emotion reached inside of him and pulled at what he'd long denied. Pulled at what haunted his nights and had driven him to this solitary life.

When he'd decided to invite her to stay for a bit, it had been because he enjoyed the idea of showing her how much pleasure she'd been missing. He'd chosen the pace. He'd been in control.

As they neared the barn, he didn't see her horse as he'd expected to and hated the emotions that rushed in. It didn't help that he felt her breasts pushing against his back with each shuddering breath she took. Something that normally would have turned him on instead revealed the depth of her fear and made him want to pull her into his arms and comfort her.

She's here for a night of fun—maybe a week tops.

I don't care about her or her damn horse. He grunted at the falseness of his desperate claim.

David walked out to meet them at the door of the barn.

"Have you seen the Paso?" Tony bit out the question.

David shook his head.

Tony turned his horse back to face the open field. He issued an order over his shoulder. "Send the men to do a perimeter check. I want a helicopter up in the air and every inch of the valley searched. No one comes home without that horse."

In his often irritatingly calm manner, David drawled, "He couldn't have gotten very far. With some on horseback and a few in trucks, we'll find him before nightfall. You sure you want to involve Dean?"

As a tangle of emotions battered him, finding the horse was the only thing he *was* sure about. Spinning his palomino, he was on David, barking out his command. "I want that horse found. Now."

David shrugged. "You're the boss."

Tense beyond what such an event should have made him, he snapped back, "I am." With that, he urged his horse to move with more force than normal. Sarah clung to him even tighter as they surged forward into a gallop. He finally slowed at the top of a small hill that gave them a better vantage point, letting out a long sigh.

"Thank you," Sarah said quietly from behind him.

"We haven't found him yet."

The grateful squeeze she gave him had nothing to do with holding on and sent his heart thudding painfully in his chest. "No, but we will. If anyone can find him, it's you." The faith she placed in him filled him with guilt. She deserved better.

He laid one of his hands over hers on his stomach and said harshly, "I have nothing to offer you outside of what we shared earlier. Don't start thinking this is more than it is. When you find your horse you should probably go."

He felt her take a shaky breath before she asked, "Is that what you want?"

He searched the open field and the edge of the surrounding wooded area as he answered, "No."

They rode in silence down the side of the hill and headed toward the tree line. A helicopter flew overhead. The pilot tipped the aircraft in their direction. Tony directed him to the other side of the woods with a wave.

"I'm sorry that you have to do all of this for me."

He didn't answer her. What could he say? It's not a bother? He wasn't one to lie. He could only imagine what Dean had thought when David called him. The local TV news would love the story, too. He could hear the sound bite now: *Carlton loses mind, now horses. Details on how far this reclusive horse trainer has sunk at eleven.*

Oh yes, he couldn't tell Sarah that she wasn't a bother.

She'd been trouble since the moment he'd found her in his shower.

But, God help him, he didn't have the strength to warn her to leave again.

What did I expect him to say? It's a flipping joy to disrupt my ranch and chase down your horse for you?

He said he doesn't want me to leave, but he also doesn't want me to stay.

What's a woman supposed to do with that?

As she and Tony entered the shaded covering of the woods, she felt another wave of panic overtake her. And as they often did, her thoughts scattered and tangled as she tried to calm herself. *I am so sorry, Scooter. I never considered that you could be the price of a wild adventure.*

But that's me.

I can't be trusted to care for anything . . . or anyone.

It always ends badly.

Tears filled her eyes, making it impossible to see past the plaid of Tony's shirt. *I don't know why I thought Texas would be different. That I would be different here.*

They say you should write what you know.

I should stop trying to write a romance and write a fucking tragedy.

Images of the intimacy she and Tony had shared just a short while ago rushed back to taunt her.

Okay, not all of this trip has been bad.

At least now I know that my bits and pieces work.

If I had tied Scooter to a tree, I could be having mind-blowing sex right now.

Oh my God, I'm a bad person. My horse could be hurt and calling for me, and all I can think about is how I'd like to be pressed this closely to Tony but without all these clothes.

No wonder he keeps suggesting I leave.

I'm a loon.

A loon who may have just killed her horse.

She hugged Tony's strong back and said, "You're probably wondering why I got so upset when we'll likely find him and he'll be just fine."

"No."

Her voice went up several octaves. "No, he won't be fine?"

"No, I wasn't wondering."

Sarah stiffened in response. "Well, that's not nice."

He tensed beneath her touch. "I told you, I'm not a nice man."

Sarah bit back an instant desire to agree with him. If she believed him, she'd leave the moment they found Scooter. But that was the problem: No matter what Tony said, she saw something in him that she couldn't walk away from. Like on TV when people sit and talk to family members in comas, believing that they can be heard even when doctors tell them they can't be.

Tony's trapped inside this gruff man, but that's not him. I know it isn't. You could judge a person by what he said, but Sarah had always believed that a person's true nature was revealed in his actions. Tony had taken her in when she'd needed a place to stay. He'd been unselfish in lovemaking and now was on a full-on hunt for an animal that meant nothing to him.

His tough talk was just that—talk.

Although she couldn't see them at the moment, she could picture his soulful eyes looking down at her. *I don't believe you, Tony Carlton.*

You and I were meant to find each other.

"Thank God," Tony said, and for a moment Sarah's heart soared until he added, "There's your damn horse."

Deep in the woods, quietly munching away on the short brush in the coolness of the shade, Scooter paused and looked up as they approached. He whinnied to the horse beneath them and received an answering call. Tony swung a leg forward over the head of his horse and slid to the ground, turning to help Sarah down.

"He looks unhurt. Does he come when you call?" Tony asked without taking his eyes off Scooter.

"When I have grain." Tony turned to look at her and she said a bit defensively, "It was never an issue before."

With no softening to the harsh set of his jaw, he said, "I could help you work on a few things with him."

Hope welled within Sarah, but she fought to conceal it. She looked at him boldly and asked, "How long would that take?"

Desire lit his eyes and ignited a responding heat within her as she waited for his answer. "Could take a day." A hint of smile pulled at one side of his mouth as they continued to stare into each other's eyes. "Could take a few weeks."

And there it was—an offer of an extended stay.

An opportunity to learn something entirely different from what they were discussing.

A chance to see what was behind all that talk.

All she had to do was agree.

Leaning forward onto her tiptoes, she put a hand on his shoulder and said yes with a kiss that left them both shaking and gasping for air. A part of Sarah registered the sound of a helicopter nearby, but she was too absorbed by the look in Tony's eyes to give it more than a passing thought. Sarah had kissed men before, and certainly done more than that with Doug, but she'd never felt out of control—experienced a desire for a man that was so strong it made everyone and everything else disappear, with nothing mattering beyond the touch of his lips and the feel of his skin.

A deep male voice pulled them harshly back to earth. "You might want to grab that horse before he runs off again. Guess I don't have to ask how you lost him the first time."

Tony straightened with a curse and turned toward a tan-uniform-clad man who, although he looked slightly older than Tony, shared enough of his physical features that Sarah wondered why neither seemed happy about seeing the other. With a noticeable lack of gratitude in his tone, Tony said, "I appreciate your help today." *Now leave.* He didn't have to say the words for his meaning to be clear.

The other man smiled—an action as lacking in warmth as Tony's words had been. "You're not going to introduce me?"

When Tony made no move to do so, Sarah took a step away from him and put out her hand to the tall stranger who, no matter what, had come to help her that day. "Sarah Dery." She noted the silver star on his shirt. Sheriff? Tony had called in the big guns for her. She looked back at him and would have thanked him again, but Tony's expression was stone cold.

He needs to learn how to relax. That much anger can't be good for you. Is it wrong that I can think of at least five ways I'd like to try to help him with that and all of them would require privacy?

Releasing her hand, the man said, "Dean Carlton. I'm the local law. You sound like you're a long way from home. Are you here on vacation?"

Carlton?

Tony stepped in front of her, his aggressive stance a warning in itself. "Like I said, I appreciate you coming by."

Even though the two men looked on the verge of either a yelling match or coming to blows, Sarah felt for both of them. She placed her hand on Tony's lower back and felt his muscles clench with tension beneath her light touch. She looked back and forth between them and felt a real sadness for whatever had happened that neither could seem to put aside long enough to see the other was hurting.

Dean leaned in and snarled, "One day I won't."

Tony shrugged dismissively, an act that appeared to anger the other man more.

Sarah understood their relationship even without knowing the details of it. Something causes a rift between two people, and time coupled with pride only increases it. It took driving hundreds of miles away from her problems, but now she saw them for what they were, and she felt grateful for the clarity she was gaining. It was that growing understanding of herself that made her say, "I appreciate your help, Dean. Maybe we could all have dinner together tomorrow night as a thank-you to everyone who dropped everything to help me find Scooter."

Two shocked Texans turned to stare down at her as if she'd suggested they both wear dresses and do a jig.

"No—" Tony said.

"That's a mighty kind offer," Dean said at the same time, and turned to challenge Tony. "Better watch out, Tony, or your little lady will teach you manners." He tipped his hat to Sarah and said, "I'm tempted to accept just to see if you could make the impossible happen."

"Get the hell off my property," Tony grated.

"With pleasure," Dean answered, and strode back to his helicopter.

Watching him go, Sarah asked, "Is Dean your brother?"

Tony turned his full attention back to Sarah, and she took an instinctive step away from the intensity of his glower. He pushed a hand beneath her hair and hauled her to him. His hand closed on her behind and lifted her onto her tiptoes against him. "I don't want to talk about him. In fact, what I want has nothing to do with talking, but you need to understand something. I'm not one of those city boys who will do what you ask just because you bat those sexy brown eyes. You stay here, you stay on my terms, not yours."

Sarah gulped. Normally she would have said there was nothing sexy about a domineering man, but her panties were soaked with evidence to the contrary. *Domineer me all the way to the bedroom, cowboy.* She rubbed herself against his already bulging erection. *Unless this location would work for you, then I'm totally okay with that option, too.*

His mouth had just descended to claim hers when David's voice announced, "Never mind, boys, it looks like they found the horse. Let's go." There was a small commotion followed by the sound of trucks starting, and then horses and vehicles departing.

Sarah groaned.

What does a woman have to do to get a moment alone with Tony on this ranch?

Hopefully, we'll need more than a moment.

She laughed at the thought, and once she started she couldn't stop. Maybe it was a release after the emotional roller coaster she'd been on. Maybe it was temporary insanity because of excess sexual frustration. Whatever it was, she hid her forehead in Tony's chest and gave in to a fit of laughter. She laughed until tears were running down her face, then settled back onto her heels to wipe a hand across her wet cheeks.

When she peered up, Tony was glowering down at her again. Sarah raised a hand and touched one of his cheeks gently.

He inhaled sharply and covered her hand with one of his own. Then he turned away, took her horse by the reins, and handed them to her. "Might as well head back."

Sarah swung herself up onto her horse and waited for Tony to join her on his own. As they rode side by side back into the open field, she couldn't help but say, "If you want, you can threaten me again when we get back to your house. I thought it was really hot."

A slight flush spread up his neck and across his cheeks before he turned his face away, and they rode again in silence.

Which was a good thing, because he missed the huge smile that spread across Sarah's face.

You might fool everyone else, Tony Carlton, but I'm onto you.

Chapter Eight

A few hours later, Sarah sat in a swing on Tony's porch with her notebook and pen on her lap. After helping her check that Scooter hadn't been hurt by his excursion, Tony had announced he had a few things to do that afternoon—alone. David said he'd headed into town.

Not exactly how I thought our return would go.

She smiled as she imagined them galloping to the porch, both coming to a sliding stop just in time. He'd jump down, pull her from Scooter, toss her over his shoulder, and, taking the stairs two at a time, whisk her into his bedroom.

Not scowl at me and announce you'll be back later.

Jerk.

Texas, you are a big fat tease.

What am I supposed to do? Sit here, revving my private engines and wait?

I hate you, Tony Carlton.

I still want to rip off your clothes and kiss every one of those muscles I clung to during the ride, but that doesn't mean you can dump me at your house like I don't matter.

I'm going to teach you a little lesson when you get home. Sarah's breath caught in her throat at the thought. *Anger is sexy.*

She whipped open her notebook and turned to the first scene of *Ridden Hard.* The scene was missing tension, the building passion of push and pull between characters. No wonder the heroine didn't orgasm.

Sarah closed her eyes and imagined she was in the scene with Tony. She pulled from how she'd felt since she first met him and began to write.

I park at the end of Holt's driveway and curse the heavy rain that makes it impossible for me to see if his car is there. I should come back later. I should wait for him to invite me over, but he's all I can think about. Right. Wrong. It doesn't matter.

I can't stay away. My Jimmy Choo stilettos fall victim to the mud, but I don't care. I step out of them and place them beside the door. The rain has plastered my white cotton dress to my body, the transparency of it only increasing the heat between my thighs.

As soon as he answers the door he'll instantly see my nipples pushing through the wet material in anticipation of his touch. I won't have to tell him how eager I am to feel his mouth on them.

I knock once.

No answer.

I knock twice and eagerly push my long red curls back from my face.

I shiver from the pleasure of knowing that I'll be in his arms in seconds.

Still no answer.

I try the door and find it unlocked. I step inside, leaving small puddles in the hallway. The clock on the wall ticks away in an otherwise silent house. Five thirty.

He should be home, but he's not.

I should leave, but I've come too far.

I step out of my dress, letting it fall to the floor in a wet heap in the middle of the hall. I walk toward the main-floor bathroom and shed my wet bra and panties along the way: a trail of crumbs for him to follow.

And he will.

Holt wants me as much as I want him, even though he tries to deny it.

I step into the bathroom I'd once used for a much more innocent purpose, when I'd attended a party at the house. The shower is just as I remembered it, when I'd pictured the two of us passionately entwined within.

I turn on the faucet and step beneath the hot spray, closing my eyes from the pleasure of it. Even alone, I can feel him with me. I know just how his kiss would feel on my exposed throat. I run my hands over my hard nipples, pinching them lightly and imagining how they would feel between his teeth.

The hot water cascades over my breasts, down my stomach, and tickles the small patch of hair between my thighs. I spread my legs wider, enjoying the warmth of it and imagining how his tongue would feel following the same path.

I run a hand down my side and to my pulsing . . .

Sarah hesitated and sought the right word. *Slit? Vagina? Lips? I can't write* pussy. *Can I?*

She avoided the decision and wrote: *(insert right word later).*

I slip a finger between my lower lips and imagine that it's his tongue. There is no need to rush when something feels this good. I softly run my finger back and forth, feeling my (clit?) grow beneath my touch.

I use two fingers to spread my lips wider, and a stream of water rushes in and warms me as I imagine his breath would. I raise a leg so I can open myself more fully to the spray, to my fingers, to him.

I slide my middle finger inside myself and clench involuntarily. I'm soft, wet, and so ready. I delve deeper, pumping in and out with a rhythm as old as time itself.

I'm fucking myself and it's good.

Oh, so good.

I circle my clit with my thumb, still pumping as I rub. One finger isn't enough now. I insert another and lean back against the coolness of the shower wall as I picture his (penis? staff? cock?) thrusting inside me. The steam of the spray is his hot kiss on every inch of my skin.

I come on my hand, shuddering and gasping for air. Unwilling to end the pleasure, I bring my wet fingers to my mouth and suckle my juices as if they were his. I lick my fingers lovingly, imagining they are his cock. I take them deep within me, deeper than I ever thought I could, and I love how he fills me.

My mouth is his for the taking, and his pleasure is my pleasure.

I clutch one wet breast while I imagine him pushing his hands into my hair so he can hold my head there, ensuring his release is welcomed deeply.

I come again, this time claiming his orgasm as my own.

An orgasm he would have had.

Had he been fucking home.

Sarah slammed her notebook shut, feeling pleased with how her writing was changing—and also about the jab she'd written for Tony at the end.

She cocked her head to the side mischievously as an idea came to her that instantly began an inner debate.

I couldn't.

That would take serious balls, and I'm . . .

See, that's the problem. If I do what I've always done, how can I expect things to be any different than they've always been?

With a fortifying deep breath, Sarah stood, opened the door to Tony's house, and headed upstairs. Instead of going to her room, she went to his and placed her notebook on his pillow.

He'd read her notebook earlier when he should have respected her privacy.

It would serve him right to read this.

Back in the hallway, Sarah leaned against Tony's closed door. She had no idea how he'd react to her latest entry.

But a woman can hope.

She pushed away from the door and decided she'd have to find something to distract herself with while she waited for Tony to come home or she'd lose her mind.

Maybe it's time to call my brother. He's not going to be happy when he finds out that I'm not at Lucy's house, but I'll tell him I needed to stay for research purposes.

Sarah chuckled to herself as she descended the stairs. *I'm not a sex-crazed woman chasing a fantasy night with a cowboy. I'm an author researching my first novel.*

She stopped at the mirror at the bottom of the stairs and blushed at the burning desire evident in her eyes. *I should try to look cool and unattainable, but all I can think is . . .*

Bring on the research.

Sarah squared her shoulders and headed into the living room to call Charlie. She picked up the phone and dialed quickly. *I'm an adult. He's my brother, not my keeper. He'll understand.*

"Charles Dery, please."

"I'll put you right through," his secretary said, so cheerfully Sarah wanted to smack her.

"Hello?" The male voice was crisp and impatient.

This trip was all about finding her voice—in her writing and in her life. She cleared her throat and said, "Charlie, it's Sarah."

"It's about time you called." His voice boomed through the line. "Mom and Dad are worried sick. You were supposed to call when you got there. What happened yesterday? We called Lucy and she said you're not staying with her."

"It turned out that I couldn't stay there."

"She said you're at someone else's ranch? I didn't know you knew anyone else down there."

"You don't know everything about me," Sarah said defiantly. *Thank God.* She covered her mouth with a shaky hand. A nervous laugh escaped. *I can barely justify this to myself; Charlie would never understand.*

The hiss of his angrily indrawn breath was more evidence that she was correct to keep some aspects of this trip to herself.

"Who the hell is Anthony Carlton?" he demanded.

"Who?" Sarah asked lamely. *How does he know about Tony?*

"You must know him since you're calling from his phone."

Shit. Why didn't I block caller ID?

"I'm fine, Charlie. You can tell Mom and Dad to relax. This trip is the best thing I've done in a long time. I'm actually writing again."

He made some noncommittal sound that spoke volumes about his disapproval. "Where is this ranch?"

Please, please do not come here. Sarah reluctantly gave him the information. She knew him well enough to know that he wasn't going to let her hang up without it.

She wanted to tell him more about what she was doing there and how everything about Texas was healing her, but talking about that would mean mentioning the past—and that had always been taboo.

Does he still blame me? Is that why he doesn't believe I'm capable of making the simplest decisions on my own?

Maybe I don't deserve this second chance, but I'm going for it, anyway. In Texas, I don't have to be who I've always been. I don't have to apologize for what I failed to be. Here, I'm simply me. Just a woman on a journey.

How do I make my brother see that?

"Charlie, I need this. I know you don't understand it, but can you give me time?"

If you do, I may even find the courage to tell you the truth.

"I should fly down there . . ."

Sarah held her breath.

"But I won't."

"Thank you."

A flash of movement behind Sarah made the hair on the back of her neck stand up.

"I sure hope you know what you're doing," Charlie said.

Me, too, Sarah thought as she hung up and looked around. The living room and foyer were empty. For a moment there she'd been convinced that someone had been watching her.

First sex-starved, now paranoid.

Just remember, Texas, I'm writing a romance novel, not a thriller.

I'll be fine with just a few weeks of memorable sex.

No need to scare the shit out of me.

This was a mistake.

When he'd chosen Fort Mavis, he'd done so for the acreage of the ranch he'd found and not much else. He'd considered the small population of Fort Mavis, even in the town's center, a perk. The fewer people around, the less there are to avoid. In his years of traveling to train horses all over the world, he'd forgotten the problem with small communities: Everyone knows everything. Instantly.

Bad enough that the afternoon's madness had been witnessed, but the amused looks from ranch hands who normally feared him were enough to set his temper boiling. David had ordered some parts for one of the tractors from the local mechanic. Tony'd hoped that going into town would give him a chance to clear his head. But he could tell by the way people watched him park his truck that the story had already spread to town.

He wasn't two steps out of his vehicle when a group of three young men, all appearing to be in their late teens, approached him.

Shit.

One of them leaned against his truck while the other two flanked him.

There's a reason I hate people.

"What kind of trainer loses horses?" one of the boys sneered.

Without turning to look at the boy, Tony growled, "Get off my truck."

One of the boy's sidekicks scowled and said, "You think we're afraid of you. We aren't."

He recognized two of the boys as the sons of Russell White, a man he'd fired the season before when he'd heard that he'd sold photos taken from Tony's barn to the tabloids. The man hadn't left without a fuss. What was it about successfully silencing one man with a punch that made others want to test if you could silence them, too?

"I won't warn you again." When none of the boys moved, Tony half turned and grabbed the one who was leaning on his truck by the neck, pinning him to the vehicle and lifting the boy onto his toes. He looked the other two squarely in the eyes and both took a step back.

"Let Keith go, Tony," Dean said from a few feet away.

Tony let the kid slide down the side of the truck and released him.

Gasping for air, Keith said, "Did you see that, Sheriff? He tried to kill me."

Another of the boys jeered, "He won't do nothing about it. They're brothers."

Pointing at Tony, Keith said, "When I tell my father that you tried to strangle me, he'll kill you."

Tony shrugged.

Dean said, "We'll have no talk of killing in my town, Keith. The only thing you'll get from your dad if you tell him this story is a butt whupping. Funny thing about trouble is that if you go looking for it, you'll always find it. Shouldn't you and your friends be painting Mary Karen's house? I heard that's what you told your father you needed time off the farm to get done."

Despite the scowl the tallest boy gave Dean, he said, "Yes, sir."

"Then y'all get along now."

Shooting a final glare at Tony, Keith said, "Come on, guys, he's not worth the trouble."

Tony let out a sigh as his adrenaline ebbed. He shook his head and started walking away as if nothing had happened.

Dean fell into step beside him. "That temper of yours will get you killed one day."

Without looking at his brother, Tony said, "You warning or hoping?"

"If I wanted you dead, why would I keep saving your hide?"

Tony narrowed his eyes at Dean. "No one asked you to."

"You are the hardest son of a bitch to like, do you know that?"

"Then stay the hell away from me."

Dean put a hand on Tony's shoulder to stop him. "When are you going to look around and realize that everyone is not against you? Your worst enemy is yourself. This is a nice town. You'd see that if you let yourself."

Tony brushed his brother's hand away and kept walking. "Yeah, they prove how nice they are every time I visit. That right there was a fucking lovefest."

Dean stopped and called after him, "You can't be an asshole every day of the week and expect people to open their arms to you. Those boys have been working odd jobs ever since you fired their dad. Russell's wife is sick. No one agreed with him selling photos of your place, but he's struggling financially what with trying to pay for his wife's doctor bills."

Tony stopped midstep and turned to face his brother. He said quietly, "I didn't know that."

"You wouldn't because you don't talk to anyone."

Uncomfortable with the information he'd just received, Tony grated, "Are we done now?"

Dean folded his arms across his chest. "Almost. You know that girl you have out at your place?"

Tony gave a curt nod.

"The whole town knows what you're doing with her up there. She doesn't appear to be the kind of woman who would welcome that reputation."

A wave of anger swept through Tony. "What happens on my ranch is no one's business."

Dean shook his head. "In a town like this, it's everyone's business. It just seems to me like she's the type of woman you might want to treat with a bit more respect."

"She's nothing to me."

Dean lowered his arms, stepped back, tipped his hat, and smiled a bit sarcastically. "My mistake. Then I guess it doesn't matter to you what people think of her."

Tony strode off toward the garage, hating the way his brother's words echoed in his head as he went.

Chapter Nine

Time is extremely subjective.

A day of lovemaking and excitement flies by too quickly, but waiting for a man to return is sweet torture that the slow tick of the clock on the wall does nothing to alleviate.

I'd write that down if I had my notebook, but where it is promises that I'll have much more to write about tomorrow.

Afternoon turned to evening. Sarah moved from the front porch swing to attempt nonchalant pose on the couch in the living room. She dug a book out of her luggage and tried to escape into another world but failed. As night darkened the windows, she returned to swing on the porch.

With their previous excursions in mind, Sarah had changed into a mint-green sundress with thin straps, made from a material thick enough to conceal that for the first time in her life she'd gone commando. Her flimsy sandals were easy enough to slip off if the right situation presented itself. There was a lot she didn't know about men, but she was fairly certain that after the day she and Tony had shared, he'd quickly forget whatever had taken him to town and come for her.

Figuratively and then, hopefully, literally.

She stood when Tony's truck pulled into the driveway. She was at the top of the steps waiting for him. A perfect moment, marred only by the harsh lines of his guarded expression as he approached the house. Still, he walked up the steps toward her and came to a stop within inches of her. Her body vibrated with a welcoming shudder.

There was a hunger in him that ignited a heat that spread within her. They stood, eyes locked, neither moving nor reaching for the other, barely breathing.

"I've been thinking," he said gruffly.

Hopefully, about what has been on my mind all day.

"Yes?" Sarah replied, just above a whisper.

He opened his mouth to say something, then closed it. "It's been a long day, but tomorrow we need to talk."

"Okay." *Seriously? Talk? Isn't that supposed to be the woman's line?*

"I have to speak to David, then I'm calling it an early night."

Alone.

He didn't have to say the word—it was stated loud and clear in his tone.

Fine.

Some of her irritation must have shown in her face, because he asked, "Did you need anything?"

Salt to the wound, Texas? Between tight lips she said, "Not a thing."

He stepped back and tipped his hat to her. "Then good night."

She watched him turn, walk down the steps, and head for the barn. She wanted to throw one of her sandals at his head as he departed. She fought against the temptation to stomp her feet in frustration.

Tony Carlton, you are the most irritating man I've ever met. I should take my notebook back while I can. Now, before more happens and I toss my pride aside and just tackle you.

In the light of the barn doorway, he turned and looked back at her. Despite the distance, she felt their connection slam through her. She put a hand on the railing beside her to steady her suddenly weak knees.

He'll change his mind when he reads my notebook.

Sarah straightened as a thought occurred to her. *What am I going to wear? This isn't just any night—this is the one I'll base all my future naughty fantasies on. Our first time.*

Sarah sprinted upstairs and stripped. She paced back and forth, buck naked, in front of all her open luggage. *Lingerie? Too eager. A T-shirt? Too casual. The virginal cotton nightgown my parents bought me for this trip?* She buried it beneath some shirts. *Naked?*

Definitely a time-saver.

She closed the luggage and moved it all back to the floor, pushing the pieces beneath the twin-size bed. She perched on the nervously on the edge of the bed, then lay back against the coolness of the quilt.

Too scary.

She stood, then slid beneath the covers and pulled them up to her neck.

Too clichéd.

In the quiet of the house, she heard the front door open and close. She tensed with each footstep on the stairs.

He hasn't read it yet.

I forgot about my hair.

I probably should have showered.

I want to look beautiful, but not too eager.

Then maybe I shouldn't be naked.

In a panic, she slid out from under the covers, grabbed her luggage, and rummaged quickly for a long nightshirt with a plunging neckline. While eyeing herself in the mirror on the back of the bathroom door, she heard Tony open the door to his bedroom.

This is it.

She heard the thuds as each of his boots hit the floor and grabbed her makeup bag. A dash of concealer and quickly applied eyeliner and mascara, and Sarah felt a bit more confident. She ran a hand through her hair and touched up her lip gloss.

He can't catch me waiting for him by the door like I'm desperate.

Sarah sat on the edge of her bed again and cursed Tony for not having even a television in the guest room to distract her. The quiet did, however, allow her to hear him open and close the drawers of his bureau.

Maybe hunting for condoms?

Sarah smoothed the hem of her nightshirt. *Who am I kidding? If he read my entry, he knows I want to be with him. Why hide in a tent of a nightgown? This trip is about finding myself. Being bold.*

She dropped to her knees beside the bed and began to rummage for her lingerie. It was a pink-satin baby-doll set, definitely sexier than what she was wearing.

Dressed again, Sarah perched on the edge of the bed and waited.

And waited.

Tony dropped his jeans and shirt to the floor beside his bed and slid tiredly beneath the cool sheets in just his boxers. If someone had told him that he'd end the day alone while the woman he wanted to fuck rustled around in a room just one door down the hall, he would have laughed.

But Dean was right.

Sarah deserved better than the way he'd treated her. She was innocent and she trusted him, two things that weighed heavily on his conscience. Earlier that day, he'd put aside what he knew was right and found his own pleasure with her. The memory of her orgasm brought him painfully to rock hardness in his boxers.

He could still remember how sweetly she'd spread her legs for him. The taste of her. The scent of her. He'd withheld his own release to give her time to get to know her own. He had told himself he wouldn't rush her, but when they'd kissed after finding her horse, he'd lost all control and would have forgotten his early resolve had they not been interrupted.

She could leave if she wanted. No one is making her stay here. I should take what she is so openly offering me and let her deal with the consequences.

He closed his eyes, and images of her warm smile and trusting eyes twisted his gut. *Guilt is available in abundance without inviting more.* Before coming into the house, Tony had gone to see David regarding what Dean had said about Russell's wife. "You should have told me," he'd boomed at his manager.

David had shaken his head sadly. "A man hears only what he's ready to hear. Russell's troubles were no secret."

"He got himself fired. He betrayed my trust," Tony had growled.

"And paid a hefty price for it. You're one of the few steady employers around. A man would have to be desperate to risk a job in this town."

"That's no excuse."

"There's not a person on the planet who hasn't made a mistake, Tony. Some greater than others. But sometimes knowing why a person did it makes the forgiving a whole lot easier."

Dammit to hell. David had a way of reasoning a man right out of a fit of anger. Tony pushed his hat back from his forehead. "How sick is his wife?"

"She has cancer. Doc says she might have a chance if she goes into Dallas for treatment, but who can afford that?"

I can.

I don't have much of anything else in my life, but money has always come easy.

Tony rubbed one of his temples angrily. "You know that barn we've been thinking about building in the far back?" David looked at him blandly, mercifully not addressing the fact that this was the first mention of it. "We'll need someone to build it. I don't expect anyone to pay for the material out-of-pocket. Give Russell an advance and tell him there's no rush on building."

After a slight hesitation, David said, "I'll call him tomorrow."

Tony nodded and started out the door, then stopped. "I don't want to talk to him about it."

"Understood."

"And I'll kill the first man I hear speaking poorly of Sarah—here or in town."

"I'll pass the word," David said seriously, then in a lighter tone added, "but if you want some privacy, you may want to stop calling for search parties."

Tony had glared at David over his shoulder, but David had merely smiled back at him. The man had a point, but that didn't make hearing it easier.

Lying in his bed, staring up at the ceiling, Tony admitted the ugly truth to himself. *I'm making a fool of myself over Sarah and ruining her reputation while I do it. Nothing matters as much as tasting those sweets lips again. All I want to do is sink my tongue into her wet pussy and lose myself in the scent of her.*

He had some serious thinking to do before he spoke to Sarah tomorrow morning, but there was something he'd have to do first. He freed his erection and resigned himself to another night of easing his frustration himself. He emptied his mind of everything except Sarah and how they would have spent the night if he'd chosen to join her in her bedroom instead.

Chapter Ten

I'm over this adventure.

Sarah dressed in simple jeans, a plain navy blouse, sneakers, and lace underwear. *Oh yes, today is definitely an underwear day. If I had granny panties, I'd be wearing them right about now.* After collecting her makeup and shampoo from the small bathroom attached to the guest room, she placed the toiletries in plastic bags, which she then threw into her suitcase.

I don't belong here.

It's time to realize that the reason I haven't written anything of substance yet is because I'm not a writer. And the reason this trip has gone from the shower to the toilet is because I'm not the adventurous type.

Sarah picked her cowboy boots up and held them sadly before putting them down beside the bed. *I'll leave them behind along with all of my ridiculous fantasies about Texas. Look at them. They don't fit in here any more than I do. How did I not see that?* Sarah turned and zipped one suitcase closed, continuing her inner rant as she did. *How could I have been so stupid? He doesn't want me.*

What about the orgasm? All those hot kisses?

Curiosity? A challenge? After all, he knew that I hadn't had one yet. Maybe he just wanted to see if he could.

Sarah sighed as she remembered the pleasure he'd brought her, then angrily zipped another piece of luggage shut. *Well, now he knows that he can, and the mystery is gone for him.*

Gone like I will be in just a few minutes.

It took her two trips to get her bags into the front hall. She heard Melanie in the kitchen but didn't ask her for help. *Although she'd probably love to help me load up my SUV, now that she doesn't have to figure out how to get rid of me.*

Sarah dragged her large suitcase out the front door, down the steps, and to the side of her SUV, in the shade on one side of the driveway. She didn't bother to wave to the men she saw in the doorway of the barn. It wasn't like they'd wave back, anyway.

How could I have thought that spending any amount of time here would be good for me? With a forceful swing she flung the heaviest bag into the back of her vehicle, using anger to fuel her strength. When she turned to head back to the house for the second bag, she walked right into a wall of muscle.

Tony.

He steadied her with a hand on either arm, but she shook free and took a step to the side to get past him. He sidestepped with her, blocking her way. "Want to tell me what has you all riled up this morning?"

She glared up at him. "No." *I don't owe you anything. I already paid for this trip with my pride.*

"Did something happen?"

Nothing happened, you big buffoon. A big, fat nothing. How can you think that's okay when I took a risk and shared everything with you? Hands on her hips, Sarah gritted her teeth and said, "I have to get my other bag."

He suddenly looked as angry as she felt, but she didn't care. As soon as she hooked up her trailer and collected Scooter, he and his mood swings could have Texas all to themselves.

"Did someone say something to you?" he demanded, gripping one of her arms.

She ripped her arm away from him, red embarrassment spreading up her neck. *Oh my God, tell me he didn't share my stories with anyone. Tell me he and David didn't have a laugh over how pathetically desperate I am. Oh no, there will be no evidence left behind when I peel out of this place.*

As her anger grew, she continued, "I want my notebook back."

Those deep green eyes searched hers. "I don't have it."

Liar.

"Do you think this is funny?" she accused.

Tony scratched at his jaw as if trying to unravel a puzzle before answering. "Maybe if you calm down we can . . ."

That's it.

Something within her snapped. She put a flat hand to the middle of his chest and pushed him back a step. "Calm down? Calm down? I trusted you. Even if you have no interest in me at all, that doesn't give you the right to treat this like a joke. If you don't hand it over, I'll . . . I will . . ." *What do you threaten a huge cowboy with?* Nothing sufficient came to mind, so she pushed him again. "Just give it back so I can get the hell out of here."

He grabbed her hand as it left his chest and held it, pulling her closer until she had to tip her head back to look up at him. His eyes burned with what she *had* labeled as desire for her, but maybe it had been nothing more than the enjoyment of making her look like a fool in front of the men who'd stopped working to watch their exchange. "Let go of me," she snarled.

"Not until you tell me what has you all wound up."

"Really? You need me to say it? Fine." She lowered her voice and glared at him. "I left you a message in my notebook last night. I put it right on your bed. Are you telling me that you didn't see it?"

A glimmer of a smile stretched his lips. "A message? In your notebook? *The* notebook?"

He's not pretending. He really doesn't know what I'm talking about. Sarah took a few deep, calming breaths. *How could he not have seen it? I put it right in the middle of his pillows. Notebooks don't walk away on their own, and we're the only two in the house.*

Besides Melanie.

Sarah angrily stomped a foot. *Score two for the angry housekeeper.* Sarah's blood pressure skyrocketed when she peeked past Tony and saw Melanie standing in front of the porch's screen door.

Pulling out of Tony's grasp, Sarah stormed up the steps to confront her nemesis. "What did I ever do to you?"

Melanie looked past her and drawled, "Tony, call off your girlfriend. She looks rabid."

The snide comment fed Sarah's fury. "I'll show you rabid. If you don't hand over what you have of mine, you'll discover why the North won the Civil War."

In the background, she heard David say, "It's better to let them sort it out, Tony."

Melanie went nose to nose with Sarah. "I don't have anything of yours, but if you think your scrawny Yankee ass can take me, try it."

After a lifetime of peacemaking, Sarah readied herself for her first real fight. Embarrassment about the night before combined with the anger she'd cultivated this morning and swirled through her, making it impossible for Sarah to see past her own fury.

The screen door opened and shut behind them, and a small male voice asked, "Mama, what are you yelling about?"

Not taking her eyes off Sarah, Melanie said, "Go back in the house, Jace."

Oh sure, bring out a kid so I can't slap you.

Wait, Melanie has a kid?

Sarah looked down at the brown-haired, tanned four-or-so-year-old boy. Beneath one of his arms he held the very thing she was looking for. With a mouth suddenly as dry as the Texas desert, Sarah asked, "Where'd you find that notebook?"

Jace clutched it to his stomach and asked, "My new coloring book? I found it while we were cleaning yesterday."

"You help your mom clean?" Sarah asked as wave after wave of new embarrassment threatened to drown out his answer.

"Sure," he said, then he looked up at his mother guiltily. "Tony doesn't mind if I use his stuff as long as I don't talk to him. I can keep it, right, Mama?"

Sarah turned away from Melanie and covered her face. *Oh my God. Please tell me he can't read.*

All aggression gone, Melanie dropped to her knees beside her son and touched his cheek with one hand. "It's not yours, baby. You have to give it back."

Jace hugged his new possession close. "I already drawed in it."

Feeling about as low as a person could, Sarah turned back and said, "Normally, I'd let him keep it, but I can't." She went about three shades of red as her eyes met Tony's.

This is not funny. She glared at him.

His lips twitched with amusement, but he was smart enough to keep his thoughts to himself.

Melanie eased the notebook out of her son's grasp as she promised, "I'll buy you a nice new one next time we go to town."

Unhappy, her son spun and stormed into the house. Melanie handed the spiral notebook to Sarah, all the warmth she'd shown a moment ago gone along with her son. She said, "He won't touch your things again."

Add being an asshole to my list of failings.

What do you say when everything you've said so far has been wrong?

"Melanie . . ."

Without a word, Melanie turned away and entered the house. It didn't help that Sarah noticed she still had a full male audience.

If I wasn't sure what they all thought of me before, there isn't much need to guess now. Sarah tucked her notebook beneath one arm, picked up her smaller pieces of luggage, and walked down the porch steps.

Tony said something to David, who nodded in agreement and headed toward the barn. With a flick of his head, Tony sent the ranch hands scattering.

"Stay," Tony said softly as she walked past him to her vehicle.

Sarah stopped in her tracks and closed her eyes. "Since I can't think of another way to embarrass myself here, I thought I should try a new location."

In a suggestive tone, Tony said, "I have a cabin a couple of hours from here. It's nothing fancy, but no one goes there except me."

His offer sucked the air from her lungs. Sarah opened one eye cautiously. "Are you asking me to go with you?"

Standing before her, he tucked a loose tendril of hair behind one of her ears, and a hint of a smile softened his features. "You could go alone, but you're not real good at finding places on your own."

Sarah dropped both of her bags at her feet and searched his face for answers to the myriad of questions rushing through her. "I'm not ready to laugh about this yet."

He pulled her to him and whispered in her ear, "That's good, because there is nothing funny about what I want to do with you at my cabin."

Sarah sagged against him, reveling in the strength of him as he held her. "You still want me after seeing me like this? I don't normally run around and threaten everyone I come across."

He smiled for the first time that day, and it transformed him from attractive to knee-meltingly gorgeous. "Give me five minutes to gather a few things, and I'll take you where we both want to be." With one parting kiss, he added, "And I'll read your message."

She would have answered him, but his kiss emptied any remaining coherent thoughts. She was lost in the heat of his lips on hers, the feel of his tongue in her mouth. Every place their bodies touched was burning with anticipation.

He left her standing there against her SUV as he sprinted back into the house. Sarah touched her throbbing lips with a hand that shook.

Now that's what I'm talking about, Texas.

I forgive you for last night.

Sarah was pretty sure she didn't start breathing again until she and Tony were driving down the dirt road that led away from his ranch. She was surprised when he took the passenger seat. Yes, they'd decided to take her SUV since she'd already loaded her luggage into it, but she'd expected him to demand the car keys like every other man she knew would have—including her brother.

The mundane act of driving was soothing to her frayed nerves. Emotionally, she'd been all over the place that morning. Her thoughts still hadn't settled in the aftermath of what now ranked among the top three most embarrassing moments of her life. She wished she could claim it stood out as her worst one, but it didn't.

"You'll be on this road for about an hour before we hit the highway," Tony said.

"That long?" she asked without looking away from the path before them.

"And then another hour after that."

Sarah cleared her throat nervously. *That sounds like a long time to think about how wise it is to disappear into the woods of Texas with a man I hardly know.* She sneaked a quick look at his profile. *What am I doing? I've spent the last few days fantasizing about this happening. This is not the time to second-guess myself.* "Have you done this before? Brought someone to your cabin?"

Like Melanie?

Is that why she has a son?

I really am an idiot.

Why can't I turn off my stupid internal dialogue and enjoy this?

Sarah gripped the steering wheel as she chastised herself silently.

He reached over, pried one of her hands off the wheel, and held it in his left hand. "You're the first." He placed her hand on his jean-clad thigh and said, "Relax."

Her hand shook beneath his. "That's easy for you to say."

"It's not, actually. Nothing about this makes any sense, but . . ."

Sarah glanced at him quickly again, and her stomach clenched at the tortured expression in his eyes. *How can I want to ravish him one moment and then the next want to pull the car over and hug his pain away?* "But?" she pushed softly.

His hand tightened on top of hers. "I couldn't let you go. You're all I think about. Tasting you again. Finishing what we started up in that field. No more interruptions. Just you and me and however much time we need."

Oh boy.

He turned in his seat and slowly unbuttoned her blouse, sliding his open hand beneath one of the lace cups of her bra and teasing her instantly hard nipple with his fingertips. "I want to fuck you again and again until I'm all you can think about."

She let out an audible sigh of disappointment when he removed his hand and then gasped when he used it to tug her shirt from her pants waistband with one strong move. Deftly, he unsnapped her jeans. Her stomach shuddered against his hand. He unzipped her jeans and slid his hand in to cup her now-soaked silk crotch. "You want it just as badly, don't you?" He teased the inside seam of her panties, hinting that he'd like to push them aside, but not yet doing so. "Say it, Sarah."

Keeping her eyes on the long straight road ahead, Sarah said, "I want you."

He fingered the seam again. "I want to hear you beg for it. I'll teach you, but only if you give yourself to me totally. I told you if you stay, you stay on my terms. You're mine, Sarah. For this trip. For however long I want you. Say it."

His hand rested possessively over her wet lips, already claiming what he demanded she surrender. This was her fantasy—the adventure she'd never dared to believe she could have. He wasn't asking for forever and he wasn't allowing her to do this halfway. He wanted to be in control, to own her, if only for a short time. Another woman might have resisted the idea, but the pleasure Tony had already brought her made surrendering a temptation Sarah didn't even try to resist. "I'm yours."

He rewarded her by pushing the silk aside, finding her wet clit with his thumb, and circling it ever so slowly until she was rubbing against his hand. "Now tell me what you wrote in your notebook for me."

Sarah froze. "No."

His hand did, too. He leaned over and grazed her neck with his hot lips. "The deal is everything or nothing. Turn the car around if you can't handle it."

Damn him. He wouldn't settle for less than everything. With a flush of embarrassment spreading across her chest and neck, Sarah admitted, "I wrote a masturbation scene."

His fingers began their sweet, sweet torture again. His tongue lapped at the sensitive area behind her neck. "Describe it."

As she did, his fingers explored her, delved within her, played with her until she pulled off the road, parked, and threw her head back from the intense pleasure of it. She could now barely remember what she'd written, but he pushed her to share more, to describe each graphic detail. When she got to the part where she was tasting her own fingers and imagining it was him, he sat back, freed his eager dick from his pants, released her seat belt, and pulled her head toward it.

"Show me."

She did without hesitation, taking him deep within her mouth. Alternately sucking and stroking him with her lips. She'd tried going down on her ex-boyfriend once but hadn't found pleasure in it. With Tony, every touch brought her as much pleasure as it brought him. The breadth of him was stimulating.

Already larger than she'd ever experienced, he continued to grow and harden against her attentive tongue until all she could imagine was how he'd feel in her later. She circled his tip with a teasing flick and gasped with pleasure as his hand fisted in her hair in response. She welcomed him deeper into her mouth, slowly opening her jaw wider until he was moaning with pleasure and she wasn't sure she could take in more of him.

His free hand sought her nub again and her arousal soared to meet his. Lost in the pleasure of her mouth, his touch was rougher, more demanding. His middle finger sought the G-spot she'd given up ever finding and sent her into near convulsions as a new level of heat flamed through her. He held her head and thrust deeper into her mouth. She cupped his balls with one eager hand, then felt them tense and tighten as he neared release.

And still his finger fucked her, in and out, pushing her to a frenzy of writhing against it and sucking wildly on him at the same time. He held her head in place as he came with a deep, satisfied groan. His pleasure was now her pleasure. Heat shot through her, and she shuddered from the intensity of it as she came on his hand.

He raised her head and kissed her still open mouth. When his hand began to move again, she pulled back and huskily admitted, "I came, too." And waited for him to pull back.

He kissed her neck hungrily, slid her blouse off her shoulders, and began to suckle her through the lace of her bra. He eased her back against her car door. His mouth was everywhere as his hands impatiently removed her clothing, both seeking entry into every crevice of her body. Unbelievably, the heat began to build again.

"This is only the beginning," he murmured against her skin.

Half out of her mind, she spoke her thoughts aloud in wonder. "It gets better?"

He chuckled against her stomach, pausing on his path to lick her intimately again. "Oh, Sarah, you have no idea." What his fingers had possessed, his lips now claimed. He parted her lower lips, arousing her with his talented tongue. He rolled his tongue, teasing her outer folds, then ramming it inside her again and again, reaching deeper with each thrust. Wet, hot, and demanding. He ran his tongue over her nub again, flicking it before diving back inside.

Sarah tensed against the door as her body again approached the unthinkable. Laid out before him, she gave herself over to the pleasure, calling out his name as she came and clutching at him as he'd clutched at her. He lifted her and pulled her onto his lap. Spent and safely tucked into his arms, Sarah rested her head on his chest and listened to the slowing beat of his heart as they both came back to earth.

A while later, dressed again, Sarah pulled out onto the road and was shocked when a car skidded and swerved around them. *This would be awkward to explain to my insurance company. I was temporarily in an orgasmic daze. Sure, I saw it coming, but I was too relaxed to care.*

She hadn't considered how public the setting had been until another car flew by, impatient at her inability to determine the speed limit. "Do you think anyone saw us?" she asked.

"The press doesn't stalk me anymore, thank God, so no."

"The press?" *Wow, cowboys are big news down here. Who knew?*

He looked irritated with himself for his spontaneous comment. "I don't want to talk about it."

"You brought it up."

His face tightened with a guarded expression she was getting used to seeing. "Drop it."

Sarah relented temporarily. "I don't mean to pry. I'm just trying to get to know you."

One of his eyebrows raised and he said, "I'd say we know each other just fine."

"That's not what I meant."

His expression darkened again. "Don't get confused about what we're doing together."

Sarah looked straight ahead. Pride made her say, "This is research to me. Nothing more."

"Good, because when this is over, I don't want you thinking I led you to believe differently."

You really are a bastard sometimes, Tony.

What am I doing with you?

Her nether regions tingled in memory and she thought, *Besides that.* "You couldn't be more clear," Sarah said sarcastically. "But then, I wouldn't expect much from a man who won't let a kid talk to him."

"How I run my ranch is none of your business," he said coldly.

Sarah threw her hands in the air. "I get it. I get it. You don't have to take out a billboard." The car swerved into the left lane, which luckily had no oncoming traffic.

Tony grabbed the wheel, correcting their path, and said, "Pay attention to where you're going."

Sarah took the steering wheel back and said, "You weren't worried about that earlier."

One side of Tony's mouth curled in a hint of amusement. "Why are we fighting?" he asked huskily.

Heat spread through Sarah's stomach at his coaxing tone. Still, she couldn't stop herself from saying, "Because you're an ass?"

Too seriously, he said, "I'm not going to change. Not for you. Not for anyone."

"And what if I told you that I like a little ass in a man?" she asked, giving them both an out from the awkward turn the conversation had taken.

Fire leapt back into his eyes, and in a flash he went from defensive to persuasive. "Then I'd say we have better things to do than argue." He slid a hand between her thighs and rubbed her through the material of her jeans. Sarah couldn't think of anything besides how good his hands felt and how soon she could pull over again.

What he thought could wait for the cabin became a feverish necessity on the side of the road. She was already wet and ready when he yanked her pants off and his cock needed no coaxing, it sprang upright as soon as he freed it. He sheathed it in a condom and pulled her from her seat to straddle him.

And slowly, ever so slowly, lowered her, hot and wet, onto his cock. She rested her forearms on his shoulders and threw her head back, exposing her neck once again to his eager mouth. She was so small, so tight. He lifted her effortlessly up and down on him.

The pleasure he'd experienced earlier paled in comparison to how it felt to finally be beneath her, inside her. All his senses surrounded by the sweetness of her. He tried to take his time, but they soon found the frantic rhythm of new lovers. He pounded upward and she ground herself greedily down onto him. When he thought he could go no deeper, she opened herself wider for him and he groaned from the pleasure of it. He was normally a methodical lover, ensuring that he gave as much pleasure as he took, but this time he couldn't wait. He couldn't think. All he could do was try to slow her down. Her desire was destroying his ability to hold out.

The honk of passing cars barely registered. She was his. Completely his. Nothing else mattered. A fire spread through him, so intense he gripped her hips desperately while he came within her, loving that she cried out and collapsed onto him only seconds later.

He kissed her damp forehead.

The siren of a police car pulling up behind them set them both to scrambling for their clothing. Sarah shimmied into her underwear in record time, but was halfway through pulling on her jeans when the officer started pounding on the window. Tony had disposed of the condom in a small bag of trash on the floor and was zippered and presentable even as Sarah double-checked her shirt to make sure it was still buttoned.

"Do they arrest you in Texas for this?" she asked in a rush, seat-belting herself back into the driver's seat.

"I don't know," Tony said, his senses still full of her sweetness. "I'm not sure I care."

The officer banged on the window again.

Sarah reluctantly turned the ignition and pushed the button to lower the window.

Shaking his head at the two of them, Dean said, "If you're going to do shit like this, could you at least do it where no one knows you?"

Fuck.

The mocking lecture continued. "How about over the county line? Anywhere but here. Do you know how many calls I received?"

Sarah met Tony's eyes and shook with a nervous giggle. She choked on the next, and then bit her lip and sounded like she was wheezing as she tried to contain another burst of amusement.

Her laughter was as irresistible as she was, and Tony found himself fighting back a chuckle, too. She caved first and laughed out loud. He joined her until they were both laughing so hard they couldn't speak.

Dean leaned in and said something, but Tony didn't hear what he said and didn't care what he'd missed. He'd never seen anything more beautiful than Sarah, mussed from sex, laughing until she was crying. Gasping for air, she said, "I wasn't sure I could pull off anything worse than this morning, but I think this tops it."

Normally, the shocked expression on his brother's face would have made Tony defensive, but he was already laughing, and somehow the stern expression only made the situation more amusing. He felt giddy. "I promised myself I would be more discreet with you, so no one would know."

Sarah let out another peal of laughter. "Good plan, poor execution."

Dean said, "Should I ask if you two are fit to drive?"

Sarah looked up at Dean and said, "This is not chemically induced."

With one final measured look, Dean banged on the side of her SUV door and said, "I'm sure I don't want to know, then. Just get to where you're going before you cause an accident."

For the first time in a long time, Tony was grateful that his brother was the local law. He leaned across Sarah and said, "Thanks, Dean."

Dean's jaw fell open and he shook his head in amused disbelief. "You're welcome. I guess. Get out of here."

Sarah started the car and as they pulled back onto the road, she pointed to a sign. She said, "He's right. We didn't even make it out of the county."

"You know what that means?" he asked as a wonderful thought came to him.

"No," she answered, glancing over at him, her laughter finally subsiding.

"We still have a long drive ahead of us."

The heated look she gave him knocked all thought clear out of his head. "Good," she said softly, and he marveled at how one simple word could make him want to throw away years of carefully staying out of the public eye and take her again on the side of the road.

Sarah Dery is one dangerous woman.

Chapter Eleven

Tony parked Sarah's SUV in the driveway of a small, secluded cabin. Neither of them moved at first. Tony unbuckled his seat belt but didn't open the driver's door. He leaned back and looked over at her, apparently as relaxed as she was.

Sarah undid her own belt and smiled at him, not rising from her reclined pose. The afternoon sun was hidden deep in the tree line. "I thought you said it was a two-hour drive."

Humor lit his eyes. "It always has been. We might've never gotten here if I hadn't taken the wheel. You're far too much of a distraction."

Me? "I have never taken off and put on jeans so many times in my life."

A smile spread across his face. "I believe that's why man invented the dress."

"Really? You're claiming that one for Team Men?"

"Wear one for me sometime and I'll demonstrate the genius of it."

Sarah shook her head with amusement. "You're incorrigible."

He leaned across and kissed her lightly on the lips. "And you're addictive. Let's go inside."

The kiss he gave her was so tender, so sweet, that she had to remind herself of his earlier warning. This wasn't the beginning of something. This wasn't even the end of something. This was just two people stepping outside of their normal lives to appease a mutual hunger.

Believing for even a second it was anything more than that would only lead to heartache. He'd stated what he could offer her and she'd accepted. *Only a fool would start hoping for more.*

He broke off the kiss and exited the car. Before she had time to even fumble for the door he had opened it and was lifting her into his arms. He carried her up the steps, paused briefly to unlock the door, then carried her over the threshold—like a bride.

She kicked herself mentally for the image.

For once can I just enjoy something without overthinking it?

He closed the door behind him with a kick and carried her up the stairs to the bedroom, where he laid her down on the soft covers of a full-size bed. Wordlessly, he began to remove her clothing.

He paused to admire each section he exposed and then kissed it—more an act of possession than foreplay. When she was completely nude before him, he ran a finger down her jaw, across her collarbone, and then over the aroused nipple of one of her breasts, circling it lightly. "You are so beautiful."

Sarah held her breath. When he looked at her she felt alive, vibrant, and unable to deny him anything.

He continued his soft caresses across her stomach, moving down to tease her legs open by outlining one of her inner thighs. "Too beautiful for clothes." He rolled up her clothing and threw it in the corner of the room. "While you're here, I want you like this."

He bent and kissed the area just below her bared navel. "Just like this."

Tony stood and shed his own clothing before lifting her in his arms again, sliding her beneath the covers, and joining her. He pulled her into his deliciously naked embrace and rolled her beneath him, his arousal boldly nudging against the inside of one of her thighs.

"And what about what I want?" she asked huskily.

Instead of answering, he sheathed himself in a condom.

I should tell him to go to hell.

I should demand he drive me back this very instant.

Tony took both of her hands in one of his and raised them above her head, holding them there effortlessly and then claiming her neck with his hot mouth. With one firm move, he slid a knee between hers and eased her legs wider. He poised himself above her, the head of his pulsing erection teasing the outer folds of her lips. Slowly he moved himself back and forth against her. Everywhere their bodies brushed ignited with consuming heat.

She opened her legs wider, exposing more of herself to his intimate strokes. The length of his dick rubbed up and down her clit until she was wild and wet with desire. He raised his head and stared down into her eyes, still holding her hands above her head while his free hand explored every part of her he could reach.

Then he concentrated on her breasts. He lapped at one while he lightly pinched the nipple of the other. Sarah moaned and squirmed, which excited him more. He moved his hand to lift her ass for his deep thrust. Sarah bit her lip to hold in a cry of pleasure. He took her deeply, each thrust boldly claiming her while sending intense hot sensations through her. She wanted to hold him, kiss him. She struggled to free her hands, but he held them easily.

She gave in to the pleasure of being taken, completely taken. She closed her eyes, threw her head back into the pillows, and came with a shudder.

And still he moved within her. His attentive mouth turned less gentle as he suckled her breast. The hand beneath her ass gripped her and squeezed. Pleasure and pain mixed and brought a renewed passion to their joining. He grabbed her chin and held it firmly. "I told you, all or nothing. You're mine now."

Arrogant bastard.

He withdrew for a moment, let go of her hands, and adjusted their position so he could raise both her hips off the bed. He claimed her mouth with his, savoring the depth of it with his tongue while entering her again with one deep thrust, then another. Sarah found herself spiraling toward a second orgasm. She gripped the sheets on either side of her, turned her head to one side, and cried out as she peaked again, loving that with one final, shuddering pound he joined her.

He rolled to the side, disposed of his condom, then pulled her to him and tucked her into his side. Sarah closed her eyes and caught her breath.

Tony ran a hand gently up her spine and kissed her lightly on the lips. Sarah enjoyed the warm afterglow of the touch, then opened her eyes and met his, drawn again into their green depths.

Which one is the real Tony? The controlling man who makes rules and pushes everyone away, or the gentle, tortured soul I glimpse when he lets his guard down?

Both are amazing in bed, but which one will send me packing when this is over?

And could either of them love me?

As if he heard her question, he kissed her lightly on the forehead, then rested his chin on her hairline. She fell asleep to the sound of his deepening breaths and the steady beat of his heart beneath her ear.

Tony held her to him and tried to sort the day out.

She leaves as soon as I get her out of my system.

Even after their wild ride and his recent release, his cock stirred at the thought of having her again. *It may take a while, though.*

He'd been far from celibate over the years, and he was comfortable with his routine. Sex was a natural function that two consenting adults engaged in without much drama. A leisurely fuck, a promise to call that neither believed, and the occasional repeat if the sex was good enough. Too much sex with one woman led to expectations that he had no intentions of honoring, so he kept it simple and brief.

So what was this?

Even if by some miracle the story of what we did today stays out of the paper, there isn't a person in Fort Mavis who hasn't already heard about it. Was that why I did it? Some primal need to pound my chest and stake my claim?

What happened to wanting to save Sarah's reputation?

A realization sent his heart pounding in his chest. *I wasn't thinking about what this would mean for her or for me. I wasn't thinking at all.*

Sarah nuzzled against his chest in her sleep and he wanted to wake her, to warn her again that her trust in him was misplaced. Instead, he held her to him and joined her in the escape of slumber.

The windows were dark with night when he sat up in bed, gasping for air, his cheeks wet from tears he shed only in his dreams. Sarah sat up and cupped his face in a move of comfort. Her hands stilled when she felt his tears.

He pulled back from her and turned away, lowering his feet to the floor on the side of the bed. She followed him and wrapped her arms around him from behind, laying her head against his back.

"I don't want to talk about it," he said harshly, fighting both the memories of his dream and a wave of shame.

"You don't have to," she said softly, and held him tighter. Bare skin to bare skin, normally a source of excitement, brought him comfort this time. Her acceptance calmed him. They sat there while his breathing returned to normal within her embrace.

Eventually, he covered one of her delicate hands with his own. "You are a good woman, Sarah. You deserve a man who can treat you better than I will."

"I had a good man. We bored ourselves into a breakup."

Tony chuckled lightly, further distancing himself from the tortured images of his dreams. "I never know what you're going to say."

Sarah kissed the base of his neck, then hugged him again. "I'll take that as a compliment." When he didn't respond to her joke, Sarah said, "Everyone has scars, Tony. If yours were on your skin and not in your heart, would you hide them from me? Would you be ashamed?"

Tony rolled onto his back and pulled her to his side again, looking at the dark ceiling instead of her. "If they were as ugly, I might."

While rubbing one hand on his chest, Sarah said, "I killed my younger brother."

Tony tightened his around her, knowing that although she believed that, a woman like her never would have done that.

She said, "We were at my family's lake house. My parents were cooking. Charlie went to ask them a question. I was supposed to watch Phil, but I didn't notice that he'd stopped making his sandcastle. I don't remember which daydream to blame. They found his body a few hundred feet away. He'd drowned. Not a sound. Not a scream. Just there and then gone. He was only three."

"How old were you?" Tony asked, feeling her pain entwine with his own.

"Eight. Old enough to know better." Five words, but they were heavy with years of self-recrimination.

"Too young to be responsible," Tony growled.

Sarah shrugged and shook within his embrace. "That's what everyone said, but I know the truth. It was my fault. I was supposed to watch him."

He hugged her to him. He sought the words that would ease her pain, but he had never found such words—not even for himself.

"Whatever you did, Tony, has keeping it inside made you feel better? Or has it festered? I would give anything to go back and undo what I did that day, but I can't. All I can do is face it and try to go on."

"Go to sleep, Sarah."

She leaned up and kissed his jaw. "Okay, but think about what I said."

He did.

Long after she fell asleep again, he stared into the darkness and thought about what she had shared and why hearing it had touched him so deeply.

Chapter Twelve

Sarah woke up in Tony's arms and froze. Her cheeks warmed as she remembered the drive to the cabin. Normally, she would have said that most displays of affection were best kept private. She and Doug had shared quick public kisses at the beginning or end of a date, but they'd both agreed that more than that was inappropriate.

She and Tony had no such agreement.

In fact, it was a little unsettling to consider what she'd agreed to by coming with him to his cabin. *All or nothing.*

I agreed to "all" without reading the fine print. What if "all" exceeds my temporary throw-caution-to-the-wind-to-discover-the-real-me comfort zone? Desire sliced through her as she remembered how good it had felt to feel so out of control and safe at the same time.

She ran her hand over Tony's chest and followed the trail of hair to his navel. She and Doug had always gotten dressed after sex, perhaps a habit left over from a lack of privacy in college. They'd never slept nude together.

Funny thing to be sad about. I hope he finds someone who shows him all the joys that neither of us thought to try. There was something wonderfully innocent about sleeping together in this natural state. No barriers. Trust in its most elemental form.

I do trust you, Tony. I don't care what you did, I know you're a good man. What happened to you? What can't you forgive yourself for?

She cringed when she remembered how she'd blurted out what had happened to her younger brother. None of her friends knew. No one in her family spoke of it after that summer. None of the family photos included Phil, and there were times when she tried to conjure his face and couldn't. That was when she felt the most guilt, when she could almost forget.

Denial, even when unanimously adopted, never cured the heartache—it only hid it. And pain that is not faced festers, just as Tony's had. *I was living a lie. I needed to come here to see why I'm so unhappy. I don't want the perfect life they crafted for me. I don't want to forget it happened. I want to carry a photo of Phil in my pocket. I want to remember him on his birthdays. I want to apologize to him for not understanding how quickly a life can be lost.*

All because I'm a daydreamer with stories in my head as vivid as reality sometimes. Characters who feel like friends. Worlds I build whether I write them down or not. Is that why I couldn't write? Was I holding myself back because I blamed my stories for Phil's death?

That's not what he would want.

I'm so sorry, Phil. Sorry that it was you and not me. Sorry that we moved on like you didn't matter. Sorry that I'm so tired of being sorry.

Some say that nothing is random. People come into our lives for a reason. Maybe Tony and I need to learn the same lesson. He shut himself away from the world so he wouldn't feel the pain. My family stayed in the world, but locked the pain away.

We've all been hiding.

I don't want to hide anymore.

She would never forget feeling tears on Tony's cheek. She wanted to hug him again as she remembered how he'd turned away from her, not wanting her to see them. Did he fear she'd think less of him?

If so, he couldn't be more wrong.

That glimpse past his tough exterior proved what I've been afraid to admit to myself.

I could love this man—no matter how many times he warns me not to.

Tony held himself immobile beneath the soft caress of Sarah's hand on his chest. As soon as he opened his eyes, he'd have to face what he'd prefer to pretend had only been an extension of his reoccurring nightmare. This was the reason he never stayed overnight with a woman.

Women tended to romanticize shit like this. She'd confuse his subconscious weakness with feelings he simply didn't have. *I haven't felt anything in a long, long time.*

Liar, an inner voice countered. His mind spun with images of the woman beside him. Sarah smiling at him in just a towel. Sarah laughing up at him in triumph when she'd beaten him in a race on her horse. The wonder of watching her orgasm for the first time. The image of her taking him into her mouth on the side of the road, oblivious to everything but them.

That's just sex.

The best sex I've ever had, but not more than that.

Too vividly, he remembered her naked body pressed to his back as she'd wrapped her arms around him after he'd turned away from her. Her gentle embrace had confused and shaken him. He'd wanted to push her away even as he fought the urge to turn around and lose himself in her kisses.

He didn't want to know about her brother or her past. She was under the misconception that sharing would get him to open up to her. He was angry.

She's a good fuck, not a therapist. Want to make me feel better? Talk less, suck more.

Cuddled to his side, Sarah kissed his shoulder lightly, and Tony's dick sprang to life, tenting the sheet. His heart thudded wildly in his chest. *I need to regain control of this situation, of myself.*

He rolled on top of her, pinning her hands beneath his on either side of her head. Her eyes widened with surprise and pleasure. "I've been thinking about how I want to spend the day with you." He spread her legs beneath him and loved how wet she instantly became against his seeking cock. Her breaths increased as her arousal intensified. He rubbed himself against her outer lips and said, "And none of it includes speaking."

Sarah opened her mouth to say something, and he covered it with one hand. "I'll tie and gag you if I have to. Or is that what you want? You want me to find some rope and restrain you on this bed? Have you ever done that before, been laid out spread-eagle for a man's pleasure whenever he wanted?" She didn't try to speak, but they both knew the answer. He kissed her neck and whispered, "Face up or down, both have benefits." A look of apprehension entered Sarah's eyes and she shook her head. "You may find that you enjoy it more than you think."

She shook her head again and he smiled in concession. "Understood." Those beautiful brown eyes stared up at him, desire overtaking her fear, and he felt bad for teasing her. "I don't need more than you willingly give, angel. Today is about pleasure, for both of us. That's why you're not allowed to speak."

Her eyes narrowed and he laughed. "Take it or leave it. Stay on my terms, or say the word and I'll drive you back to the ranch. You can call your boring ex to pick you up."

Sarah's chest heaved angrily. Tony was pretty sure those lovely brown eyes cursed at him, but he didn't care. She wasn't going anywhere, and they both knew it.

He removed his hand from her mouth. "So, are you staying or going?"

She pressed her lips together angrily, but didn't say a word.

He rewarded her obedience with a deep kiss and reveled in the heat her anger brought to it. She was on fire beneath him, and he soon lost himself in more than her kiss.

An hour later, Sarah shivered beneath Tony's finger as it absently traced one of her nipples, marveling at how it hardened and sprang to life for him. She'd had more sex in the past twenty-four hours than she normally had in months, and somehow she was ready for more.

She blushed as she remembered how wantonly, wordlessly, she'd begged him to enter her after a torturous amount of foreplay. His fingers had teased what his mouth had gloriously tasted and suckled later. He'd brought her to a passionate frenzy, then kissed her back and neck while rubbing his rock-hard dick across her clit from behind.

Faced away from him on all fours, she'd lifted her ass for him, opening herself completely to him with a mix of desire and trust. He'd buried one hand in the back of her hair to hold her in place while he'd thrust into her, again and again until they both found release in a glorious explosion of sensation.

They'd collapsed into each other's arms.

Normally, Sarah would have chattered about something to fill the silence, but she honored their agreement and kept her thoughts to herself. Instead of being awkward, the quiet seemed to extend their intimacy.

Which doesn't mean I agree with his rule, but I'll give him his day of silence. It's better than the alternative: going back to Fort Mavis.

Besides, he doesn't fool me.

He doesn't like to talk because he thinks that he can't get hurt if he doesn't let anyone close.

He's trying to control whatever is between us.

But he can't any more than I can.

The only disappointment so far is he hasn't got the rope.

She gurgled to hold in a laugh, and he looked down at her in question. She smirked up at him. *I'd tell you, but you won't let me speak.*

"There's food in the kitchen. Go make us breakfast, but stay naked."

Sarah cocked her head to one side at him. *Really? You're enjoying this a bit too much, buddy.*

He slapped her bare rump with a force that made her jump. She met his eyes again and opened her mouth to say something.

His eyes dared her to.

She snapped her mouth shut. *I'll make your damn breakfast, but I'll also remember this. You'll be at my mercy one day, and I'll enjoy every moment of making you pay.*

She stood near the bed, stretched her arms out, and arched her back in a yawn, loving how quickly burning desire replaced all smugness in his face. *Oh yeah, you can pretend to be in control all you want, but I know the truth.*

She took her time crossing the room to the door, stopping to look over her shoulder at him. He didn't attempt to hide how aroused he was. She smiled back at him.

Times like this make me wish I knew how to cook.

The kitchen was surprisingly well stocked considering he'd said he never came here. *No, wait. He said he never brought anyone else here. He could come here all the time for all I know. Does he have help cleaning? Buying groceries?*

More questions for after the silence game.

Sarah took two pieces of bread and put them in a toaster oven. *Who doesn't have a regular toaster?* The dials offered too many choices. *Temp. Timer. All levels of toast darkness. I just want to press a lever down and see toast when it's done.* She turned the dial for toast halfway and walked to the refrigerator.

In movies, everyone knows how to whip up sophisticated postsex omelets. Tony would have to deal with simpler thanks-for-the-orgasms scrambled eggs. She preheated the pan, searched for non-stick spray, then settled on a pat of butter to stop the eggs from sticking.

As her confidence grew, Sarah began to hum a pop tune and dance, loving how free and uninhibited she felt. *I could get used to cooking naked. This is fun.*

She navigated his coffee machine with relative ease, danced her way over to save the slightly burned toast, and hummed her way to the quickly cooking eggs. *Crap, my mom always added milk. Is it too late?* She poured a bit in the pan and wrinkled her nose when the milk and eggs didn't mix.

Oh well. I'll drain it.

A hunt through the cabinets below the sink produced a serving tray. Sarah placed two plates of food, some silverware, and two cups of coffee on it. She added a small bit of milk and sugar to hers and hesitated before adding any to his, then smiled mischievously.

I'd ask him how he likes his coffee, but oh damn, that silence thing again.

She gleefully added three teaspoons of sugar to his cup. It was difficult not to laugh at his expression when she approached the bed and placed the tray on his lap. He studied the burnt toast and the watery eggs and demanded, "Did you do this on purpose?"

Sarah pointed to her closed mouth and gave him a sarcastic wish-I-could-tell-you shrug.

He took a sip of the coffee and spit it out, glowering at her.

Oh, poor baby. I guess you don't like it sweet.

When he put the tray to one side, she stepped away from the bed instinctively and sprinted toward the door. He moved with the swiftness of a hunter and blocked her retreat. He reached out to grab her, but Sarah beat him to the punch and threw herself in his arms, leaving him no choice but to catch her. She wrapped her arms around his neck and pulled his mouth down to hers. The heat that sprang between them rocked all thought out of her.

He lifted her by the waist and crushed her hungrily against the wall. Without clothing to remove, there was just the instant feel of their mutual excitement. "God," he said against her neck, "what are you doing to me?"

Sarah silenced his question with another deep kiss and let her actions be her answer. She wrapped her legs around his waist and arched to give him access to all of her, which he quickly and extensively took advantage of.

When he finally rammed inside her, it was without comment, control, or a condom. Just when Sarah thought it couldn't get better, she felt the unobstructed intimacy of him bared, and the heat of his release within her.

He kept pumping after his release so she could have hers and then carried her back to the bed. He sat her on the uncluttered side of the bed and covered his face with his hands. "Tell me you're on birth control."

Sarah stood and placed a hand on his tense arm. "I am," she said softly.

His muscles quivered beneath her touch and he shook his head, fighting some inner demon. "I'm sorry."

"It's fine. I'm an adult, Tony. This is just as much my responsibility as it is yours."

"It can't happen again. I don't want children—ever."

Ouch. After the initial desire to slap him passed, Sarah tossed back a barb of her own. "Because you'd have to talk to them, right?"

When he didn't say anything, she lowered her hand and shook her head.

Wordlessly, he walked to his pile of clothes and started getting dressed. "Bringing you here was a mistake."

Arms akimbo, Sarah waited for him to turn around. When he did, she stood there, still proudly nude before him. *He might be afraid, but I'm not.* "I'm not running away from this. I'm choosing life—all of it, the good, the bad, the scary parts. I'm done hiding."

His face tightened with anger. He growled, "What do you want from me?"

In that desperate question, she heard what kept her heart open to him. She understood his pain and his journey in a way she doubted many others could. Giving up on him was like giving up on herself in a tangled, impossible-to-explain-even-to-herself way. "I want you to tell me whatever it was that made you like this. I want to know you."

Their eyes clashed across the short distance between them.

When he spoke, his harsh tone was in direct contrast to his words. "Get dressed, then, because I doubt we'll get much talking done with you standing there like that."

Sarah turned her face to the side and hid a smile behind her hair. *Score one for the Yankee.* She quickly slipped into her clothing and went to stand next to him, boldly taking his hand in hers.

He turned away and walked out the door, but his hand tightened on hers as he dragged her behind him down the steps and out into the bright late-morning sunshine. They walked together down a rugged path that made Sarah glad she'd chosen to wear sneakers instead of boots. He stopped when they reached a small clearing that boasted a crystal-clear mountain stream.

"This is where I come when I need to think . . . or forget."

Tony let go of her hand and picked up a rock to throw angrily into the stream. "You know that feeling you get when you first start driving a car on your own? At first you're nervous, then you get more and more confident until you feel invincible. That's how I'd describe my career until about five years ago. I came from nothing, you know? No one expected anything from me. I moved out of my father's house at sixteen. I was working on a cattle ranch when I won a green horse in a poker game. The ranch owner let me keep him at his place and watched me work with him. Pretty soon, he had me training all his horses. I quickly gained a reputation for taking horses from green to champion in everything from racing to the rodeo circuit. People wanted to see what I did, so I booked shows at expos and fairs. Before long, I was getting offers to work with high-profile horses. Some went on to win their owners millions."

Sarah joined him by the water and simply listened.

"The money came fast and easy after that. Rich people like to win. It made for a very profitable exchange. By the time I was in my early twenties, I was getting jobs all over the world. Racehorses. Barrel racers. The foundation is the same. A willing horse can be taught anything. I've always been able to bring a level of trust out in a horse that others couldn't."

"Because you care about them," Sarah said.

"No, because I understand them. I always have. It's not something I can put into words."

Sarah wanted to ask more about the topic, to debate his claim about not caring, but she was afraid he'd shut down if she did. She let him tell his own story, at his own pace.

"People said there wasn't a horse I couldn't gentle, and I started to believe my own press. I met a family with a teenage daughter as headstrong as any animal I'd ever met. She had bought a Canadian warmblood. A seventeen-hand gray stallion with a dangerous reputation and a violent past. There were all sorts of rumors where that horse had been, but whoever had abused him, they hadn't left a mark. He was stunning and enough of a challenge that he was exciting. I accepted their money and never doubted that I could fix that horse."

His face whitened as he continued. "I thought I had him ready for her. I was blinded by my own confidence. Something in him was broken in a place I couldn't reach, but I couldn't see it. I told them he was safe. I told her father she'd be fine. For a while, I was right. Near the end of their first riding season, someone was lunging a horse in the same ring and cracked a whip against it. I don't know what that stallion had seen or endured, but it came back to him with a vengeance. Those who were there said he went wild. He threw her and, before anyone could stop him, he stomped her to death."

Tony threw another rock into the water. "I knew he was dangerous, but I thought I was gifted. I'm not. I'm cursed. She was only sixteen."

Sarah whispered, "What happened after that?"

Tony closed his eyes. "The father took me to court. I hired some fancy lawyer who told me that any apology would be an admittance of guilt and I could go to jail." He opened his eyes and the depth of his remorse was almost unbearable to witness. "We won the case and the court documents say I wasn't guilty, but I know the truth. I am guilty, and I never did tell the father that I was sorry."

Sarah wrapped her arms around his waist and held him tightly. *I understand, oh, so much more than you know.* It was because of that understanding that she knew there wasn't anything she could say right then that he'd be able to hear. So she held her tongue and gave him another piece of her heart.

The questions Tony braced himself for didn't come, and the sincerity of the hug she gave him robbed him of further speech. She wasn't demanding that he give more, nor was she smothering him with pity. In her embrace, he felt understood and accepted.

And it was more terrifying than any nightmare he'd ever had.

He put an arm around her waist and rested his chin on top of her head, releasing a shaky breath as he did. Outside of initial lawyer consultations and his testimony in court, he'd never spoken of that time in his life. People had thrown accusations his way, both in private and in public, but he'd never defended himself.

There was no defense for what he'd done. He'd been young and cocky. Then young and afraid. If either of those combinations were a valid excuse, prisons would be less full.

At first he'd tried to weather the character flogging he received in the press. Everywhere he turned, there was a reminder of what he'd done, who he'd hurt, what he'd taken from the planet. The news played the story over and over until there wasn't a person on the street who didn't stop to talk to him about it. It didn't matter if they were damning him to hell or excusing what he'd done, each encounter left him feeling raw and filled with a guilt so intense he'd considered taking his own life to even the score.

So he'd bought the Double C and retreated there. Drinking heavily and eating next to nothing, Tony probably wouldn't have lasted long had David not wandered onto his property. The memory of their initial meeting was muddled by the drunken haze of his first months on the ranch, as were the details of exactly how David had become Tony's manager. Had David bought the first horses with his own money or Tony's? He couldn't remember. They'd just started appearing.

At first David had worked them while Tony continued to binge drink, deliberately ignoring the changes at his own ranch. Eventually, boredom, curiosity, or both had driven Tony to watch David train.

Then to work with a horse on his own. Before long, working with the horses replaced drinking, and he and David came to an agreement. Tony didn't want to meet prospective buyers or hear about the horses after they left his ranch. David could hire whomever he thought necessary to keep the ranch running smoothly, as long as they respected Tony's privacy and kept their distance from him.

Somewhere along the way, anger replaced fear. Indifference replaced regret. He found peace in the distance he placed between himself and those around him.

Peace everywhere except in those fucking dreams.

And now with Sarah.

Nothing in his life had prepared him for the whirlwind of his little blonde intruder. Pushing her away was about as easy as trying to stop high tide with a spoon. She played by her own rules and challenged every one of his.

For the first time in years, he felt something besides anger, and part of him hated her for it.

She thinks she can save me. She's too innocent to understand that some people, like some animals, are damaged beyond redemption.

Hand in hand, they walked back to the cabin. Tony asked, "Do you need anything from inside before we leave?"

Those dark brown eyes searched his face before she nodded. He opened the door, fighting temptation and winning by the merest margin.

Sarah closed the door and pulled her shirt off over her head. Her bra followed. His jaw fell open a bit as she stepped out of her shoes and the rest of her clothing. What normally would have been an act of seduction was charged with a different emotion. "I saw a deck of cards in the kitchen. I've never played cards naked. Have you?"

He shook his head wordlessly.

"Want to play?"

A man didn't need to be asked that question twice. Tony stripped bare and, despite his arousal, went to retrieve the deck of cards. They sat across from each other on the rug in the living room. He shuffled the cards and asked, "What do you know?"

She smiled at him and blushed. "I don't mind learning something new."

He caught her double meaning but asked a safer question. "Have you ever played poker?"

"No, but I've always felt that I would be good at it. Maybe I was a cardsharp in a past life."

He couldn't help but return her smile as he dealt. "I didn't bring much cash with me." He fished out some dollar bills and change from his jeans pocket.

"Let's play for something more valuable than that."

He didn't try to guess what she wanted, because there was really no way of knowing with her. "Such as?"

She sat straighter and crisscrossed her legs, giving him an unbelievably distracting view that sent his blood pounding southward. "Time. Each one of those quarters can be an hour and every dollar could be a day. The winner gets to choose what we do with that time. You could win a few more hours of silence." The teaser at the end was unnecessary because he'd already lost the ability to do anything but agree to whatever she suggested. When he didn't respond, she prompted, "I have no idea how to play, though, so we will have to speak."

She listened intently as he explained the game, and he was torn between throwing his cards down and taking her again and again until his fascination with her ebbed and demanding that they end the game now, before it was too late.

Don't trust me, Sarah.

People don't change.

I don't want to be the one to teach you that harsh lesson, but God forgive me, I can't stay away from you, either.

She won six days and three hours from him, which was all the money he'd brought, but he conceded to himself that his attention had been divided. He expected her to gloat when she pulled the last of the winnings to herself, but she didn't. He waited for her terms, certain that they would exceed what he would honor.

She counted the days on her fingers and said, "Six days. That brings us to Tuesday."

He hated that he had to know. Hated that he couldn't charge forward as uninhibited as she'd been since the moment he'd met her. "Six days of what?" he demanded.

She smiled at him gently and shrugged. "Of whatever we want to do, but let's stay here at the cabin."

"We have to go back eventually," he said gruffly, not wanting her to know how much he wanted those extra days alone with her.

"I know," she said a bit sadly. "But we don't have to go today."

Six days and three hours.

He could give her that.

All seriousness fell away as a huge smile spread across her face and she announced, "And we stay naked!"

He raised one eyebrow at her. "Are you a nudist now?"

She shrugged those beautiful shoulders again and said, "No, but I may have been one in a past life, because I would love to play Ping-Pong like this."

The image of the two of them attempting such a feat made him chuckle and then give in to a hearty laugh. "I don't have anything like that here."

"Well, who stocks your food? Maybe they could drop a few games by."

"I can think of better ways to occupy our time," he said suggestively.

She placed her hands on her hips, lifting those lovely breasts up and down with the move and countered, "You're just afraid you'll lose again."

He stood up, walked to the phone, and called the man who lived a mile or so away and cared for the cabin. "Carl, I need you to pick up a few things for me in town. You may have to go to Dallas to get some of them, but I'll make it worth your while." Although Carl was an older gentleman, Tony knew he had sons living with him who could help. "Leave everything in the driveway. I'm here for about a week, but I don't want to be disturbed."

The old man cackled loud enough that Tony held the phone away from his ear for relief. "You finally brought one of your lady friends with you, have you? I'll tell my boys to be real discreet-like. Now what do you two lovebirds need?"

On any other day, with anyone besides Sarah looking sweetly up at him, he would have told Carl what he could do with his sense of humor. Instead, Tony gritted his teeth and said, "I'd like a Ping-Pong set. You know the ones you can put on top of a table?"

Carl said, "I'm sorry. I have an old man's hearing. Did you just say *Ping-Pong*?"

It didn't help Tony's mood that Sarah heard his question and was covering her mouth to stop from laughing.

She jumped to her feet, a movement so tantalizing that it temporarily wiped all coherent thought from Tony, and gripped his arm. "And backgammon—I love that game. Oh, and Monopoly?"

Carl lowered his voice and said, "Son, if your lady friend is that bored, you may want to meet me in the driveway for a bit of advice. Never too late to learn a few tricks."

Tony covered his eyes with one hand and groaned. "I appreciate that, Carl, but just bring the games."

"Your call, Tony. The offer stands, though. I've been married over fifty years. I know a thing or two about the workings of the female mind." When Tony didn't acknowledge his offer with a response, Carl said, "I should have the stuff by tomorrow. Until then, don't be afraid to get a bit more creative. There's no shame in asking a woman what she wants."

Tony hung up the phone and turned to Sarah. "He thinks I've bored you into seeking alternative recreation."

Sarah ran a hand playfully down his arm. "Poor Tony, do you want me to call him back and reassure him that I'm completely satisfied?"

Tony caught her hand beneath his and held it. "No, but I have to warn you that I've never enjoyed playing games, Ping-Pong or any other type."

The impish grin she gave him sent his heart racing in his chest. "That's because you've never played them naked."

He conceded that point. He'd always enjoyed poker, but today was the first time he hadn't minded losing. The idea of watching Sarah's lovely breasts bounce as she leapt to make a shot or glimpsing her delightful ass bent over as she retrieved a stray ball was beyond tempting—creating a fantasy that rocked his control.

Familiarity normally lessened his desire. Sarah was different. The more he was with her, the more he wanted to be. He hoped to God six days would be enough to change that. For now, he had another fantasy to address. "The games won't be here until tomorrow, but I'm pretty sure I have some rope around here somewhere."

Instead of looking nervous as he'd expected, she said, "I've always wanted to tie a man to a bed and have my way with him."

He shook his head. "I'd never let that happen."

She raised herself up on her tiptoes and wiggled her eyebrows at him. "Is that a dare?"

He tried to look down at her sternly, but the evidence of his arousal sprang to life between them, making it difficult to argue that the idea had no appeal to him. "It's a fact."

Sarah leaned forward until her nipples brushed his chest. She took his throbbing dick in one hand and caressed it while she pulled his head down to whisper in his ear. "I've always dreamed of being in control just once. I'd rub my body all over you and take things at a slow pace. Instead of enjoying your hands on me, I'd lick every inch of your body. I'd take you in my mouth and bring you to the brink and then, only then, I'd let you taste me. They say that a postponed orgasm is a stronger one. I'd test that theory. I'd bring you close again and again, taking my orgasms but delaying yours until you couldn't take it anymore. You'd threaten me, beg me, want to drag me on top of you, but still I'd make you wait. Then, when we're both in a place where neither of us could wait a second longer, I'd lower myself on your . . ." She paused over her word choice, and he smiled despite how excited she'd made him.

"Cock," he suggested. "You'd lower yourself on my cock."

Her hand tightened on him and she echoed the word in a whisper. "Cock."

The mixture of innocence and siren drove him wild. He jerked and almost came in her hand, cursing that he could be so close so soon. "I'll go get the rope," he said in a rush, stumbling a bit as he stepped back from her. She'd done it again, bulldozed through what he considered a nonnegotiable line in the sand.

Some things were worth keeping an open mind about, though.

And he was sure there wasn't a man alive who wouldn't agree with him.

Chapter Thirteen

A few days later, Sarah catnapped beside Tony on the couch, snuggled beneath a light comforter. Time was passing too quickly—a blur of showering together between games they often didn't finish because one of them lost patience and leaned in for a heated kiss that would lead them both astray.

Although Sarah had left her notebook in the car, she knew that when she returned to it, her writing would be stronger. Plus, she wasn't worried that she would forget the wonder of one kiss, one touch, or a single moment they'd spent together.

Especially the unexpected revelations.

Even days filled with passion and laughter can be enhanced by the use of a toothbrush and a dash of deodorant. I'll leave that tidbit out of my romance. No one will want to hear about how fast the heroine's leg stubble can grow or that unsuccessful attempts to pretend she can cook may lead to a condition called "the nervous fart that must be held in at all costs."

If romances were a bit more realistic, I may have looked less maniacal about the latter discovery.

One definite perk of remaining unpredictable with Tony was that he didn't question her need to do a naked, solo, outdoor lap around the house before they had sex the night before. She'd waited for him to ask, but he hadn't.

Smart man.

She closed her eyes and chuckled as she remembered the contents of the care package Carl had left along with the supplies they'd ordered: a huge box of condoms, all the fixings to make an ice-cream sundae except the ice cream, and vitamins. She and Tony had burst out laughing at the sight of the last item, but decided not to question the wisdom of a self-proclaimed expert.

When she opened her eyes, she found Tony watching her.

"What do you do for your parents' business?" he asked, surprising her. They had avoided personal questions since their talk near the stream.

"I file, bill people, set up appointments."

"You like it?"

"I hate it."

"I didn't take you for someone who would tolerate doing something you didn't like for very long."

"You'd be surprised. But I'm working on that. That's what this trip is about—figuring out what I really want."

"And then you'll go home." It was a statement, not a question.

Not if you ask me to stay. "Maybe, maybe not."

"A woman like you would never be happy out here."

A woman like me? His words stung like a slap. "What is that supposed to mean?"

He held up her perfectly manicured nails, running his work-roughened thumb over the soft palm of her hand. "You don't have a callus on you, do you?"

She snatched her hand away. "I didn't know they were a prerequisite to visiting Texas."

"Don't get all riled up by an observation."

"Then don't try to tell me where I could or couldn't be happy. A callus or lack of one doesn't mean a thing."

"I've seen your horse."

She huffed. "What's wrong with Scooter?"

"Probably nothing where you come from. But most people down here don't put glitter on hooves and bows in manes."

"So the extra time I take grooming my horse is proof that I wouldn't fit in here?"

"I never said that."

"Then what are you saying?"

He sighed. "It's just a different way of looking at things."

"You think it's better to not even know the name of the horse you ride?"

"I know my horses."

"Do you? I never hear you talk about them. I can't believe you can have all those horses and not love one."

"No need to get attached to something that's not staying."

Like me? Sarah thought with a shudder. "What a sad way to live."

Tony looked up at the ceiling, shifting so he could tuck an arm beneath his head. "Not sad, just practical."

Sarah moved so that she was above him, blocking his view. "Look me in the eye and tell me you never had a horse you were attached to."

For a moment he looked cornered, angry. His whole body tensed, but she didn't back down, she just raised her eyebrows and waited.

"I had a mare when I was twelve. My dad had gotten her for free from someone who couldn't handle her. He'd hoped to train her a bit and sell her for a profit, but he couldn't stay on her long enough to teach her anything."

Sarah laid a hand on Tony's chest, felt the heavy thud of his heart, and knew from the tension in him that she'd stumbled on another of his scars. "But you rode her?"

He nodded. "I did. She taught me about patience and how to listen to a horse. I hit the dirt a lot that summer before we worked things out."

"What happened to her?"

"My father sold her." His even tone might have fooled others, but Sarah heard what he didn't allow himself to say.

"Even though you wanted her."

Tony looked her in the eye and said harshly, "It was the right thing to do. We needed the money, not an animal we couldn't afford to feed."

"Where did she end up?" Sarah asked softly.

"I don't know. My dad left me to do chores while he took her to auction."

Sarah's heart broke for him, but she kept the depth of her sorrow to herself. There was too much more she wanted to know to risk shutting the conversation down. "What was her name?"

Tony closed his eyes for a moment, then opened them and said, "Missy. She was nothing special, just a grade horse, a mixed breed for sure."

"But you loved her."

He didn't deny it.

"Do you ever take in troubled horses now?" she asked.

There was that wall again. She felt him withdraw emotionally even before he answered. "I don't have time for other people's problems."

Sarah looked into his eyes, past his irritation with her questions, and saw the hurt he tried to conceal from her. He was afraid to care about a horse that wasn't his. He didn't want to love and lose again. She felt compelled to show him how it could be.

She laid her head upon his chest and said, "I know you don't think much of Scooter, but I've had him for seven years, and he's part of me. There were times when he was the only part I liked. I let guilt hold me down. I let my life get smaller and smaller until it nearly suffocated me, but whenever I would take Scooter out on the trails behind the barn, we would run. He's so smooth it felt like we were flying. And for just a few minutes, I was free and anything was possible." She peered up at him and admitted, "You make me feel the same way."

She could have sworn that he'd looked down at her in agreement, but the moment passed and his expression turned into a scowl. "I suppose it's a compliment that I'm on level with your horse."

Sarah pinched him lightly. "He's easier to get along with, though, so sometimes he ranks higher."

In one strong move, Tony rolled over on top of her. "Is that so? Well, let's see what I can do to improve my standing a bit."

Loving the feel of his arousal growing against her stomach, Sarah wrapped her arms around his neck eagerly and joked, "Standing, sitting, rolling around on the floor—I've enjoyed all of your ideas so far."

"That's good," he said between hot kisses to her neck, "because I can't get enough of you."

Even as her body began to hum with desire for him, her mind raced at his words. *Could this be it? Is Tony the man I'm meant to be with?*

Is this how forever starts?

Tony moved his attention lower to brush his lips tenderly across the tips of her breasts, and Sarah buried both of her hands in his hair.

If so, I'm all in.

On the sixth day, during the third hour, Sarah rolled over to face him in their bed. He smiled warmly at her and her heart filled with worry. They hadn't talked about what would happen next. Neither had mentioned their self-imposed time limit on their paradise.

I thought I was done hiding, but isn't that what we've done all week?

Our lives haven't changed. Everything is the same back there—in reality.

Why did I give myself six more days of him?

Five more than I needed to know there was no avoiding this heartbreak. Like a movie that you know ends badly, but you can't stop watching.

What if this is it? We go home and it's over?

Why did I think more time together would make things better?

"It's Tuesday," she said sadly, waiting for the reassurance she needed.

"I know," he replied, his jaw tight and his expression guarded for the first time since she'd practically dragged him back into his own cabin.

Worry turned to panic. *No, this isn't how it's supposed to go.* "I don't want to go back," she admitted hoarsely.

He didn't say anything, but she saw the torment in his eyes before he lowered his lids to conceal it from her.

Give me something, she pleaded silently. *Anything to hold on to.*

I'll go first, if that's what it takes. "I never knew it could be like this," she said.

"You got your research for your book, then," he said blandly, dismissively.

Quick, hot anger filled her. *Bastard.* "Is that how this will end? You become an asshole again?"

"I'm the same man you came here with, Sarah. I haven't changed." He met her gaze coolly.

She wanted to shake him, hit him, force him to admit he cared. Instead, she said, "Would it be so bad if you did? Can't you give us a chance?"

You're so close. I know how hard it is to face the past, but I've done it and you want to. And when you do, you'll see how we were sent to help each other. I've never believed anything more strongly.

"I told you that I have nothing more than this to offer you."

I don't believe you mean that. "So, what now? Do you want me to leave as soon as we return?"

"You can do whatever the hell you want to. Most people do." He turned away and gathered his clothing.

Sarah would have thrown something at his head if she'd had anything to throw. Instead, she pulled the sheet around herself and went to gather her own clothing. Wordlessly, they gathered the toiletries they'd brought into the cabin and took them back to her vehicle.

He chose the driver's seat, and nothing about the tense set of his jaw and the way he refused to look her in the eye implied the ride home would remotely mirror the ride there. They had driven about halfway back when she could no longer keep her thoughts to herself.

Staring straight ahead, Sarah said quietly, "Sometimes I think you're the man I've waited my whole life to meet. You're gorgeous, you're great in bed, and you have a tortured side that helps me feel less alone in my own hell. We could be more than lovers, we could be friends, too. I feel safe when I'm in your arms. But then, sometimes, like now, I wonder if I'm completely wrong and you're nothing more than a coward."

Red spread up his neck and across his face, but he didn't snap back at her as she'd expected him to—half hoped he would. She was afraid of losing him, but his silence was proof that he was already gone.

She crossed her arms over her chest and said, "Shit happens, Tony. You can't let guilt destroy your life. We both have to live with what we've done. No, we can't bring them back, but there has to be something we can do—some way to heal. I'm going to find that something. When you stop feeling so sorry for yourself, maybe you should do the same."

In my novel, this is where the hero will melt, take the heroine in his arms, and beg for forgiveness. He won't stare at the road ahead pretending he didn't hear her, once again demonstrating why fiction trumps reality any day.

When they pulled into the driveway at the ranch, Sarah could no longer hold her tears back. She let out a sob as she fumbled for the door handle. He reached across her to open the door, then kept his arm in front of her as he said, "I'm sorry, Sarah."

She pushed at his arm, but he didn't move it. She snapped, "Just being sorry isn't enough. Get out of my car. I'll hook my trailer, get Scooter, and you'll never have to see either of us again."

He held her captive by blocking what would otherwise have been her escape route. "You can't leave in the middle of the day without setting up places to stop along the way, and you shouldn't drive while you're upset."

She hated that he was right, but that didn't stop her from spinning in her seat and snarling, "You don't get to tell me to leave and then sound like you want me to stay."

His jaw tightened, and his admission sounded as if she'd wrung it from him. "I didn't tell you to leave."

Sarah's blood pressure rose and she shook her head angrily. "You think I'll stay with you, knowing you have no feelings for me? Are you hoping for a bit more cheap sex before I go?"

He didn't look pleased, but he said, "You can have the guest room again."

Sarah's breath caught in her throat. *What is he saying? What does this mean?* "And what? We act like nothing happened?" *I can't do that.*

"Or you make the phone calls you need to and leave when you're ready."

I can't do that, either.

I can't go back to where we were, like the last week didn't change everything for me.

And I hate you for being able to.

How can you close me out like this?

"No."

"I'll ask Melanie if you can stay with her for a few nights."

Brilliant idea, because that's the only place I can imagine I'd be less comfortable.

I should peel out of here, letting the smell of burning rubber express my feelings.

Sarah searched Tony's expression for any sign that he cared for her, but he had his walls firmly back in place. *There are about a million reasons why I should tell you where you could shove that last suggestion.*

And only one reason not to.

Because I'm not ready to give up on you yet, Tony.

"Fine, ask Melanie. I'm sure she'd love to have me."

"You want Sarah to stay here with me and my son? Are you serious?" Melanie asked from the doorway of her house.

He looked her in the eye without answering her question. He didn't need to. She knew he wasn't the type to joke.

Melanie held the doorknob with one tense hand. "Did you not see how she was with me the day you two left? We don't get along."

Tony wasn't asking. He wasn't budging until she agreed. "Sarah needs a place to stay while she sorts out how to get home."

Melanie hedged, suggesting, "How about a place in town?"

Tony shook his head, unwilling to even consider the option.

Pursing her lips in irritation, Melanie said, "I don't see why she can't stay with you. It's not like the whole town doesn't know how close you've gotten."

He was about to tell her that the house she lived in was his, not hers. Anger swept through him and he'd barely opened his mouth when Melanie spoke before him in a rush. "I shouldn't have said that. Whatever happened between the two of you is none of my business." When he didn't say anything, she said, "I need this job, Tony. Sarah can stay here."

A wave of shame swept over him, rocking him back on his heels. *When did I become the man that single mothers believe would throw them out in the streets with their children?* He rubbed his forehead angrily. Her house was the only home her son had ever known. He removed his hat and said, "You're not fired, Melanie."

Melanie nodded, visibly relaxing in response to his quiet tone. He hated the tears that came to her eyes as she said, "Thank you. I don't know where I'd go if I was."

Tony shook his head, his remorse deepening, and although he strove to distance himself from it, he couldn't muster anger or indifference. All he felt was a deep regret that she had lived so long in a state of desperation that he'd never even noticed. Why didn't she have savings? She didn't pay rent. Where was her money going? He felt worse when he realized how very little he knew about a woman who had worked for him for the past four years.

He turned to walk away. The screen door slammed behind him, and he figured Melanie had gone back inside until he heard her call his name. "Tony."

He looked back over his shoulder.

"Send Sarah over. I have an extra room just sitting here, and it might be nice to have another woman to talk to."

"You don't have to do that," he said gruffly.

She squared her shoulders and put on a bright smile. “I know I don’t, but I want to do this for you. Send her. It’ll be fine.”

He settled his hat deep on his head and nodded without returning her smile. “I appreciate it,” he said, and realized that he sincerely did. Those two women were like oil and water, and Melanie’s instincts were probably right that mixing the two wasn’t wise, but he wasn’t ready for the alternative.

He wasn’t ready for Sarah to leave.

Chapter Fourteen

In her wildest imagining of how her first day back on Tony's ranch would go, Sarah had never dreamed it would include an invitation from Melanie to stay at her house for a couple of days. Sarah searched her face for a sign of sarcasm but found none. *What did Tony threaten her with that made her willing to stand there and pretend she doesn't hate me?*

Instead of feeling triumphant in the face of her rival's humility, Sarah felt profoundly sorry for Melanie, and she knew that before addressing her housing offer, there was something that needed to be said. "I am so sorry for what I said to you last week. I was wrong and I was rude. I felt awful about asking for my notebook back from your son. If it wasn't full of personal information, I would have let him keep it."

Melanie's eyes locked with hers in surprise. "He knows better than to take what's not his."

"Could I buy him a few coloring books before I go?"

Melanie stiffened with pride. "We don't need anything."

Sarah suppressed a grimace. No matter how hard she tried, she and Melanie just didn't click. "I know, but it would make me feel better about how I behaved."

Lips tight, Melanie said, "I'm not going to poison you. You don't have to be nice to me."

Sarah smiled nervously. "That's a relief." *Crap, I can't believe I forgot about that.* "Listen, your offer is nice, but we both know it's not a good idea. The sooner I leave the better."

Melanie took a piece of paper out of her pocket. "A friend of yours has been calling all week. Maybe you should call her back. She might be the solution you're looking for."

Sarah took the paper and her lip curled slightly in distaste. *Lucy? Seriously?* She crumpled the paper in her hand.

Melanie said, "She called almost every day."

She can call until the end of eternity and I won't call her back.

"I have to go make lunch. I'll be in the kitchen if you need me."

Still feeling badly about the last time she'd seen Melanie, Sarah couldn't help but ask, "Is your son with you today?"

Melanie shook her head and looked away. "He was tired today, so he stayed back at the house with David."

"I'm sorry to hear that. Is he okay?"

"I don't want to talk about it." Melanie answered shortly and walked away, disappearing into the hallway that led to the kitchen.

That seems to be a theme around here.

Sarah foraged through her purse and found the list of places where she'd stayed on the way down—all horse-friendly bed-and-breakfasts. She called the closest one. No availability for at least a month. *Crap.* The same answer from the second place she called. Full up.

I could call Charlie. He'd know what to do. No, I need more time before I face him, before I even begin to try to regain what we've lost.

And I can't stay here and pretend last week didn't happen.

Melanie walked into the living room again, this time with a cordless phone. She handed it to Sarah. "It's your friend again."

Shocked into silence, Sarah took the phone and held it to her ear.

Lucy gushed a greeting. "Oh my God. I can't believe I finally reached you."

Before this goes any further, it's time for a bit of honesty. "I don't want to talk to you."

In a much more subdued tone, Lucy said, "I deserve that, I know, but please don't hang up."

Sarah sighed and didn't.

Lucy continued, this time sounding a bit desperate. "You don't know what it has been like here. I had no idea how badly we were doing until right before you arrived. We could lose everything, Sarah. My brother missed five months of mortgage payments. The bank is threatening foreclosure. We've been scrambling to sell whatever we can to hold them off."

Sarah sat down in the chair behind her. She didn't want to feel anything but anger toward her old friend. "You should have told me. I could have helped you figure it out."

After a quiet moment, Lucy said, "I didn't want you to see me like this. I was embarrassed."

Rubbing a pounding temple, Sarah said, "So the better option was to leave me stranded in a part of the country I've never been in before?"

"Stranded?" Lucy's voice sharpened. "You said you were staying with friends."

I lied, Sarah wanted to scream. *Pride makes people say stupid things, apparently. It can even kill what I thought was a solid friendship. Maybe it's time to just pack up, admit this adventure is a complete disaster, and call Charlie.*

"I had no idea you knew Tony Carlton." Lucy said his name like he was famous or something. "Do you know what most people would do to visit his ranch just once? He's a big deal around here." After another awkward pause, Lucy said, "I know you're still angry with me, but I need your help. My brother and I both do. Maybe the bank wouldn't care, but could you ask Tony to call and ask them to give us just one more month? I'm working a deal with someone to buy our herd. It would be enough to bring us up to date. I just need one more month."

Dismay filled Sarah. "I can't do that." *Because there's a good chance we're not talking to each other anymore.*

"Please, Sarah. Don't say no." Her friend's voice broke a bit with emotion. "My brother would kill me if he knew I was asking you, but this ranch has been in our family for five generations. Steven gave up everything to keep it going after my parents died. I didn't know how much it meant to me until I came back to it, and now we're going to lose it. I can't tell you how sorry I am about what happened when you first got here, but I was in shock. I had just gotten the news. Please, one phone call. I made a mistake, and it's one I deeply regret. Haven't you ever done something you wish you could undo?"

Low blow, Texas.

"How would a call from a horse trainer convince a bank to do anything?"

"I'm only guessing, but a man with as much money as he has must have it spread around. If he has a good portion of it at our bank, maybe they'd bend the rules to try to keep his business?"

Resigning herself, Sarah said, "I'll ask him, but I doubt he'll say yes." She remembered his words earlier: *I don't have time for other people's problems.*

Lucy let out a shaky sigh that was laced with tears of relief. "Thank you. Thank you. Thank you."

"I'm not promising anything," Sarah warned.

Lucy's voice was thick with tears. "I understand and I know this doesn't mean that everything is okay with us again, but I really am sorry."

"I'll call you when I know something," Sarah said, and hung up.

That might take a while, though. I'm not sure I know anything anymore.

Sarah found Tony outside, giving Scooter fresh water in his paddock. Her heart warmed at the sight until she remembered the many reasons she wanted to kick Tony in the shin.

He said, "Did you sort it out with Melanie?"

Sarah nodded. "She was very nice and seemed to sincerely want me to stay with her, but I said no."

There was a beat of silence, then Tony asked, "You staying in the spare room, then?"

Shaking her head, Sarah said, "No, I can't see how that's a good idea, either. I'd head out tonight, but the places on the way back are booked for now. I'll probably leave Scooter here for a few days if that's okay and find a place in town. I'm sure I can find something if I can use your phone.

Tony looked as grim as she'd ever seen him but said nothing.

What do I have to lose? "I do have something I wanted to ask for, though. A favor. I know you don't like getting involved, but this could really help someone I know."

Amazing how those green eyes can look right through a person and hide so much at the same time. Sarah looked down at her white sneakers in a protective move of her own. *Okay, here goes nothing.*

"Remember my friend Lucy?"

"The one who ditched you the first day you were here?"

"Yeah, that one. Well, we talked, and it sounds like she did it because she's in a rough spot financially. I don't know why she thinks that a phone call from you would convince her bank to give her and her brother more time to settle what they owe, but she asked me to ask you." Sarah raised her eyes from studying the toes of her sneakers to meet his. "So, I'm asking you. Would you do that for me?"

Let's play a game.

How many ways can a cowboy say "I don't care about other people?"

In five, four, three . . .

Tony closed the gate behind him. "I'll make that call for you."

Sarah almost sank to her knees in shock, but she steadied herself by holding on to the railing of the paddock.

Tony pulled her away from the railing and into his arms. His lips hovered over hers, his eyes glittering with a passion she'd begun to believe had died when their trip had ended. "On one condition."

"Yes?" Sarah asked, and licked her lower lip.

He buried a hand in the back of her hair and tipped her head up until her lips parted for him. "You stay. In my room, in my bed. Mine, whenever I want you."

Sarah swayed in his arms, wanting to deny him even as her body begged for his touch. He was so close to being the man she knew he could be. Softly she said, "You could simply ask me not to go."

His hand tightened in her hair. "I don't want to date you. I don't want to discuss what we have. But I do want you. You're all I can think about."

Sarah stiffened in his arms. *Or you could continue to be a complete ass.* "The only way you could make this worse is if you offered to pay me."

"I can if that's what you want. I could pay off whatever your friend owes, and it wouldn't make a dent in what I still have from my old career."

Sarah saw red. "How can you be so nice one minute and then such a jackass the next?"

His kissed her with such need that she forgot why she was angry. She forgot everything except how it felt to be with him, on him, beside him in his bed. Her body quivered with want and her hands clung to him feverishly.

He pulled away from her and smiled, a devilishly cocky smile. "I'll call your friend and get the details. I'm sure her number is saved on the phone."

He walked away, heading to the house, looking happier than she'd seen him since their return. She called after him, "I didn't say I was staying."

His laugh echoed back to her, and she made a silent promise to his retreating back.

She muttered to herself, "Mine. In my room. In my bed. Whenever I want you." *What an asshole. A hot, sexy, blow-your-mind-because-the-sex-is-so-good asshole.*

So why am I still here? Why not throw his conditions back in his face?

Because I want more than anything to believe that regardless of how he asked me, he did so because he doesn't want to lose me.

Because the more I understand myself the more I believe I can save him.

He wants more time and I don't have the strength to deny him.

Chapter Fifteen

Sarah looked around the bedroom and was happy to see her high-heeled cowboy boots. Tony had brought all her things to his room, and from the near grin on his face when he'd rejoined her on the porch, it seemed he'd enjoyed the act immensely. Then he'd given her some lame excuse about having to get some work done but added he'd see her that night.

She could just imagine him now, gloating to the other men. *"For all of you who think I don't understand women, don't worry. I got this one."*

She had fumed and stomped into the house and up the stairs. *Feeling pretty proud of yourself, aren't you, Tony?* She whipped open the zipper of another piece of luggage. *Think you have the upper hand?*

She smiled when she came across the denim shorts she'd impulsively purchased for the trip, imagining she might one day have the confidence to wear such a revealing pair.

She searched through Tony's closet until she found a blue-plaid cotton shirt and tied the bottom of it in a knot just below her breasts. She buttoned it, then smiled mischievously at her reflection in the mirror and unfastened two more buttons than she'd ever dared to.

You shouldn't have taught me poker.

I'll see your blackmail and raise you one deliberate seduction.

In your bed whenever you want me? Sarah arched her back and widened the open collar of the shirt a bit more, revealing just a tease of her lace bra.

Really?

Oh, you'll want me.

And then I'm going to help you.

Whether you want me to or not.

No ponytail—this called for a bit of hair tousling. She teased and sprayed her long curls until they hung wild and free in a casual, sexy style that looked natural, slept on. She applied just the right amount of makeup, including pink lipstick to accentuate her full lips, and studied her reflection again, kicking up one heel in mock flirtation. She put a hand over her mouth and rounded her eyes with forced innocence. *Perfect.*

She made a quick phone call, then with her head held high, she walked down the stairs, past an openmouthed Melanie, and out the front door of Tony's house. She saw him in the distance, talking to David near one of the round pens. Without sparing them more than a glance, she walked into the barn.

Her ego received a boost as all activity instantly ceased. All five young men stood absolutely still, as if they were animatronics whose power source had just been pulled. She walked to where they were working, and hid a laugh when one of them dropped the pitchfork he'd been holding and didn't take his eyes off her to retrieve it.

She'd never felt particularly beautiful, but the past week had brought a side of her alive that she'd never expected. For once, she was aware of the power of her femininity.

"I'm looking for Tony," she lied huskily, almost bursting into laughter when none of them moved except for one red-haired young man who pointed wordlessly toward the side door. *I've spent twenty-five years dressing fashionably and have never gotten this reaction. No wonder women do a little flash-and-tease now and then. Holy crap, men are easy.*

"Sarah," Tony growled from the main door of the barn.

Sarah didn't turn to face him. Instead, she bent slowly at the waist to pick up the pitchfork that the redheaded man had dropped. She was fully aware how high her shorts rode up her ass cheeks during that move and the view it probably gave him.

He was beside her in a heartbeat, and Sarah smiled up at him before slowly straightening. His eyes were flashing with a mix of passion and anger. She leaned against him, loving how his eyes were drawn to the cleavage she'd purposefully revealed. "I was looking for you," she said, laying a hand on his tense forearm. He knew she'd seen him outside before she'd entered the barn. Her words hung like a playful taunt between them. "But luckily, you found me. Now we can invite them together."

His eyes narrowed and between gritted teeth he asked, "Invite who—where?"

Sarah looked around at the rapt audience. "Do you remember how we talked about how nice it would be to have a dinner to thank everyone who helped search for Scooter the day he got loose? Why not tonight? Melanie and I can throw something together." Sarah asked the young men around her, "Would you be able to make it on such short notice?"

The men looked to Tony as if their responses depended on his reaction to her offer.

And for a painfully long pause, everyone waited.

Tony's hired hands all knew that he didn't want them in his house. Hell, some of them had worked at the Double C for years without being this close to him. This was the exact opposite of the way he ran his ranch, and his temper rose even as he bit back the initial impulse to shoot her idea down without discussion.

It wouldn't change anyone's opinion of him in the slightest if he gave Sarah a verbal thrashing right in front of everyone for suggesting this. In fact, that was the behavior the men expected from him.

And Sarah knows it.

This is her attempt to stick it to me.

Let her have her one dinner. It won't change a thing.

And it won't bother me because it doesn't matter.

She's here until I work her out of my system, until I dull the edge of my need to kiss those pink lips she's pursing so seductively at me right now. Let her invite whoever she wants to dinner. Knowing that I can sink my teeth into that ripe little ass she's deliberately wagging in my face right now will more than make up for the aggravation.

Stone-faced, Tony addressed the men. "Y'all be at the house tonight at seven."

"Yes, sir," they said, practically in unison, then continued to stare at him wordlessly.

"Now get back to work," Tony ordered and almost smiled as the men scrambled to do just that. One paused in front of Sarah as if he were about to ask her for the pitchfork, then changed his mind and hurried off.

When they were alone, Tony pulled her into his arms, his hands instantly claiming the curve of her ass just above the high hem of her shorts. Her soft flesh felt just as good as it had looked, and he claimed her mouth hungrily, impatiently wishing they were somewhere more private. She wrapped her arms around his neck, pressed herself wantonly against him, and moaned in pleasure. He kissed the side of her neck and threatened, "You put me in a difficult position there. You'll pay for that tonight."

She rubbed herself against him, sending a throb of need through him in a punch of lust. "I'm counting on it," she murmured, throwing her head back and moaning softly.

He bit the lobe of her ear in gentle chastisement and said, "You need to learn who is in charge here. I don't mind putting time into training you." She froze in his arms, then relaxed, and he chuckled. "Good girl. You're starting to understand, Sarah. Don't challenge me again. You won't win." He kissed her deeply, not stopping until she was sagging with need against him. Then he said, "I'm going to enjoy making you beg for your orgasm tonight. Beg until I forget how deliberate this setup was."

Sarah pulled back a bit and flipped her lush mane over one shoulder. "Sounds like it's going to be a long night, especially since I invited your brother."

"You did what?" Tony boomed, grabbing her arm.

She smiled impishly up at him and said, "I know how to use redial, also. His number wasn't that difficult to uncover."

This time she's gone too far.

"Not going to happen. Call him back and tell him dinner is off."

Sarah ran a hand playfully down his cheek. "Yeah, about that. I'm going to need considerable training before I jump when you use that tone with me." She pulled her other arm out of his grasp and said, "If you don't want your brother to come, call him and tell him he's not welcome. I have a dinner to organize."

Taking advantage of his moment of shock, Sarah flounced out of the barn. Tony rubbed a hand roughly across his face while he attempted to recollect the thoughts she'd just scattered from his brain.

David entered soon after her departure. "So, we're all eating at your place tonight?" he asked, his tone heavy with amusement.

Tony glared at him but kept his profanity to himself. He wasn't sure he'd be able to stop swearing if he started.

Chapter Sixteen

Why did I think I could do this?

What if tonight is a disaster?

Standing on Tony's front porch, Sarah saw David walking by and waved him over to talk. He looked back at Tony, who was glaring at both of them from the doorway of the barn, then headed in her direction, stopping just a foot before the steps leading up to the porch.

Sarah bit her bottom lip and looked across the driveway at Tony. Their eyes met and held for a hot moment. David, the ranch, everything else disappeared, and she could feel his need for her pulsing through the air. She wanted to run to him. He looked like he was considering the possibility of closing the distance between them, swinging her over his shoulder, and taking her straight to his bedroom without a care for who was watching—until he turned abruptly away and strode back into the barn.

Sarah let out an audible sigh of longing and sagged against the top of the railing. In the quiet that followed, she whispered, "Will you help me?"

David took off his hat and brushed it against his jean-clad thigh. Quite blandly, he said, "Depends on what you're asking."

Sarah gave him a funny look, then continued, "I can't cook. I invited more people than will fit in his dining room. And I don't even know where the damn town is to go buy what we need. Why did I think it was a good idea to invite everyone to dinner tonight? Why didn't I think this through? Is there any way this is not going to be a complete disaster?"

"Sounds like a conversation to have with Melanie."

With a shrug Sarah said, "In case you haven't noticed, she hates me."

David shook his head. "Melanie has too much on her plate already to care about much else, so I doubt that."

Remembering what Melanie had said earlier, Sarah asked, "What's going on with her son?"

David said, "Not my place to talk about it."

Sarah walked down the steps to stand in front of David, not wanting her questions to be overheard. "Does Tony know?"

Looking uncomfortable with her line of questioning, David hedged. "We've never discussed it."

She attempted to explain her motivations, as much to herself as to David. "David, I don't know if Tony and I are going to work out, but I do understand why he bought this place. He told me about the girl who died." David's eyebrows shot up, the only sign that her words surprised him. "I know what guilt can do to a person. You can't run from it. You can't hide from it. If you try, you lose a piece of yourself to it every day. I was lost before I came here. Now I see that I am strong enough to face what I did. I don't want to hide anymore. I don't think Tony does, either."

David looked past the barn to where Tony was still watching them and said, "He'd tell you that some creatures are damaged beyond help."

Sarah followed his line of vision and said, "You don't believe that, do you?"

David said, "I wouldn't be here if I did."

Setting her shoulders determinedly, Sarah said, "Where is this town that everyone talks about? Looks like I have some shopping to do."

David coughed into his hand and asked, "You going dressed like that?"

Sarah's smile widened as she met Tony's eyes across the distance. "Oh yes." After David gave her the directions, she said, "Could you have some of the men put two tables together under the tree on the side of the house? Make sure there are enough chairs for everyone here and Tony's brother."

David asked, "You invited Dean?"

"I did."

"And Tony knows?"

Chin held high, Sarah said, "He does."

David whistled and raised his hat in admiration. "Tony needs someone like you."

Truly surprised, Sarah said, "Thank you."

David replaced his hat and said, "I just hope he's not too much of a damn fool to realize it." He walked away and left Sarah standing there, thinking about what he'd said.

I hope so, too.

Unable to concentrate enough to work with the horses, Tony tried to release some of his frustration through good old-fashioned manual labor. He cleaned, he stacked—anything to keep his mind off Sarah. When he saw her talking to David, his stomach clenched with an emotion he refused to acknowledge.

I'm not jealous.

She can talk to whoever she wants to.

He watched as David leaned down to hear something she said and they both smiled. *Oh, hell no. Find your own Yankee.* Tony fought the urge to stride over there and punch his manager. Fortunately, David walked away.

Sarah headed toward her SUV. *Where the hell is she going?*

The question had barely registered when Tony realized he'd dropped the bale of hay he'd been holding and then practically sprinted over to her vehicle. She was already in the driver's seat, lowering the automatic windows to cool off the car. He grabbed the handle and opened the car door next to her. "What are you doing?"

She kept both hands on the steering wheel. "I told you that I have to organize things for tonight. We need some supplies, so I'm driving into town."

"Not alone, you're not." He hadn't planned to say that and he wasn't entirely sure why he had.

She rounded her eyes innocently and asked, "Should I ask one of the ranch hands to come with me?"

"No," he growled. The idea of her spending the day with another man was enough to set his heart pounding in his chest angrily.

"Did you want to come with me?" She asked so sweetly he knew she was deliberately trying to push his buttons. Going to town was the last thing he wanted to do. He wanted to run his hands down the long expanse of bare thigh that her shorts revealed. Too vividly, he could imagine sliding his hand into the open neckline of her shirt and beneath the pink lace of the bra it displayed. "There is no way in hell you're going to Fort Mavis dressed like that."

Sarah's lovely breasts heaved with irritation. "I don't remember giving you the right to tell me what to wear."

"Do you want people to think that you're a . . ." He stopped before he said the word.

Sarah jumped on his omission and snapped, "Whore? You mean like someone who would stay with you as your own personal sex toy? Someone you could buy with a favor or a promise of cash? Someone like that?"

Between gritted teeth, Tony said, "That's not how I see you."

With cheeks red with anger, Sarah said, "Yes, it is. If you think you can trade favors for sex with me, that's exactly what you think."

Tony removed his hat and ran a hand through his hair in frustration. "You have me so crazy, I don't know what I'm saying half the time."

Sarah unclipped her seat belt and turned toward him, her legs dangling out of the open door. "That is the nicest thing you have said to me so far."

He buried a hand in the back of her hair and claimed her mouth with all the emotion swirling between them. So close to her, he could barely think. He thrust his tongue between her lips and savored how she eagerly welcomed him. His other hand went to her hip to edge her closer to him. He hungrily kissed her exposed collarbone and the curve of her neck. "Let's go inside and forget about everything else."

With a hand cupping either side of his jaw, she raised his face from her and said, "No."

Aroused, confused, angry—he would have been hard-pressed to describe how he felt in that turbulent moment. He bent down to claim her lips again, sure he could change her mind, but she scooted away from him.

She folded her arms across her chest. "This is important to me. You can come with me or I can go alone, but I'm going into town."

When he didn't say anything, she softened a bit and said, "I will gladly put on jeans and a T-shirt if you ask me to."

Why did women have to make everything into an issue? Couldn't she simply go change because she knew it was what he wanted? Apparently not, since she sat there, out of his reach, waiting for him to speak. Frustration rumbled in his chest.

Still, she waited.

He caved and ordered, "Go change."

Suddenly excited, she leaned forward and rewarded him with a quick kiss on the lips. "And you'll come with me?"

Hell no.

Then he tasted her and nodded wordlessly, forgetting everything in the fire of their kiss. Too soon, she broke it off and stepped away, saying, "I'll be right back."

I'll be right here, Tony thought angrily. *Trying to figure out exactly what the hell just happened.*

Chapter Seventeen

Tony drove into Fort Mavis, and Sarah thoroughly enjoyed everything they passed to get to the center of town. The streets were wide and flanked with a mixture of historical and renovated buildings. The tall doors on the storefronts were freshly painted in white and black. Through their glass windows, Sarah glimpsed a variety of wares: jewelry, clothing, and hardware. There was even a bookstore inside a historic theater whose billboard promised vintage movies once a month.

They parked in front of what looked like a general store. Tony walked around the SUV to open Sarah's door, and the guarded look in his eyes pulled at her heart. He slammed the door after she stepped out and stood protectively beside her. Sarah looked around and understood his earlier reluctance. People on the sidewalks stopped and stared. Faces peeked out from inside restaurant windows. She touched Tony's arm, felt the tension building within him, and slid her hand down to hold his.

His eyes flew to hers, their green turning dark with emotion. She entwined her fingers with his and gave a supportive squeeze. He looked away, but his hand tightened on hers. He cleared his throat. "I'm not well-liked in this town." His warning melted her heart.

"I don't believe that."

They stepped up onto the sidewalk together. "It may have something to do with how many times I've told them all to go to hell."

Sarah held in the chuckle that his self-revelation inspired and said, "Then today, try saying hello instead."

He stopped walking and halted her, waiting until she looked up at him before he said, "I don't want you to get hurt."

Putting on her brightest smile, Sarah said, "I don't care what these people think of me, Tony. I'm done apologizing for who I am. It's a beautiful sunny day, and I'm with you. There isn't a thing anyone could say that could ruin this for me."

Two teenage boys stopped when they saw Tony and set a course straight for him. Tony pulled Sarah closer to him and said, "I'm not so sure about that."

One of the boys stopped several feet away; the other, who looked older, came much closer. He stood right in front of Tony and said, "Mr. Carlton."

Sarah felt a defensive tension pulse through Tony's arm even though his face remained expressionless.

The young man said, "My dad told me what you did. Thank you."

Some of the tension left Tony and he gave a curt nod.

Sarah took advantage of the opportunity to introduce herself. "Hello, my name's Sarah."

The young man took off his hat and briefly shook her hand. "Keith. Nice to meet you, ma'am."

When the awkward silence dragged on too long, Sarah said, "Well, we're here to get some things, so we have to run, but hopefully, we'll see you again soon."

Walking away, hand in hand with Tony, Sarah said, "See, that wasn't so bad."

Tony made a noncommittal sound deep in his chest.

"What was he thanking you for?"

"Nothing," Tony answered automatically.

Sarah tugged on his hand until he looked down at her. "The amazing thing about conversations is they help people get to know each other better." *Except in this town*, she wanted to say, but took another tack instead. "I can keep asking you until I drive you so crazy you tell me to shut me up, or you can just tell me now. Your choice."

He rubbed his chin in slow deliberation.

Losing patience, Sarah warned, "I am also not above a swift kick to the shin if warranted."

Tony threw back his head and laughed out loud, the last of his tension falling away and real amusement filling his eyes. "You would do that, wouldn't you?"

"In a heartbeat," Sarah joked, and hugged him, laughing along with him. They passed more than one person whose mouth dropped open in shock at the sight of the two of them, which only set the two of them laughing more.

Sarah felt young, alive, and in love for the first time in her life.

Love. Her gut clenched at the word, and the laughter died on her lips.

I love him.

He stopped walking and turned her to face him, suddenly concerned. "What's the matter?"

Even if I could say it, you're not ready to hear it.

Instead, she said softly, "Tell me about Keith and what you did for his father."

"I don't want to talk about it."

She laid a hand on his cheek and said, "Why? It sounds like you did something wonderful."

He shook his head. "Only to make amends."

Sarah bared her inner pain to him and asked, "Do you believe that I deserve to be happy after what I did?"

His jaw tensed beneath her hand. "You were young, innocent. It wasn't your fault."

"That wasn't my question. A thousand people can tell me I was too young to know better, and it won't change what happened or bring him back. It'll never lessen the guilt I feel. But how should I spend the rest of my life? Hiding from it? Denying it? Or making amends for it and finding a way to go on?"

He hugged her to him, publicly, right in the middle of the sidewalk. "I don't know," he murmured against her hair. "I don't know."

Sarah found a comfort in his arms that she'd never found elsewhere. For a man who gave reluctantly, he gave her everything. He kissed her, not in the heated way they'd done so often in the past, but gently, reverently. Then he pulled her tighter into his arms and rested his chin on the top of her head. The deep breath he took was as shaky as Sarah's knees felt.

Eventually, awareness of where they were seeped in and Sarah said, "Maybe we should talk about this later."

Tony stepped back with a grim expression. "I don't know if I can be the man you need me to be."

Sarah wanted to tell him that he already was, but she couldn't.

He wasn't.

Not yet.

Instead, she lightly kissed him on the lips and said, "Let's go shopping before your brother orders us off the sidewalk. We're stopping traffic."

Tony looked around, but this time he didn't seem to resent the attention. "They'll have to get used to it, because you're not going anywhere anytime soon."

It'd be nicer if you said . . . ever.

But we'll work on that.

Chapter Eighteen

Tony took his place at the head of the somewhat makeshift long table his ranch hands had put together while he and Sarah were in town. He wasn't much for decorating, but he had to admit Sarah had set a beautiful table: a light-blue linen tablecloth, nice plates he hadn't known he owned, and floral centerpieces she'd insisted were necessary.

David and Melanie had quickly taken over the job of cooking after Sarah had asked if the grill required an extension cord. Had the question come from another woman, Tony might have thought she was joking, but he'd tasted Sarah's cooking a few times during their week in the cabin. Sarah was an amazing woman, but a man might decide starving was a viable option if forced to live on what she whipped up in the kitchen.

Sarah took the seat to his right, and it was the first time he'd seen more than a blur of her since they'd returned from town. The way she'd fussed about the house and then retreated to the guest room to primp made him feel like an ass for wishing the meal were already over.

He took a moment to appreciate her effort. She'd piled her blonde curls in a loose knot and changed into a summer dress. A memory of their earlier conversation about the advantages of dresses sent his blood rushing southward.

She caught him looking at her and smiled—so beautifully he temporarily forgot to breathe.

She leaned in and whispered, "Nervous?"

Not exactly. He shifted, the crotch of his jeans suddenly uncomfortably tight. He shook his head, trying to clear his thoughts of visions of how she'd look later that night when he showed her how much fun dresses could be.

Sarah laid a reassuring hand on one of his, proving quite definitively that women cannot read a man's mind. Still, the sweet look on her face reminded him why he'd agreed to the meal in the first place. She wanted this, and when it came to Sarah, he had a real problem saying no.

He didn't notice how the food arrived on the table. He couldn't have cared less if his glass was filled with lemonade, sweet tea, or beer. Sarah had woven her fingers through his and was absently caressing the back of his hand with her thumb. Nothing else at the table mattered.

She leaned toward him again and said, "You should say something."

He frowned at her but she didn't relent, so he stood. The guests fell quiet and all present turned to hear what he would say. David, Melanie, and her son were seated on Tony's left. Five young men sat on both sides of the table at the far end. He realized he should know their names, but he didn't. He always preferred not to know. It made firing them easier.

One seat was empty.

Dean hadn't come.

Good.

It had been a long time since he'd addressed a group of people he wasn't threatening. He felt like a fraud making a speech to people who knew he'd rather they were all anywhere but there. His attention was drawn to the serious expression on the young boy's face. *He should be running circles around the table while Melanie warns him to calm down.*

I should know his name.

Noticing the sustained attention of her boss, Melanie tensed and put a protective arm around her son's shoulders, as if she believed Tony was preparing to order for the child to be removed from the table.

I'm not that much of an asshole.

Not anymore, anyway.

Tony's free hand clenched in a fist on the table. *When did I become a man even I don't like?*

Tony realized he was scowling at Melanie and the boy, and he tried unsuccessfully to defuse their anxiety with a smile—a sad attempt at one if her continued grip on her son was anything to go by. He winked at the boy and felt infinitely worse when he sat up straighter and smiled—his hero worship obvious to all.

I've never said two words to that kid.

He should hate me.

Sarah squeezed his hand gently. He looked down into those loving brown eyes of hers. Was she right? Was it time to let go of the past and salvage what he had left before it was too late? Could he ever deserve the faith she had in him?

Tony cleared his throat. "I know I'm not an easy man to work for, but I appreciate y'all joining us tonight. Thank you for the work you put into setting it up. Let's eat."

He sat down, both relieved and surprised at how good he felt. During his short-lived career, he'd spoken to crowds of all sizes and enjoyed it. Until now, he'd put those feelings behind him. It surprised him to discover that a piece of him missed public speaking. He missed the rush of adrenaline he'd always felt just before stepping out in front of a crowd and the sense of accomplishment that followed his speech. He spontaneously lifted Sarah's hand to his lips and gratefully kissed the back of it. If the move shocked anyone, he didn't notice.

"I never would have believed it if I hadn't seen it with my own eyes," Dean said from a few feet away, referencing the group in front of him. Tony stood, releasing Sarah's hand.

David stood and walked over to shake Dean's hand. "Sheriff."

Dean shook his hand. "David, always good to see you." He tipped his hat at Melanie and said, "Melanie, Jace gets bigger every time I see him. What are you feeding him? He's growing like a weed."

Melanie smiled at the compliment. "What *don't* I feed him? He's a bottomless pit."

Jace left his seat and ran over to hug Dean's legs. "I'm near all grown up, Sheriff. Watch your job. I'm fixin' to take it."

Dean ruffled the young boy's hair and said, "By the time you're ready for it, I may give it to you gladly." He nodded a greeting to the other men.

Sarah put a hand on Tony's arm and said, "I'm so glad you made it, Dean."

Tony stood silently.

Sarah elbowed him, causing him to expel his breath harshly. He caught David's amused expression and glared at him. Then he looked down at Sarah intending to express his displeasure, only to have the breath knocked out of him for the second time. When she wanted something, she had a way of looking up at him with the widest, sweetest eyes he'd ever seen. A man could lose himself in eyes like that.

Or make a fool of himself because of them.

Tony shook his head to clear it and offered his brother the warmest greeting he'd likely ever given him. He held out his hand and said, "Dean, you're late. Sit down before everyone's food gets cold."

Dean shook his hand briefly, then nodded at Sarah. "It's nice to see the two of you fully dressed."

Anger flared, but before Tony let his heated thoughts fly, Sarah chastised Dean gently. "Let's have a nice meal together. You two can go back to fighting tomorrow, but I put a lot of work into making tonight nice. Behave."

To Tony's surprise, his brother's face reddened slightly and he removed his hat. "Yes, ma'am."

Something about her tone and his compliance tickled Tony's sense of humor, and he laughed out loud, all his anger dissolving as quickly at it had come.

Dean shook his head in awe of the sight and then smiled. "Sarah, don't let my brother run you off, you hear? You marry him just as fast as you can."

Sarah laughed his comment off and sat back down. Dean found his seat and everyone started eating again. Everyone except Tony. He felt a bit sick.

It wasn't Dean's comment that had struck the hunger from him—it was how close he'd come to agreeing to the idea.

Some people weren't meant to be happy, and Tony had long ago accepted that he was one of those people. Believing that things could be better, that he deserved more, was how he always felt just before life intervened and proved him wrong.

Sarah would stay as long as she wanted to stay. They'd find pleasure in each other's bodies while she was there, and when she left, he'd find another willing woman to replace her.

That was all they could have, because that's all he had to offer.

He met her eyes and knew she was upset by his sudden change of mood.

Good.

It's better if she doesn't forget the kind of man I am. Even if she makes me wish things were different.

Sarah pushed the slab of steak around her plate. *It's not every day I watch a man turn green and lose his appetite at the idea of marrying me. You're lucky I didn't throw this drink in your face and walk away. But I'm not going to, you know why? Because you're so close. All you have to do is open your eyes and see that these people care about you. Even your brother. They're here, waiting. Just like I am. How can I make you see them?*

And me?

Sarah put on her brightest smile. "David, I'm embarrassed to say that I don't know the names of everyone at this table. Will you introduce me?"

Like Tony should have, but he'd have to want them to like me to do that, and he doesn't believe I'm staying. Maybe I'm not, but does he have to treat me like I don't matter in front of his men?

David said, "Yes, ma'am. You've met Jace, Melanie's son." David pointed to each of the men around the table, and each stood in greeting as he did. "Lucas is the one with red hair. He helps out with most of the exercising and has been here the longest. Sawyer's sitting on his left. He can stay on a horse better than any man I've ever met. Really should be in the rodeo, but he says there's too much left to learn here. Then Austin and Gunnar. They are brothers, and if you want to have some fun, ask them which one was born first. They're fraternal twins and their mama won't tell them who is the older. Then there's Travis. He's new this year, which means Tony hasn't fired him yet."

Tony frowned at his manager. "Are you saying you keep rehiring the same people?"

David shrugged. "Some. You never noticed, and they're hard workers."

Sarah took a sip of lemonade to hide her smile. She didn't dare look at Tony, because she knew she wouldn't be able to contain the laughter bubbling within her.

Tony didn't appear as amused. He said, "So, you all think this is a fu—"

Sarah laid a hand on his arm and shook it, stopping him mid-word. She looked at Jace and back at him, raising both of her eyebrows with meaning.

"Damn joke," Tony finished, growling out his amendment.

Dean roared with laughter and David said, "It's almost sad to watch, isn't it?"

Dean said, "Sad or entertaining? It's a tough call."

Tony stood. "I'll entertain you with my fist in a minute if you don't shut up."

Dean also stood and took off his badge and gun, laying them on the table beside the steak he'd barely touched. "It might be time for you to try it, Tony. Instead of pretending you want me here, why don't you give throwing me out your best shot?"

Oh no you don't, Sarah thought. She couldn't take it anymore. It was all going wrong. They weren't supposed to be laughing at Tony. The dinner was supposed to bring them all together. If she couldn't make the dinner work, how could she ever make things between Tony and herself work? Sarah jumped to her feet and threw her napkin down beside her plate. The whole evening was a huge disappointment. "Stop it right now!" Everyone froze at her harsh tone. "No wonder Tony doesn't eat with you people. They say Northerners are rude, but you have us beat. I don't know how you think you should behave toward your host, but you should all be ashamed of yourselves." She spun and focused her irritation on Tony. "And you. Did you really just threaten to punch someone over a stupid remark? You know how much I wanted tonight to be nice. Melanie won't have to poison me to get rid of me. I can't imagine staying here another day. So, go ahead, kill each other or spend another five years not talking. I don't care. I'm done."

She walked back to the house, head held high, and slammed the front door behind her.

Melanie was the first to speak after Sarah left. "Well, I feel like an ass."

Her son said, "Isn't that a bad word, Mama?"

She ruffled his hair and smiled. "Yes, it is. Don't say it when you go to school or your teachers will give you the same lecture Sarah just gave us."

Tony watched the light in his room go on, followed by the light in the spare bedroom, and he knew his plans for that night had just changed. He wasn't going to chase her, but that didn't mean he didn't feel badly about how it'd turned out.

In the quiet late-evening air, no one spoke. Then Melanie interrupted the silence, saying, "Just for the record, I never actually threatened to poison her. I only implied I might."

Dean said, "You sure picked a high-strung one, Tony."

David leaned back in his chair, noting the upstairs activity as Sarah continued to move back and forth between the two bedrooms. "We may have driven her to it a bit."

In the face of the truth, Dean's stance softened. He looked at Tony and said, "I didn't mean to ruin the evening."

Tony let out a slow sigh. "I don't actually want to punch you."

Dean crossed the short distance between them and stood shoulder to shoulder with his brother. "Don't let her leave."

Across the table, David chimed in. "She did bring us together. We may need a woman around here."

Melanie punched him in the arm. "And what am I?"

David rubbed his arm and said, "You know what I mean."

Temper rising, Melanie snarled, "No, I don't know what you mean."

Tony practically jumped when he felt a small hand touch his. He looked down and found Jace, Melanie's son, at his side. "Just tell her you're sorry. That's what Mama tells me to do when I do something wrong."

Shaking his head, Tony looped a thumb in his jeans pocket. "It's not always that easy, son."

Jace mimicked Tony's stance, right down to watching Sarah's shadow go from room to room as she moved her things down the hall. "Yes, it is. You say you're sorry and she says okay. That's how it works."

Dean added his opinion from Tony's other side. "I'm with Jace on this one."

Jace puffed up with pride at the endorsement from his other idol.

Squaring his shoulders, Tony said, "I'm not real good with words, but I owe her that much, I suppose." More gruffly he added, "She's right about our behavior. We're out of practice when it comes to being civil. We might need to eat together once a week so y'all don't embarrass yourselves like this again." After a moment, he added, "You, too, Dean. You're the worst of the bunch."

He didn't wait for their response to his announcement as he had much more pressing matters on his mind. Like how to get his little blonde angel's pink-and-green checkered luggage out of the guest room and back where it belonged.

Sarah was still fuming ten minutes later when she heard the sound of Tony's heavy boots on the main stairs. She peered out the small window in the guest room and saw Melanie and the men gathering up the plates and clearing the table.

The door behind her opened and shut.

Without looking away from the window, Sarah said quietly, "If you're here to say anything except you're sorry, do yourself a favor and leave now."

After a pause, Tony replied, "And if I am?"

Sarah turned slowly toward him, clasping her hands in front of her to stop them from shaking. She was angry, hopeful, scared. Maybe this was one day that should end the same way it started, with them not talking to each other. She looked up at him and waited.

He stood there, frowning at her for a painfully long time.

When she couldn't take it anymore some of her frustration burst out. "Do you know what the worst part about the whole thing was? You didn't even introduce me."

Tony looked a bit cornered when he admitted, "I didn't know all of their names."

Sarah's mouth fell open. "Are you joking?"

"No."

She shook her head in wonder. "You honestly didn't know their names? So, David was serious when he said you didn't notice he rehired men you'd fired?"

Tony's steady look was as much of an affirmative as she was going get.

"How does that happen?"

Tony shrugged. "I don't want to know them. David deals with them. All I do is train the horses."

Sarah sat on the edge of the bed, absorbing the enormity of what he'd shared. "I knew you distanced yourself from everyone, but I didn't realize the extent of it."

He leaned on the doorjamb without responding.

In a near whisper, Sarah asked, "What are you afraid of?"

Tony straightened from the door. "I'm not afraid of anything."

Sarah stood and moved to stand directly in front of him, searching his face for signs of what she suspected. "Are you sure? You can't be happy with your life the way it is."

He glared down at her. "I was happy before you came."

His comment hit Sarah like a punch, knocking her momentarily off balance. Then a thought occurred to her, and she set her mouth determinedly. *He wants me angry. That's how he keeps everyone at a distance.* She countered his jab with a smack of reality. "No, you weren't." *You were hiding, numb. Too afraid to even get to know the names of the people who work here.*

He pushed a hand through the back of her hair and dragged her closer to him, tipping her head up toward him. "You're not the first woman to think she can change me." When she gasped and struggled to pull away, he held her there, with her chest heaving against his own. He ran the finger of his free hand down the exposed arch of her neck and traced the round neckline of her dress. "But I do enjoy letting you try."

Despite how her body pulsed and yearned, Sarah stood rigid in his hold. Strangle him or kiss him? Both sounded equally pleasurable. "Do you want me to hate you?"

His hands dropped away, his face tight with torment as he glared down at her. "No."

There it is, just the slightest ray of hope—the reason I can't give up on him.

Sarah took in a steadying breath and said, "Then stop pushing me away."

He dragged a hand through his hair, leaving it mussed in a sexy way that Sarah cautioned her libido to ignore. He met her eyes with an openness she hadn't seen since the cabin and said, "I'm sorry about dinner."

Sarah touched his tense jaw with one soft hand. "It's okay. Part of it was my fault. I knew you didn't want it, but I thought that once we were all together, you would see how it could be. I didn't mean to make things worse."

"You didn't."

Really? Then why do you look so miserable? What is holding you back from being happy? "When we were at the cabin you laughed. You smiled and joked. Why can't you do that here?"

At first, she didn't think Tony would answer, but then he took her hand from his cheek and held it in his. "The cabin was different. It wasn't real, so I didn't care." Sarah tensed and pulled at her hand, but he gripped it and said, "That came out wrong."

It better have.

Tony tipped her face up again with a finger beneath her chin. "When I start thinking I know what I'm doing, really know—that's when things fall apart. It's never as good as you think it is, and if you let yourself believe it is, you're setting yourself up for a bad fall."

Sarah looked up into his beautiful green eyes and prompted, "Please tell me. Let me in."

Tony pulled her to his chest, unwilling or unable to look her in the eye as he opened up to her. "My mother left when I was real young. I don't remember her, but I do remember wanting to find her. I used to ask about her all the time. Didn't matter who I met, I interrogated them. I was sure that if I asked enough people, I'd find her. You know what I found? Dean. Seems my mother left soon after I was born because she found out my father had been married before and never told her. Neither woman wanted anything to do with my father until Dean's mother decided it was important for brothers to know each other."

"So, Dean's really your half brother?"

"Half, whole, it never mattered. We're not close."

"Did he want to be?"

"I don't know what the hell he wanted, but after I found him I couldn't shake him. He was always visiting, sometimes with the mother he got along so well with. All it ever did was set my father and me to fighting until we couldn't be in the same room anymore. My father always told me that the fewer questions a man asked, the happier he tended to be. He was right about that. I moved out at sixteen because my father and I couldn't talk without coming to blows."

Sarah hugged him as he went on. "I used to believe in what I was doing with horses. I had all the answers. I lost that and more when Kimberly died." He shuddered against her, betraying how much it had cost him to relive both heartaches.

Gazing up at him, Sarah said, "I wish I could guarantee that nothing bad will ever happen to either one of us again. If they ever do invent a time machine, I'll be the first one in line to go back and try to do most of it better. But until then, this is the only life I'm going to have and I don't want to waste any more of it. You helped me see that. It took coming here to see that I was only half alive up North. I could blame my parents. I could blame my brother. I could even blame Doug. But no one did that to me. I did it. I let my life become so much less than it was meant to be. I won't make that mistake twice."

His heart thudded in his chest as she continued.

"Life is scary, but I think it's supposed to be. If you're living it right, that is."

He hugged her tighter against him. "What do you want from me, Sarah?"

She met his eyes and dared the truth. "A chance."

He nodded and ran a finger teasingly over the neckline of her dress. "And in return?"

Sarah raised herself onto her tiptoes and whispered, "A confession."

He growled deep in his throat, "I like that. Tell me."

Rubbing herself against him, Sarah said, "When you grabbed the back of my head and pulled me to you, I liked it."

He reenacted his early move, burying his hand in the back of her hair and holding her helplessly immobile before him. "You mean this?"

She sighed through parted lips, "Yes."

He claimed her lips with his, teasing, testing, while he boldly slid a hand beneath the back hem of her dress, cupping her ass roughly. "You like it rough?"

Sarah playfully struggled against his hold, loving how easily he restrained her. "I don't know, but I'd like to try it out," she admitted.

His mouth closed over hers again, his tongue deep within her mouth, demanding a submission she gladly gave. With one strong move, he ripped her thong off. There was a sting to the move. Sarah moaned into the kiss, loving how the slight pain flooded her with want.

He growled into her ear. "I told you earlier that there'd be a price to pay for inviting everyone to dinner."

Sarah wasn't sure if his anger was fake or real, and she didn't know if she cared.

He pulled away from her and took off his belt. Her eyes rounded as she realized she should have defined rough before the game started.

He laughed and dropped the belt, along with the rest of his clothing, to the floor. "Don't worry, I would never mark what is mine."

She turned to flee, half in jest and half in response to what she was pretty sure he intended to do. He grabbed her around the waist, swung her up, and sat on the edge of the bed, settling her face down across his lap. The material of her dress softened the sting of the first spank, but then he slid it up, exposing her bare ass to his reprimand. "Do you like soft?" He tapped one ass cheek lightly. "Or hard?" The crack of his hand echoed in the quiet of the room, and Sarah gasped at the sudden pain, then marveled at how it intensified her desire.

"Both," she panted, and squirmed in his hold.

He repeated the same pattern on her other cheek. Another gasp and more pleasure. A few more spanks, and Sarah was writhing and moaning. Just when she thought she couldn't take any more, he bent and kissed the flesh he'd reddened. He ran his hand down the back of one of her thighs and pushed her legs apart wider.

With one hand, he held her head arched back by pulling on a fistful of hair while he slid one finger of his other hand inside her soaked pussy. His thumb sought and circled her excited nub. His erection jutted against her stomach. "You're not in control here, Sarah. I am." He thrust another finger inside her, pumping in and out, faster and faster. "You only come when I tell you to."

He kissed her waist, bit her lightly on the curve of her ass, and kept a steady rhythm within her. He'd stop, twirl a finger, rub her clit with increased speed, then stop again. She felt orgasms build, then retreat, only to come back stronger and fiercer in their promise.

"Oh, God"—she gripped his leg—"don't stop again. Please."

"I like it when you beg."

"Don't make me kick your ass," she threatened in a haze of frustrated desire.

He chuckled, but his hand started moving again, faster than before, while his thumb lavishly rewarded her most sensitive spot. "Now, Sarah. Come for me."

"Yes," she groaned as she wept, moving her hips against the fingers he'd paused within her.

He released her hair, removed his hand, and rolled her over in his arms, kissing her lightly as the last waves of orgasm shook through her. She laid her head on his shoulder, closed her eyes, and said, "Apology accepted."

He chuckled again, then stood, still holding her in his arms as he carried her to his bedroom. Later, spent and wrapped in each other's arms, Tony was just about to fall asleep when Sarah asked,

"Would you be upset if I quickly write a few things in my notebook before I forget them?"

He opened one eye and said, "I don't know which I should worry about more—that you have enough energy to write, or that you're afraid you'll forget what we did."

Sarah laughed and stood naked beside the bed. "Would it help if I told you that I want to capture the wonder of it all?"

He smiled and closed his eyes with a groan. "Go get your notebook. You can read it to me tomorrow, and if you forgot any details, we can repeat tonight again and again. Purely to help you with your research."

Sarah lifted his shirt off the floor and threw it at him. He caught it a few inches above his head, smiled, and dropped it to the floor.

Pulling her notebook and a pen out of her bag, Sarah headed back to the bed. *I hope he doesn't really believe I'm doing this for my book. What we have is about so much more than sex.*

Isn't it?

Chapter Nineteen

Three weeks later, Sarah was sitting on the porch in a cotton summer dress and the new cowboy boots Tony had surprised her with, hugging her notebook to her chest. Time had flown by in a happy haze of notebook-worthy lovemaking. Being with a lover who was both demanding and respectful of her preferences gave Sarah a confidence she had never imagined possible. It wasn't about what she would or wouldn't do; it was about what they enjoyed doing together and how the trust between them was growing.

She woke in his arms each morning, loving the warm kiss he gave her and how reluctant he always was to leave her. He'd returned to his training schedule and Sarah had found a comfortable rhythm to the ranch days. She helped Melanie with the morning cleanup, read books with Jace, and dragged them both to town to shop for Tony's house. At first their conversations were strained, but as trust began to build, a friendship was born.

Sarah took photos of the people who worked on the ranch and framed them, placing them on the walls and around the house on tables. With Tony's permission, she replaced his old furniture with simple but comfortable pieces that made a person want to stay for a while. The quiet of the house was replaced with soft music on most days, and Sarah had even convinced Tony that he needed not only a television but also a computer and Internet access. Slowly, Tony's house was becoming a home.

A home she felt comfortable enough to spend her afternoons writing in. Her once-empty notebook was overflowing with answered questions, drafts of chapters, revisions, characters based on people she'd met through the ranch, and steamy scenes she couldn't believe she'd been able to write. Sarah had never felt more alive or at peace.

This is where I belong.

Thursdays had become days she looked forward to. She'd been apprehensive when Tony had suggested she invite everyone to dinner again, but he'd reassured her things would be different, and he'd been right. Everyone, including Dean, had been on their best behavior, and real conversations had replaced the previous ribbing and uneasiness.

Tony would never be a man of many words, but when he'd patiently answered questions from the young men around the table regarding his training philosophy—and even praised one of them for his work with a horse—Sarah's heart had soared. Like rain coming to the desert, the change in Tony brought his ranch alive. After dinner, she and Tony often walked, hand in hand, through the barn and paddocks. Tony greeted the men he came across, and she even caught him smiling more than once.

Everything was perfect.

So perfect that Sarah accepted that Tony didn't talk about his feelings or the future. She told herself that she didn't need the words because his actions showed the world he cared about her.

Maybe even loves.

Sarah hugged her notebook more tightly.

Definitely loves.

In the main barn, Tony absently brushed down the horse he'd just exercised and fought to empty his mind of the images from his latest nightmare. Sarah didn't know he was still having them, and he wasn't about to tell her they were getting worse rather than better.

Images of the girl who had died tormented him long after he awoke. The happier he was during the day, the more pleasure he found with Sarah in his bed, the uglier and more graphic his nightmares became, until the message in them began to overshadow what should have been a good time in his life.

Kimberly Staten.

Are you haunting me or am I torturing myself?

Which one of us is convinced that I don't deserve to be happy?

His hand paused as an image of Sarah, smiling sweetly up at him during one of their evening walks, mocked him. *How can she be the best and the worst thing that has ever happened to me? Is that the hell I earned for myself? To have everything offered to me and not be able to enjoy it? To watch a good woman fall in love with me and know that ultimately I'll disappoint her?*

And Sarah was a good woman. Everything she touched was better for the attention she gave it. His house finally looked lived-in, his employees were happier than he'd ever seen them, and David said their clients appreciated the sparkly hoof polish she applied to each horse they sold. Dean dropped by the ranch a few times a week, and each time he did he mentioned how good everything and everyone looked.

So I smile and lie.

I let everyone believe that Sarah's magic has worked on me as well.

Because the truth is as ugly as my nightmares. No matter how much I want to, I'll never be the man she needs me to be.

Chapter Twenty

Sarah was sitting on the porch steps and had just finished revising a chapter in her book when a long black limo pulled into Tony's driveway. She stood up and shaded her eyes to see it better. A prospective buyer? Had Tony gotten to the point where he was willing to meet with them now? A swell of pride rushed through her. *He's come so far.*

When the tuxedoed driver walked around to open the rear passenger door, Sarah held her breath and then instantly recognized the expensive shoes and business suit before she saw the face of the man they belonged to. *Charlie!*

She sprinted down the driveway, her smile growing wider as she did. She'd wanted to tell him the details of her new life in Texas but had been waiting for the perfect time. Now she could show him instead.

He took off his dark sunglasses and looked around even after Sarah had come to a near-sliding stop in front of him. "So, this is where you've been all summer."

Despite how serious her brother appeared, Sarah threw her arms around him and hugged him. "I'm so glad you came."

The hug he gave her in return wasn't as enthusiastic as she would have liked, but she blamed fatigue. He'd traveled a long way, and no doubt his formal attire was making him miserable in the heat of the afternoon sun. He replaced his sunglasses and without smiling said, "Mom and Dad sent me after you spoke to them. They said you think you're staying here."

Sarah waved an arm behind her and said, "I'm happy here, Charlie. For the first time in forever I feel like I know where I belong. And I'm writing. I'm halfway through a book. Can you believe it?"

He didn't say anything, but his mouth pressed into a straight line of displeasure. "It's time to go home, Sarah."

Before she had time to say more, Tony appeared beside them. Country met city as they sized each other up. Two men who were used to intimidating those around them squared off in a bit of a standoff, as if waiting to see who would blink first. Sarah took Tony's left hand in hers. "Tony, this is my brother, Charlie."

Tony held out his hand and said, "Welcome."

Charlie hesitated just long enough to make Sarah want to kick him. *Not here. Not now. Don't judge this, Charlie. He means too much to me.*

"Charles," her brother said, correcting Sarah's name for him. Their handshake looked a bit brutal on both sides. "So, this is your place." He released Tony's hand and looked around.

Tony nodded once.

Trying to lighten the mood, Sarah asked, "You must be tired, Charlie. Let's go in the house. It's much cooler in there."

Her brother glanced over his shoulder at the white ranch house, then back at Sarah. His tone was arctic cold. "Is that where you're staying?"

Tony answered for her with one curt word. "Yes."

Charlie turned and said something to the driver, who nodded and reentered the limo, moving it to a place in the shade. "Then by all means, let's go inside."

As the three of them marched toward the house like it was a guillotine, Sarah searched Tony's face. It was impossible to tell from his guarded expression if he was nervous about meeting her brother or put off by his attitude. Charlie could be a bit of a pill, but he was her only brother and she wanted these two men to get along.

As they stepped into the main foyer of the house, Melanie and her son came out of the kitchen to meet them. Melanie's reaction to seeing her brother was almost comical. Her eyes rounded, her jaw went slack, and she instantly started shoving her loose tendrils back into her ponytail.

Charlie looked over Sarah's head at Tony, and in a tone as quiet as it was deadly, he asked, "Who is she?"

Sarah jumped in, "That's Melanie, his housekeeper."

"Does she live here, too?"

What are you doing, Charlie? What's with the interrogation? "She has her own house on the other side of the barn."

"Convenient," Charlie said, his displeasure and innuendo clear to all.

Melanie's face reddened. "It is since I spend most of my day working here."

"I'm sure you do."

Tony made a noise deep in his chest that sounded an awful lot like a warning growl. "Melanie, why don't you and Sarah take Jace into the kitchen and get us a drink. I'm sure Charles is thirsty."

Sarah looked back and forth between the two of them. She didn't want to leave them. She'd really wanted their first meeting to be pleasant, but her brother was being an ass, and if their past was anything to go by, nothing she could say would change that.

When Charlie made up his mind about something, he could be as stubborn as Tony.

I don't know why I thought he'd approve.

He's never approved of anything I've ever done.

He'll say this is for my own good, but it's about him. Without me around, he's probably afraid he'll have to go home and deal with Mom and Dad himself.

Don't judge me for leaving, Charlie—you left a long time ago.

That last thought convinced Sarah that Charlie deserved whatever Tony was about to say to him.

Tony took a calming breath. *I can't punch Sarah's brother.*

I'd love to, but I shouldn't. "It would mean a lot to Sarah if you pretend to be happy for her," he said.

Charles whipped off his sunglasses and glared at Tony. "I deal in facts, not fantasy like she does. You may have her fooled, but I've had you investigated, and I don't like anything I learned about you."

One corner of Tony's mouth curled sarcastically. "I'm beginning to understand why she had to leave Rhode Island."

His face red with fury, Charles snarled, "You're a violent drunk who should be rotting in jail instead of making a fool out of my sister in all the gossip rags."

A deadly calm swept through Tony. His past had found a voice at last. He went toe-to-toe with Charles, striking out at him with words in a way he knew would wipe that superior look off his face. "I haven't had a drink in four years. My guilt or innocence is my own business. But your sister, she's a good fuck." He regretted the words even as they came out of his mouth.

Charles hauled back to punch Tony, but Tony caught his fist in his hand, his strength buoyed by a rage that had simmered inside him for years. He dropped it in disgust and prepared for another strike.

Melanie's voice carried clearly in the charged quiet moment that followed. "Sarah, he didn't mean that."

Tony's head spun in time to see the two glasses of lemonade in Sarah's hands fall and shatter on the wooden floor at her feet. Shaking her head slowly back and forth, she turned and ran out the front door.

Tony looked back at Charles just in time to receive a brain-rattling punch that set him back a step. The world beneath Tony tilted and he shook his head to clear it, preparing to deliver a crushing rebuttal.

Melanie was between them before he raised his fist. She was spitting angry. She threw her glasses of lemonade in their faces, which brought them both to a shocked, temporary cease-fire. "You two just broke that girl's heart. If one of you doesn't chase after her to apologize, I'm coming back with a frying pan."

The real concern in Melanie's voice focused Tony's attention on Sarah's vulnerability. This wasn't about what her brother thought of him. He'd let the mention of his past cause him to say something he would always regret.

Melanie didn't look like she needed any help defending her honor. *She wasn't joking about the frying pan.* Tony set off in long strides to find Sarah.

She was holding on to the railing at the corner of the porch, her pale cheeks wet with tears. He went to stand beside her, searching for what to say to erase the hurt he'd caused.

She turned to him, folded her arms protectively across her chest, and said, "Is that what you think of me? What I am to you?"

He shook his head. "Of course not."

Her tear-filled eyes searched his. "I want to believe you. I really do, but I need you to give me a reason to."

"What do you want me to say?" he asked, his gut clenching painfully.

She wiped her cheeks with her hands and implored, "Tell me you love me. Tell me this is real and that this summer has meant as much to you as it has to me."

He reached for her, but she pulled back, waiting.

He wanted to say what he knew she needed to hear. He wanted to so badly that he almost did, but he chose honesty at the last second. "I care about you."

She released an audible, shaky breath and demanded, "But you don't love me. Say it. Stop pretending to be someone I could spend the rest of my life with, and just say it."

He rubbed his chin and shook his head sadly. "I want to love you."

Her eyes filled with tears, but she straightened her shoulders and said, "Okay."

He hadn't wanted to hurt her. He'd never wanted to hurt her. He grabbed her arm. "I didn't mean what I said back there to your brother. I let my temper choose my words and I'm sorry."

She pulled her arm out of his grasp and said, "It's fine. I understand. I shouldn't have left the two of you alone. I knew my brother was being a bastard. I guess I hoped you'd put him in his place." A lone tear ran down her face. "I just didn't know you'd use me to do it."

"Sarah, don't . . ."

She met his eyes and he knew that no matter what he said, he'd already lost her. She held up a hand in a request for him to stop talking. "Please. Stop. I know you said it to hurt my brother and not me, but maybe I needed to hear it. I was imagining us living happily ever after, but you can't do that, can you? Because you can't let yourself be happy."

He didn't have to say anything. She knew him too well.

"I'm going to hook up my trailer and load Scooter. If you can ask Melanie to come see me, I'd appreciate it."

She's leaving. She's really leaving.

"I can ready your trailer for you."

Sarah shook her head sadly. "No, I'll do it myself. Just get Melanie."

Tony turned and walked back into the house. Charles was headed toward the front door when they met up. The two men stopped and glared at each other.

Tony said, "She's packing up."

"Good," Charles said curtly. They both knew he'd gotten what he came for. There was nothing left for him to say.

The same couldn't be said for Tony. He took a step closer and said, "Get your head out of your pinstriped ass and say something nice to her."

"I don't need someone like you to tell me how to deal with my sister," Charles countered coldly.

Tony leaned closer and said, "From where I'm standing, it looks like you do—before you lose her, too." Having spoken his mind, Tony walked away to find Melanie.

Sarah was loading the rest of Scooter's tack into the front compartment of her horse trailer when Melanie joined her.

"The boys could have done all that for you," she said.

Sarah closed the door of the trailer, leaning against it with one hand. "I wanted to. I needed to do something while I calmed down."

"Did you talk to your brother yet?"

Glancing over at the limo she knew Charlie had returned to, Sarah shook her head. "No, I'm surprised he didn't storm over here and gloat, but I'm grateful he didn't. I don't think I could handle him right now."

"Where are you going?"

"I was hoping you'd have an idea of someplace that boards horses."

"You heading back to Rhode Island?"

Sarah leaned her back against the trailer and closed her eyes. "I don't know where I'm going, but I have some money saved so I have options."

"What about that friend who owns a cattle ranch? You made up."

Sarah opened her eyes and shook her head. "Lucy? She has her own problems. I need a peaceful place where I can finish my book. That's the important thing to me now that I finished what I came down here to do."

"You could stay with my parents. They have a place a few towns over. Very quiet. They've always had horses. They wouldn't even notice Scooter. There's an attached apartment they don't use. I'm sure they'd let you stay for free."

"I don't mind paying rent. It sounds wonderful, but if it's that great why don't you live there?"

Melanie tried to make light of something she was clearly uncomfortable discussing. "Could you live with your parents?"

"Okay, good point."

"I'll call them now. They're only about two hours away."

"Is that enough notice?"

"I'm sure it is. I'll run in and call them. Give me five minutes."

Sarah nodded. "Mel, one other thing."

"Anything."

Sarah swallowed painfully. "Could you pack up my stuff and bring it down?" Just the thought of doing it herself made her stomach twist and threaten to hurl. She covered her mouth with one shaky hand. "I can't go back in there."

Melanie smiled sympathetically and hugged her. "Sure thing, hon."

Sarah hugged her back and marveled that their friendship had blossomed despite its rocky start. "I'll miss you, Mel."

"You're only going a couple of hours away, not dying. Jace and I will come visit you. With you there, my parents may actually behave long enough for me to survive a visit."

After Melanie had gone back into the house, Sarah knew she couldn't put the unpleasant conversation off any longer. The limo driver opened the rear passenger door for her as she approached, and she slid into the air-conditioned domain of her brother.

Charlie pocketed his cell phone and said, "I can't wait to get back to civilization. My cell phone works everywhere but not here. Leave your vehicle for now. As soon as we're on the highway, I'll send a driver for it. I have a private plane waiting in an airfield just outside Dallas. You'll be home by tonight."

It was obvious that Charlie still considered Scooter no different than a vehicle. Just another item to be shipped up North and another part of her life that he didn't understand.

Bracing with a hand on either side of herself, Sarah said, "I'm not going back to Rhode Island. Not today. Maybe not ever."

Charlie gave her an impatient look. "Don't be ridiculous. Of course you are."

"No, Charlie, I'm not. I came to Texas because I wanted to find out what was holding me back from writing—from being who I felt I should be." He didn't understand, but this time Sarah needed him to. "You know what I discovered? I was all locked up inside myself. We never really talked about what happened with Phil because that's the deal we made that summer—we'd close off that chapter of our lives and pretend it never happened. But you know what living a lie does to you? It kills you slowly, Charlie. It's not healthy."

Charlie's expression hardened at the mention of the brother they'd lost. "What's not healthy is thinking that embarrassing yourself down here with some has-been celebrity is going to do anything more than hurt Mom and Dad. Grow up, Sarah."

Slapping the leather beside her, Sarah said, "No, you grow up, Charlie. Grow up and face that something awful happened to our family and none of us got over it. You're not here to save me. Admit to yourself that the only reason you want me back in Rhode Island is so you don't have to be. I'm done pretending I never had a little brother. I don't care if it upsets Mom and Dad, I'm going to ask them to send me pictures of him—pictures of all of us together. I want to remember him. I'm going to remember him. And if you can't handle that, go back to New York and hide." When Charlie remained stone-faced, Sarah asked, "Do you blame me, Charlie? Is that why you can't discuss it?"

A visible shudder betrayed how deeply her words touched him. His jaw was white with tension. "God no. I never blamed you." He didn't say more and Sarah's heart broke for him.

"It was an accident, Charlie."

In a voice full of self-hate, Charlie said, "Mom and Dad asked me to watch both of you while they were cooking. I should have stayed with you, but I wanted to ask them something. I don't even remember what was so goddamn important."

"We were kids."

"Maybe you can tell yourself that, but I was twelve—old enough to know better."

Suddenly, Sarah understood what had torn her family apart. She closed her eyes for a moment to gather her strength, opened them, and said, "I've told myself it was my fault every day since he died. Every single day. Guess what? It was my fault. And it was yours. And it was Mom and Dad's. We can keep blaming ourselves and each other, but none of that is going to bring him back. None of it will make us back into the family we might have been."

Charlie shook his head, refusing to hear what she was saying. Sarah thought about Tony and the pain he refused to let go of. In the saddest of ways, Tony and her brother had more in common than either would likely ever know. Maybe it was time to admit that both were beyond her reach. "I thought I could heal Tony, but I can't. If you want to torture yourself for the rest of your life, I can't stop you. But I'm not going to live like that anymore. I'm going to find a place where I can be happy. Good-bye, Charlie."

Sarah opened the limo door before he could say anything and closed it behind her, raising her face to the cleansing brightness of the sun. She looked around and saw Tony standing in the barn doorway with Scooter. Melanie and Travis were putting her luggage in the back of her SUV. Melanie waved the notebook in the air, making sure Sarah knew it had made it to the vehicle, and gave her a thumbs-up regarding her parents. Sarah groaned. Only she and Tony knew the subject of her novel, and now she had to face him again to get her horse.

Tony walked Scooter to the trailer. Sarah took the lead line from him and stopped just in front of him, looking up into his eyes. She wanted to hate him. She wanted to storm away with some sophisticated cutting remark that would make him feel as badly as she did.

And she wanted to hug him and tell him that she understood.

Instead, she said softly, "Do you know how little it would take to make me stay? I love you."

His face filled with a mixture of sadness and farewell. "I know."

"I don't regret any of it, Tony. Not one moment of it."

His eyes glistened, then he turned and walked away, leaving her to numbly take directions from Melanie while one of the ranch hands finished loading Scooter. Sarah stopped at the turn in the driveway, waiting one last time, hoping to see Tony appear in her rear-view mirror.

He didn't, and that was when she knew it was really over.

Chapter Twenty-One

Tony stepped out of the barn to watch Sarah's SUV pull onto the main road. Her brother's limo pulled out directly after. Tony felt the presence of David at his side, but didn't acknowledge it until they were both gone. Then, without looking away from the path they'd driven, Tony said, "Say it. Tell me I'm a fool to let her go."

In a surprising twist, David didn't. Instead, he said, "She couldn't stay. You're not ready for her. Staying wouldn't change that."

In that moment outside of time, Tony admitted, "I hurt her and I never meant to."

David took his time answering. "You've hurt a lot of people since I met you, Tony, and I've never seen you look sorry about it."

"I never felt sorry," he said. "I stopped feeling anything a long time ago."

"Until Sarah," David diagnosed.

Softly, Tony agreed, "Yeah."

The two men continued looking out over the empty driveway in silence. Finally, David said, "Five years ago I came here thinking I'd find a man celebrating his court victory. I was ready to cut you down a peg or two and shove a bit of reality in your face. But you taught me something instead."

They both knew the condition David had found him in, so Tony didn't bother to ask. He'd rather not know.

David continued, "I learned that in a tragedy there are no winners, only people struggling to survive the aftermath."

Tony nodded slowly and said, "You sure I was worth saving? I am one miserable bastard."

"And you always will be until you face your past."

"I face it every day, every night. It never leaves me," Tony said in frustration.

"I'm no psychologist, but it seems to me that when something pesters you that much you haven't dealt with it the way it needs to be."

What the hell is that supposed to mean? Tony would have asked, but David had walked away.

A week later, Dean came by around dinnertime. Tony was sitting at the small table in the kitchen, not touching the plate of food that Melanie had placed in front of him. He hadn't eaten in days. Nor had he left the house. He'd tried to go back to the way things were before Sarah, but instead of feeling nothing, he felt an overwhelming sadness.

"You look like hell, Tony," Dean said.

Tony rubbed a hand over the week's growth of beard on his face. He felt like hell. "Isn't there sheriff business somewhere that you're late for?"

"You drinking again?"

Tony shook his head, pushed himself away from the table with two hands, and stood. "No, but if I were I wouldn't need you here butting into what has always been none of your business."

"You're my brother. You are my business."

"Half brother. Consider that your ticket to freedom from any responsibility."

Dean sat back against the kitchen counter, not appearing bothered by Tony's foul mood. "I've been making excuses for you since the first time I met you. David said you haven't been feeling well."

"Is there a point to this conversation? If so, make it and get out."

Folding his arms across his chest, Dean said, "I should. I was never happier than the day I found out I had a little brother. I know you blamed my mother for yours leaving, and maybe I always felt a bit guilty about that. I never stopped hoping you'd get over it. When you bought this place, I moved here because you were self-destructing. Everyone figured it was only time before someone found you dead. I came here for you, Tony. And I stayed, smoothing over every mess you made. Keeping your ass out of jail every time you threw someone off your property with enough force to have warranted an assault charge. Now you're self-destructing again, and I can't sit back and watch it happen. I don't expect you to be grateful."

"Good, because I never asked you to get involved in any part of my life."

Dean's face whitened a bit in anger. "You're right, you never did—and you never thanked me. You're an ungrateful ass."

"Then why are you still here when you know I don't want you to be?" Tony goaded.

Dean pushed off the counter, his hands clenching at his sides. "I give up. You want to be as miserable as our father was."

"I'm nothing like him."

"Are you kidding? You're *exactly* like him. He was one cold, unfeeling bastard. Do you even know if he's still alive? I don't, and I don't care. He's going to die alone, just like you will if you don't wake up." Dean turned to leave.

"Dean," Tony said, his tone free of all its earlier sarcasm.

Dean turned back.

As close to an apology as he could voice, Tony said, "I don't know how to be anyone but who I am."

Releasing a long sigh, Dean said, "Yes, you do."

Dean had always seen good where there was none. Still, Tony felt driven to tell him what he'd been considering. "I've been thinking about going to see Kimberly Staten's father."

Dean's eyebrows shot up to his hairline. "Is that wise?"

"I never told him that I was sorry about his daughter. It's time I do."

Dean approached Tony, then stood in front of him in a show of support. "You want me to go with you?"

Tony shook his head. "No."

"Then why tell me?"

I don't know.

There was a past between them that he'd never spoken of, and maybe it needed acknowledging. "I may never be a good brother to you, but I don't blame you for my mother leaving. I can't imagine any woman being able to stay with him for very long." The past was there, vivid between them. "I always resented how happy you were, how easy your life looked. You and your mother would visit for a day, laughing and talking about where you'd been or what you'd done together, giving me a glimpse of what a family could look like, and then you'd leave again. I used to wonder what it would be like if I left with you. I doubt our father would have cared if I had."

"You could have come with us. My mother would have taken you in."

Tony didn't doubt the truth of that. Dean had gotten his giving side from his mother. "That was your life, not mine."

"It could be yours now. You don't have to be our father. Whatever path you take today is one of your choosing, not anyone else's."

Tony put his hand on his brother's shoulder, the first time he'd ever voluntarily touched him. "I want to be the man Sarah believed I was."

Dean nodded in understanding, then stepped back and said, "Then clean the fuck up, because you smelled an awful lot better when she was here."

Tony smiled, lowering his hand and releasing some tension in a short laugh. "That might explain why Melanie has been leaving my food and running away."

Dean smiled back and joked, "Probably had nothing to do with your foul mood, either."

"Me? Moody?" Tony looked across at his brother in feigned surprise.

Dean's smile widened. "Come to dinner at my mom's house this Sunday. She'd like to see you."

The automatic refusal died, unspoken, on Tony's lips. The past only had the power he gave it, and Margery, Dean's mother, was another part of it that he'd denied for too long. "I'd like that."

Dean left smiling, probably the only time Tony had ever seen him leave happier than when he'd arrived.

Two weeks after leaving Tony's ranch, Sarah had just returned from a long, cathartic ride in the fields surrounding Melanie's parents' home. Her cheeks were still flushed from the rush of Scooter's ground-covering gallop. She'd smiled through untacking and brushing him down and was cooling him off by hand, walking him on the dirt road in front of the horse barn.

She missed Tony, but she refused to let herself wallow in the feelings that swamped her when she thought of him. She couldn't hate him. He'd never been anything but honest with her. She was the one who had invaded his home, practically thrown herself at him, ignored all the warnings he gave her, and then left when she'd discovered that he was the man he'd always claimed to be.

Melanie's parents, Steve and Cindy, could not have been nicer. They set her up in the attached apartment that they said they'd made for Melanie when she was pregnant. Why she hadn't stayed there and why they had kept it empty weren't questions anyone offered to answer, so Sarah didn't ask. She understood family taboo topics.

For now, she helped their three daughters, all in their late teens and early twenties, do the barn chores and clean up after meals. It never ceased to amaze Sarah that the women in Mel's family were so friendly, happy, and feminine. The way they did their nails, carefully styled their hair, and pored over fashion magazines gave Sarah an instant rapport with them. *Vogue* was a language Sarah was fluent in.

Things were comfortable at Steve and Cindy's home, except when Melanie and Jace visited. The first time had that awkward it's-been-a-long-time feeling to it. But Melanie kept coming to see Sarah once a week and, although the atmosphere felt strained, at least everyone was civil. Sarah wanted to ask what had happened that made them all so uncomfortable around each other, but she didn't. *I haven't spoken to my brother since I left Tony's house, so who am I to judge?*

Sarah spun at the sound of gravel crunching beneath tires. *Can it be? Has he finally come?*

A slap of disappointment was quickly followed by confusion. Her brother, dressed like he was going to attend a board meeting in the city, stepped out of a stretch limo with a cardboard box so large it required both of his arms to carry. Sarah rushed to put Scooter in his paddock and returned to the driveway.

Charlie stopped, still holding the box in front him, his sunglasses too dark for Sarah to be able to predict his mood. "I brought you something," he said gruffly.

Not the warm greeting some might have offered, but considering how they'd left things, it was a promising start. Sarah pointed to the side door of the house. "Come on in out of the heat. I'll get you a drink and you can show it to me."

Inside the small apartment that she was temporarily calling home, Charlie set the box down on the table in the small living room and looked around. The furnishings were mismatched leftovers she'd thought were quaint until he stood appraising them.

"How are you?" he asked, surprising her.

"Busy. I'm writing more than I ever thought I could." *But that's not what you were asking about, is it?* She added, "Sad, but I'm okay. At least, I'm determined to be."

"Have you heard from him?"

Tears pricked Sarah's eyes, but she forced a brave smile. "No, but I didn't expect to."

Charlie sat down heavily on one of the couch's thick cushions. "He wasn't the right man for you."

Sarah went to the refrigerator and poured two glasses of water. She handed one to her brother and sat in a chair across from him. "Maybe not, but it was my decision to make, not yours."

"I know," he said, removing his sunglasses and pinching the ridge of his nose as if fighting a headache. "I'm sorry."

Had Sarah not been sitting, she would have sunk to the floor in shock. Her brother never apologized—ever. She was pretty sure he'd been genetically shortchanged on the ability to. Her voice thick with emotion, she said, "Thank you. I needed to hear that."

Pocketing his glasses, Charlie turned to face Sarah directly and said, "And I needed to hear what you said to me at that ranch. I didn't want to hear it, but I needed to."

Sarah raised a hand and covered her trembling lips. Silent tears poured down her cheeks as she watched her proud brother reach across all that had divided them. "I went home to see Mom and Dad when I flew back. I asked them for pictures of Phil and any albums they had of us all together. It's all there in that box. They saved everything."

Vision blurred with tears, Sarah rushed to the box and opened it reverently. Just as Charlie had said, it was full of photo albums and loose photos in clear plastic bags. She flipped one album open and smiled through her tears at the first photo. Charlie at nine years old and she at five, sitting on a hospital bed posing with their newborn brother, Phil. They looked happy and nervous at the same time, like they were afraid they'd break him.

Sarah wiped one of her wet cheeks and said, "Would you look at them with me, Charlie?"

He crossed the room and put an arm around her shaking shoulders. "For as long as you want me to."

She and Charlie moved to sit side by side on the couch with the box of photos wedged between them. She showed him the first photo and said, "We really were so young."

Faced with the evidence of his own youth, Charlie said, "Do you remember how everything made him laugh? It didn't matter how many times we showed him the same puppet, he was just as amazed by it."

As they turned the pages of the album, Sarah said, "I remember how determined you were to teach him to walk. And then when he learned to, you were sorry because he followed you everywhere."

Sarah stopped at one photo and smiled. She and Phil were in a wagon that Charlie had tied to the back of his bike and was pulling up and down the long paved driveway of their parents' house. "I believe you had two shadows you couldn't escape."

Charlie looked at her sadly and said, "I did."

"What happened to us, Charlie?" Sarah whispered.

His face tight with sadness and shame, Charlie said, "I don't know. I didn't want to know. I wanted to be as far away from all of this as I could get."

"We all did. But running away from it never made me feel better. Pretending it hadn't happened was slowly killing me." Sarah hugged the album to her chest, her eyes filling with tears again. "Thank you for this. Ignore the tears. You've made me really happy by coming here."

Charlie lightened the mood by referencing the mascara that was smeared across the lapel of his suit coat. "Does that mean this is the last suit Texas will ruin? My other one still smells like lemonade."

Sarah gave him a playful swat. "You deserved that."

A glimmer of a smile tugged at Charlie's mouth. "That was one hotheaded housekeeper."

Sarah sat back and slapped her leg as she realized something. "Oh my God. You like Melanie."

"No."

"She'll be here for dinner tonight with her son, Jace."

"I'm not staying."

"You're going to run away because you like her. You think she's pretty."

"She's not my type," Charlie growled defensively.

Sarah laughed. "I know, that's what makes this perfect. The business tycoon and the cowgirl. Both convinced they don't need the other. Both determined not to change. Then *wham*, they fall in love and nothing else matters."

Eyebrows furrowed, Charlie asked, "Did you hit your head on something?"

"No." Sarah clapped and laughed again. "Even worse. I started writing romances."

With a groan, Charlie reached for another album. "Let's go back to why I'm here."

The mood had been lightened with jokes; Sarah relaxed back against her brother's side and opened the second album. "I think you need a woman who is not afraid to threaten you with a frying pan."

"I think you need to drop it."

"Okay, but if I'm right, you have to learn to ride a horse."

"And if you're wrong?"

"I'll make you that double-chocolate fudge cake you always used to ask for when we were little. I'm sure Mom still has the recipe."

"I'd rather ride a horse. I've tasted your cooking."

Sarah laughed. "That's low, Charlie. Real low."

He relaxed, too, and laughed next to her. It was the first time she'd seen this unguarded side of him. "You're all about facing the truth. Hurts, doesn't it?" he joked.

No. It actually feels pretty damn wonderful.

Chapter Twenty-Two

"Mr. Staten will see you now," the secretary announced, leading the way to his office.

Tony adjusted the tie he'd worn for the occasion. He wasn't one to dress up in a suit, but the older man deserved the respect that wearing one would pay him. This wasn't a conversation Tony thought belonged in the workplace, but since it was the only place Evan Staten had offered, it would have to do.

Tall and white-haired, Evan was an imposing figure even in his late sixties. Tony stood in the doorway of the office, but his hesitation had more to do with the photos of Kimberly displayed throughout the room. Looking at those happy images reminded him of her joy the first time she'd successfully ridden the stallion that would later take her life. She'd been an intense young woman who lived 150 percent in the moment, and he had to admit that the day he'd handed the reins over to her had also been a good one for him. He'd been filled with his own sense of accomplishment, having done what many had said was impossible.

"You coming in or not? When I heard you wanted to see me, Carlton, I wasn't sure you'd actually have the nerve to show up."

Tony stepped inside and closed the door behind him. He met the older man's eyes and said, "I appreciate you seeing me."

Evan stood and walked to the front of his desk. He picked up a photo of his daughter and looked down at it as he spoke, his face twisting with bitterness. "Do you know how many times I've imagined this moment? In the beginning, I used to fantasize about simply killing you—evening the debt. Only the love I have for my wife stopped me. She couldn't have borne losing me along with Kimberly."

Tony took a few steps into the room. He stopped several feet away from Evan and remained silent.

Putting the photo down, Evan looked at Tony, his face set in harsh lines. "I would have ruined you, but you destroyed your own career. You cheated me from even that pleasure."

Tony nodded, still giving the other man free rein to verbally flog him. It was the least he could do, considering what he'd taken from him.

"When I heard that you'd called, I thought about how many ways I'd tell you what a piece of shit you are. You should be rotting in jail. You don't deserve to have a life after you took my daughter's," Evan snarled. "And you did kill her. I might not have been able to prove it in court, but it was because of your negligence that she died. Yet you sat there in court as if it had nothing to do with you. You couldn't even look me in the eye. You know why? Because you're a coward, Carlton."

Tony inhaled sharply, but he met the older man's gaze respectfully. His temper was fully in check because this was not about him. This was for Kimberly, and for the father who had loved and lost her. Besides, Evan wasn't saying anything Tony hadn't thought himself many times over the past five years.

Evan leaned back against his desk and folded his arms across his chest. "What would a man like you think he could possibly have to say that I would want to hear?"

Studying the photo of Kimberly on the wall behind Evan's desk made what Tony had held in for so long easier to say. "Not a day has gone by since your daughter died that I haven't thought of her, that I haven't regretted ever agreeing to work with that stallion."

Voice full of sarcasm, Evan said, "Sounds like a good burden for a guilty man to carry."

Tony didn't deny that charge. "I am guilty, guilty of arrogantly believing I could fix an animal that was clearly dangerous. Guilty of letting my confidence blind me to what I should have seen. Your daughter paid the price for that mistake, and I will carry that truth with me for the rest of my life. Words could never express how sorry I am for what I did."

Suddenly unsteady on his feet, Evan sank into the chair near his desk. His face went white, and Tony took a concerned step toward him, then stopped. "Should I leave?"

With a harsh shake of his head, Evan looked down for a moment. "I've spent a good many years hating you, Carlton."

"For good reason, sir."

"I waited for you to pick yourself up and try to rebuild your career. I wanted to destroy you as you'd almost done me." Evan looked up, referencing the office around him. "I used to care about all of this. I built a business and a reputation from practically nothing. What people thought of me used to matter, but I would have thrown that all away just to take you down." He gripped the arm of his chair. "My men told me you were drinking yourself to death and hiding up in Fort Mavis. Sounds like you made your own prison."

Tony met his eyes again and said, "I couldn't live with the guilt, but I suppose I was too much of a coward to take my own life."

The old man shook his head sadly. "Dying's easy. It's living that takes courage."

"I haven't done either particularly well," Tony said quietly.

Pushing himself to stand again, Evan approached Tony and searched his face with sharp eyes. Finally, he said, "Not many people do. I need you to be guilty, Carlton, or I have to face that Kimberly's death was likely my fault."

Tony started to speak, but Evan made a sound deep in his throat and waved a hand to silence him. He picked up another photo of her from his desk, one from when she was just a toddler. "Kim was our only child, and she came to my wife and me long after we'd given up thinking we could have children. She was our miracle. I never said no to her. I should have, but I never did. Spoiling a child feels good at first, but you reap what you sow, and Kimberly was impossible to deny when she wanted something. People tried to tell me about that horse's history and his reputation, but Kimberly wanted him. Hell, I fired the only man who tried to talk me out of buying him. Told him that if he didn't have what it took to break that horse, I'd find someone who could. Looking back, Harmon was the only one brave enough to stand up to me when he disagreed with me."

David Harmon? His manager? Is it possible that David had worked for the Statens and never said a word?

"The man I replaced him with hired you. So you see, I carry my own guilt."

Normally a man of few words, Tony felt that Evan needed to hear something. "Someone recently told me that there are no winners in a tragedy, only people struggling to survive the aftermath."

"Can't say I've ever heard truer words spoken." Evan nodded sadly and rubbed his hands roughly over his face. When he looked at Tony, he looked older, sadder. "Have you said all you came to say, Mr. Carlton?"

"Yes, sir," Tony said, understanding the dismissal for what it was. He turned and opened the door, feeling there was more he wanted to say, but not knowing for sure what it was. When he closed the door, he saw Evan still looking down at the photo of his daughter and the sight touched his heart.

I wish to God I knew how to ease his pain.

Instead of immediately driving back to his ranch, Tony found himself pulling into a cemetery he'd considered visiting many times but never had. He knew exactly where Kimberly was buried. He'd always known.

With his hat in his hand, he stood before her headstone and softly spoke aloud. "I'm not a praying man and I don't know if you can hear me, but there has to be more than this. It can't all be about what we've done wrong and those we've let down. Your dad says he gave you everything, Kimberly. Give me something for him."

There was no sudden breeze. No light from above. Tony replaced his hat and shook his head. *What did I expect? If there's anyone up there, why the hell would they listen to me?* He returned to his truck and headed home.

On the way, he thought about David and what it meant if he'd been fired by the Statens and then come to the Double C after Kimberly's death. *What had he said? He'd come to slap me with reality and had expected to find me celebrating my not-guilty verdict. Instead, he found me drunk and sinking fast.* It wasn't easy for Tony to look back at that dark time and how close he'd come to ending his own life.

I wouldn't be alive today if David hadn't come to find me.

He tried to save Kimberly and failed.

So he saved me.

A random thought followed and almost made Tony smile. *I hope I pay him.*

A few hours later, Tony avoided David and his ranch hands and took off for a long ride on the horse he'd ridden the day he and Sarah had raced. He remembered what Sarah had said about feeling free when she galloped on Scooter. Tony urged his palomino on until he felt the same exhilaration. For just a moment, he was far away from his past and somehow closer to the woman he'd let walk away.

He stopped his horse on the highest point of his land and admitted a truth that he could no longer deny.

I miss her.

The next few days dragged by uneventfully. Tony returned to working with the horses, and his ranch hands went back to pretty much avoiding him. On the surface, things had returned to how they were before Sarah, but Tony was beginning to understand they never really could.

He'd changed.

He didn't want to eat alone anymore. He didn't want people to look away when he approached and rush off to return to work. He knew their names now and for the first time he watched them work the horses. They were good at what they did, really good. So was David. It was humbling to realize how little credit he'd given any of them for the quality of the final product they sold.

Tony was in his kitchen drinking a glass of water when Melanie walked in and said, "There's a man on the phone for you, Tony. I know you say you don't want to be bothered with calls, but David told me to get you for this one."

Who would David think I'd want to talk to?

Evan? Does he even know I met with him?

Charles? That's a conversation with a low likelihood of being pleasant.

Tony took the phone from Melanie and raised an eyebrow at her. She took the hint and left the kitchen, giving him his privacy.

"Tony Carlton," Tony said abruptly and waited.

"Mr. Carlton." An enthusiastic male voice echoed his name. "You don't know what an honor it is to finally get to speak with you. Normally, I don't get past your ranch manager."

Leaning back against his kitchen counter, Tony asked impatiently, "Who is this?"

In a rush, the man said, "Sorry, my name is Gerry Hamilton. I represent the Dolan Children's Fund."

"David handles donations," Tony said dismissively, and prepared to hang up.

"We're not looking for a donation. Well, not exactly. We'd like you to host a horse expo we've been putting together. A big name like you would bring the crowds. All you'd have to do is a couple demonstrations. We'd handle the rest. The proceeds go to our non-profit foundation . . ."

"I don't do public appearances anymore."

"Yes, but you're still a celebrity. People remember you."

Unfortunately. "I'm sorry, I wish I could help you, but—"

"Mr. Carlton, we need you. The Dolan Fund was created by a local widow who wanted to help families with sick children. We work with hospitals throughout Texas to make sure families who need to travel with their children for treatments can afford to. We've been doing this for twenty-eight years, but in this economy it's harder and harder to find donors."

Rubbing a hand over his forehead in frustration, Tony said, "How much do you need?"

"Of course we'd take a cash donation, but this event has the potential of bringing in a significant amount, especially if you agree to host it. Please reconsider the host spot," the man said urgently.

Sarah's voice echoed in his head. *"Just being sorry isn't enough."*

"Call back and give David all the details and we'll make this happen."

"Thank you so much. You won't be sorry. This is going to be—"

Tony hung up the phone on the man.

On impulse, he dialed Evan Staten's secretary and asked to speak to him. He was put through, which he took as a sign that what he was about to ask might be well received.

"Mr. Staten, I'd like to talk to you about an idea I've had." Tony told Evan about the phone call he'd received and how he'd agreed to host the expo for charity. He paused, then added, "I'm considering some demonstrations on how to gentle a horse without violence and possibly give some riding safety tips. With your permission, I'd like to dedicate those demonstrations to Kimberly."

At first Evan said nothing, then in an angry voice he demanded, "What makes you think I'd agree to something like this?"

After inhaling deeply, Tony said quietly, "It's a good cause and her name will be spoken there regardless of who says it first, me or the press. I think she'd rather be mentioned boldly and have her death help others than be whispered about."

After a long pause, Evan said, "That's exactly what she'd want." In a much more robust tone, he said, "I'd like to be a part of this expo. If my little girl is going to be there, I want it to be the best goddamn expo the state of Texas has ever seen."

"Yes, sir."

"My wife will be happy when she hears about this. I told her that you came to see me and she cried, but she said it was a good kind of cry. She'll like this," Evan said, his voice sounding suddenly certain, like a part of him was coming back to life. "It'll be good for all of us."

I hope so.

Tony told Evan he'd send him the information, and then he hung up and placed the phone on the counter beside him.

You did good, Kimberly.

You did good.

It was as if a weight had lifted from Tony. *I can do this. I may not be able to ever bring Kimberly back, but I can do something in her name that will bring comfort to others. I can be a better man.*

A man who is not afraid to love.

A man worthy of a woman like Sarah.

With a smile on his face, Tony went into the barn to look for David, who must have heard him, because he was walking through the barn to meet him. Tony didn't stop. He walked straight up to him and hugged him. David shoved him away.

"What the hell is wrong with you? Are you drunk?" David asked.

"Better than drunk. I'm back." Tony noticed one of the ranch hands in the background, looking like he wanted—but was afraid—to laugh at the scene. Tony said, "Laugh, I won't fire you. I may never fire anyone ever again."

David turned to the ranch hand and said, "Don't listen to him. Go clean out the side paddocks." When the young man didn't immediately move, David added, "Before *I* fire you." That put some speed beneath the young man's feet.

Alone with his boss again, David studied Tony's eyes. "What are you on?"

Tony shook his head, still trying to label whatever had suddenly made the sun shine brighter and everything seem possible. "Nothing."

Looking doubtful, David pushed back his hat and asked, "Are you smiling?"

I guess I am. "I went to see your old boss the other day, Evan Staten."

If possible, David looked even more concerned about Tony's sanity. "And that put you in a good mood?"

I can see his point. But the meeting itself was only part of it. "It helped me sort out some things. Sarah was right: being sorry isn't enough. I need to do something, and I intend to. I'm going to host a charity expo for the Dolan Children's Fund. Don't look so surprised—you told Melanie to give me the phone."

"Yes," David drawled slowly. "I guess I never thought you'd agree to it."

"Well, I did," Tony said proudly.

Eyebrows furrowed together, David studied him. "I know, and I'm not sure what that means yet."

Tony stepped closer to David, suddenly serious, and said, "I never thanked you for everything you've done for me."

David took a step back. "Don't hug me again."

Tony smiled. "Invite everyone to dinner tonight at my house. I have a few things I need to say."

"I'll do it even though it goes against my better judgment."

Satisfied, Tony almost walked away but then stopped and asked, "Hey, how do you get paid when you don't have access to my bank accounts? How does anyone here get paid?" He couldn't believe he didn't know, but then again, he'd never cared enough to ask. David had always handled the business side, filed the taxes, cut the checks for everyone.

David took a moment before answering, then said, "I bought the first horses we trained here and started an account with the money we got from selling them. We've been splitting the profits since then and paying everyone from that fund."

"So you never actually worked for me."

David shrugged.

"No wonder I can't remember hiring you." The realization of how detached he'd become from his own life was frightening. "I don't know why you stayed, but I'm glad you did."

David looked away, then said, "Get your overly happy ass out of the barn and find Melanie. She deserves to meet this new you."

Tony smiled, imagining the look on Mel's face when he did. *She'll probably think I'm on drugs, too, but it doesn't matter.*

Dean had warned him to "wake up" if he didn't want to die alone like their father would.

I'm awake, and I'm not wasting any more time.

I am going to make things right.

Now where is my favorite angry housekeeper? If she knows where Sarah is, I may have to hug her, too.

Later that night, Tony, David, Melanie, Jace, and the ranch hands stood in the kitchen of the main house. The men had devoured the country-fried chicken and had moved along to the more serious matter of dessert. Plates in hand, they packed away pieces of Texas sheet cake.

The initial feeling of euphoria that had followed his conversation with Kimberly's father had passed, leaving Tony with the reality of what he would have to do to piece his life back together. He cleared his throat. "I wanted everyone here tonight so I wouldn't have to say this twice. I intend to make some changes around here."

The room fell silent, a general apprehension growing as he took a moment to choose his words. Even David looked concerned. "David has done a damn good job running this place, but I'll be more involved from today forward. I'll be hosting an expo for the Dolan Children's Fund sometime in the near future. The coverage will likely be national. Things will change when we open ourselves to the public. I've been there. The press runs with whatever you say, so keep your mouths shut. Learn the game, and you might be able to spin these events into a career for yourselves. I don't mind saying that I want y'all working on this with me. David's not going anywhere. Y'all, however, need to understand what has changed.

I'm going to try real hard to keep my temper to myself, but from this day forward if I fire anyone—there is no way back."

David looked on and nodded with approval.

"Now get out of here while I'm still in a good mood."

The ranch hands hastily put their dishes in the sink and retreated.

Melanie shook her head at his behavior and Tony shrugged, a hint of a smile pulling at one side of his mouth. "I couldn't let them think I'm getting soft."

David chuckled. "There is very little risk of that, but it's good for them to know that you'll be watching them, too. They respect your skill with the horses, and now they'll respect you as their boss."

"They won't be happy at first," Melanie said, "but they'll adjust. I'm sure the idea of working on something public like you said will be a real motivator for them, too."

"Things are going to change quickly," Tony said, then pinned Melanie and David with a look. "Which one of you is going to tell me where Sarah is?"

Melanie looked to David for confirmation that she should. He nodded. "She's staying with my family in Telson. It's a couple of hours from here."

Tony checked the clock on the wall and was surprised at how late it was. "I suppose I'll go collect her in the morning."

Throwing her hands up for emphasis, Melanie said, "She's been sitting there for weeks stewing about how it's over between the two of you. Do you really think you can just go there and pack her up like she's a horse and bring her home?"

No? Because I'm a jackass?

Yes? Because I love her?

"She loves me," Tony said.

Melanie put a hand on one hip and said, "That's not going to stop her from throwing something at your head if you don't do this right."

Remembering how beautiful his little blonde angel looked with her cheeks flushed and her breasts heaving with anger, Tony said, "I don't mind a little temper in a woman."

Melanie covered her eyes and groaned. "David, don't let him ruin what could be his only chance to bring her back. I really like Sarah."

David held up both hands and said, "What makes me the relationship expert?"

Forgotten during the postdinner meeting, Jace grabbed Tony's hand and said, "You should listen to my mama. She knows everything."

Melanie ruffled her son's hair. "You tell 'em, Jace."

David said, "My mother always said that God made kids cute when they were little so parents could cling to those memories when they turned into teenagers."

"As long as he doesn't turn out like the two of you, I'll be happy," Melanie quipped.

Tony looked down at his young adviser and said, "Jace, could you go check on the barn with David? I need a moment alone with your mother."

Jace hesitated, not letting go of Tony's hand until he clarified something. "You mad at her?"

Shaking his head, Tony said, "Not at all." He smiled down at Jace. "Besides, in a scrap, I'm pretty sure she'd win."

David said, "Come on, Jace. Let's go see how our pregnant mare is doing. She's looking ready to foal. Maybe tonight. You can name the new one if you're there." With one last look at Tony and Melanie, Jace agreed and followed David out the door.

When they were gone, Tony took out a folded piece of paper and handed it to Melanie. She opened it, gasped, and tried to hand it back to him. "I can't accept this."

"The property sits on the edge of mine. You can keep it or sell it, but I want you to have it. Jace deserves a place he can call his own and so do you. I spent a lot of time thinking over the past few weeks. This ranch has been my sanctuary and my curse—so well insulated from the world that I didn't have to face what had driven me here. I think it's been the same for you. It's not going to be like that once we start dealing with the public again. There'll be no place to hide. I'm hoping you see this as an opportunity, but if you don't, you can take the money from that house and buy a place more private."

Clasping her hands in front of her, Melanie said, "Are you firing me?"

"Damn, I'm not good at this, am I? I'm trying to tell you that you and Jace have a home, no matter what changes around here."

Eyes glistening with emotion, Melanie hugged the paper to her stomach and said, "You're a good man, Tony Carlton, and I was wrong. You don't need my advice. You just go get Sarah. You'll have no trouble talking her into forgiving you."

"I was hoping to keep the actual talking to a minimum," Tony said with a straight face, then winked.

Melanie laughed softly, then her expression turned serious and she said, "Just tell her how you feel, Tony, and you can't go wrong."

I will.

This time I will.

Sitting at a small wooden desk in the living room of her temporary apartment on Melanie's parents' ranch in Telson, Sarah wrote the two most satisfying words across an entire page of her notebook:

The End.

She'd written not only one but two short books. No, they weren't perfect. They needed revisions, but she'd done it. She'd created a world of characters she felt others would enjoy.

They say write what you know, so I did.

Tempted (in Texas)
Torn (in Telson)
By Breshall Haas

Sure, Texas *isn't as specific as* Telson, *but it sounds a whole lot better than* Mussed in Mavis. *Or* Fucked at Fort . . . *See, that doesn't even work.*

Tempted was a powerful title that described the incredible journey she'd been on. A better version of it, anyway. No midnight nervous-fart-releasing laps around a cabin.

And *Torn.* Well, any writer will tell you that the worst of what you endure can inspire the best fiction.

Book three will have to wait until I find my own hero. Or at least until I think of another title that starts with a T *besides* Tragic.

She thought back to her first impression of Tony, and the title for the last book in her trilogy came to her: *Taken.* In the cabin and for a short time following their return from it, she'd glimpsed what it would be like to belong to Tony. In the end, he just wasn't where she was—and knowing how painful it was to be held hostage by the past made Sarah feel more sympathetic than angry toward Tony. He would have loved her if he'd been capable of it.

This is not the end of my story. I will have a happy ending because I'm determined to.

Thank you, Tony.

I may never have found my voice if I hadn't found you first. She smiled as she remembered how they'd met. *Or you found me. Whatever.*

You didn't give me your heart, but you gave me confidence and courage. In some weird, twisted way, you even gave me back my family.

Hmm. Twisted. *Also a possible title.*

Sarah flipped her notebook open and jotted it down. The words on the page blurred, and she saw Tony with painful clarity in her mind. *I wish I knew you were better off because of our time together. What did I give you?* She blushed as vivid memories of their nights together returned in force. *Well, besides that.*

I chased you, cornered you, and then pushed you to be someone you're not.

No wonder it didn't work out.

You kept telling me you weren't ready, but I heard only what I wanted to hear.

Sarah thought back to their time together at the cabin and what he'd shared when he'd opened up to her. He hadn't always been incapable of love. He'd loved Missy, the mare he'd trained that his father had sold. *How old did he say he'd been? Twelve? That would have been eighteen years ago. Can she still be alive? Depending on how old she was when he'd trained her, maybe. Some horses live into their thirties and beyond.*

But how would I even begin to look for her?

Dean.

Sarah contacted him through the Fort Mavis Sheriff's Department. After all, this was sort of a community service request. It was for a member of his community.

Dean didn't require much convincing. It was a long shot and he told her so, but he promised to look into it. Unbelievably, he called back the next morning and, after checking with Steve and Cindy to let them know she'd be gone for part of the day, Sarah hitched the empty trailer to her SUV. Missy was with a family a couple of hours away, and now that the children had all grown and gone, the aging parents kept her as a pasture pet. They weren't looking to sell her, but that didn't stop Sarah.

I'm not leaving without her.

I don't care what she costs.

I'll bring her home, clean her up, and call David. He'll know the best way to deliver her to Tony.

Chapter Twenty-Three

It was late morning when Tony pulled into the driveway of Melanie's parents' house. Melanie had told him to park near the barn because Sarah was staying in the attached apartment at the back of the house.

Sarah's car wasn't parked where Melanie had said it would probably be, and she didn't answer his knock on her door. *So much for surprising her.*

Tony walked to the main house and bypassed the doorbell for a more satisfying thundering knock on the door. A young brown-haired woman, who appeared to be in her early twenties, opened the door. Her eyes rounded at the sight of him. "Oh," she said, "you're not supposed to be here."

"Where is Sarah?" Tony demanded. When he'd rehearsed his speech on the way over, it hadn't occurred to him that she might not be there.

"She's not here," the young woman said.

"That much is obvious," Tony replied, quickly losing his patience.

An older woman's voiced called out from inside the house, "Who is it, Bunny?"

"It's Tony Carlton," the young woman called back.

"What's he doing here?" the woman asked, not waiting for the answer before rushing to her daughter's side to find out for herself. The elegantly dressed woman held out a hand in greeting. "Mr. Carlton, what a surprise."

With a nod, Tony reluctantly shook her hand. "Ma'am, I came to see Sarah. Melanie told me she's staying with you."

"She is, but she went out to run an errand this morning. I'll tell her you dropped by."

"I'll wait," Tony stated with determination.

"Mom, he can't. It'll ruin everything."

"Bunny, stop. Does it really matter how he finds out?"

Tony's temper began to rise. *What don't they want me to know? Did I leave Sarah alone for too long? Did she find someone else? If so, I hope she's not overly attached to a man I'm going to kill when I meet him.* Between gritted teeth, Tony asked, "Find out *what*?"

The sound of a car pulling into the driveway caught Tony's attention. He didn't wait for an answer to his question; he strode down the steps and headed toward Sarah's apartment. It was Sarah driving her SUV with the horse trailer in tow. She parked next to the barn and jumped out, rushing to the side of his truck and looking around.

Fortunately, she was alone.

"Sarah," he said. He knew his tone had been harsh and was wishing he'd softened it when she spun toward him. He saw the joy she felt at seeing him, just before she reined her emotions in.

I'm an ass.

There isn't anyone else.

He closed the distance between them, rehearsing exactly what he'd say to convince her to give him a second chance. He'd start with an apology. He'd tell her how much he'd missed her, how much he needed her. And then, he'd tell her what had taken him weeks to admit to himself.

I love you.

She took a step toward him, and he swung her up and held her slightly above him, kissing her with all the passion that had been building within him since he'd last seen her. She wrapped her arms around his neck and settled into his arms as he lowered her slowly against his chest. Her tears mixed with their kiss. He buried his face in her hair and held her to himself.

"I was a fool," he said urgently, hugging her closer.

She pulled back so she could look into his eyes and said, "No, I was. I pushed you when I should have given you time."

He cupped her face in his hands and said, "I didn't need more time, I needed a swift kick in the pants, and you leaving me did that. I was trapped in the past. You set me free."

Still crying even though she was smiling, Sarah said, "Are you really here?"

He kissed her lips lightly, tenderly. "Yes, and I hope you can pack fast, because you're coming home with me."

She cocked her head to one side. "Pretty sure of yourself, aren't you?"

"I know what I want and that's you, Sarah."

Her beautiful brown eyes searched his face. "For how long?"

He ran a light thumb over her bottom lip. "Forever."

She launched herself onto her tiptoes and kissed him, and the world around them receded. All that existed, all that mattered, was the two of them and their hunger for each other. They kissed until the desire to rip each other's clothing off, right there in the driveway, almost won out.

Tony broke off the kiss and rested his forehead on hers, their mutual labored breathing blocking out all other sounds. "Do you have anything inside that you can't get later? You already have Scooter loaded. Let's go home. We'll come back for my truck and your things tomorrow . . . or the next day. I want you in my bed, and once I have you there, I can't imagine we'll be leaving it anytime soon."

Flushed and looking a bit bemused, Sarah said, "That's not Scooter in the trailer."

"You bought yourself another horse?"

Sarah touched his cheek softly. "No, I bought you one."

He looked at the trailer but couldn't see more than a shadow of what was inside. "You bought me a horse? Does that mean you'd decided to come back?"

"No," she said, her eyes brimming with emotion. "I was going to have David deliver her to you."

"I don't understand," Tony said.

"Go look at her," Sarah suggested.

The last thing Tony cared about right then was a horse, but Sarah seemed to care an awful lot about her gift, so he went to the back of the trailer and opened it. To his surprise, it wasn't a quarter horse or even a young horse.

Sarah opened the side door and unclipped the horse's harness. An aged white mare backed off the trailer. Tony's gut clenched painfully as he recognized her profile.

It can't be.

He put out his hand for the mare to smell. She whinnied into his palm, then rubbed her head roughly against him. His voice came out in a whisper. "Missy?"

Emotion flooded him as he tried to make sense of what he'd never dared to think possible. Sarah had found the horse his father had sold when he was twelve. The only horse he'd ever let himself love.

Did she remember him? Before Sarah, Tony would have said she couldn't. He would have dismissed her greeting and the way she was nuzzling against him as learned behavior—something she associated with any human contact. But as he looked into those wise equine eyes, he saw recognition and love.

"Where did you find her?" He put his hand out to Sarah, and his heart swelled when she took it between both of hers.

"Dean found her. The people that owned her bought her at an auction in your town from your father. They remembered him. She's been at their farm ever since. All their children learned to ride on her, but they retired her when their kids moved out. If I hadn't told them your story, they would have let her graze in their back field for the rest of her life. They loved her, Tony, just like you did. And they would like to come visit her at your ranch if you'll let them."

Whatever wall had been left around Tony's heart crumbled, and he pulled Sarah into a bone-crushing embrace. He didn't even try to hide the happy tears that ran down his cheeks. He wasn't sure he'd ever done a single thing to deserve a woman as kind-hearted and loving as Sarah, but he knew he'd spend the rest of his life trying to. "I love you, Sarah Dery," he said.

Sarah wrapped her arms around Tony's waist. *He loves me!* "It took you long enough to realize it."

He pulled her to his side, kissed her upturned lips softly, and said, "From the moment I found you in my shower, I knew my life would never be the same."

"In a good way?"

He kissed her cheek. "In the *best* way. When do you want to get married?"

Sarah laughed. "You're not going to ask me first?"

He kissed the tip of her nose. "I'm not giving you the option of saying no. But you can pick the date as long as it's soon."

"You are one pushy cowboy," she teased.

For a long moment, he looked down into her eyes, and she glimpsed the sadness that had originally drawn her to him. "I love you, Sarah, and I am a better man because you came into my life."

Sarah hugged him possessively. "Well, don't change too much. I have a few things left on my list, and I don't think they are nice-guy approved."

A huge smile spread across Tony's face. "List?"

Looking down at his chest, Sarah said, "It's a bucket list." *Or more accurately: My Fuck-It List.* Sarah chuckled at the thought that she wasn't quite brave enough to share out loud. *I should write that down.*

Tony held her just a little away from himself and waited until she looked up at him. "Tell me."

My notebook can wait.

"Let's go home," Sarah said playfully, then whispered seductively against his lips, "I'd rather *show* you."

Chapter Twenty-Four

The next morning, dressed only in one of Tony's plaid shirts, Sarah left him sleeping in their bed and slipped away to the bathroom for a moment. She looked in the mirror and smiled. Her hair was loose in a tangled mess. The makeup she hadn't taken the time to remove was smudged beneath her eyes.

I look like we spent the night doing exactly what we did. Eventually, one of us will have to go downstairs for food, and I can't look like this if there is any chance it might be me.

She turned on the water and slid out of Tony's shirt. A few moments later, Sarah closed her eyes and sighed as she relaxed in the full tub. She smiled as she replayed every wonderful, hot moment of the night before. They'd barely made it in the door before they'd ripped each other's clothing off and had sex on the stairs while heading to his bedroom.

Eventually, temporarily spent, they'd cuddled in his bed and talked. He told her about the changes he wanted to make at his ranch, and she told him about her plans to self-publish her stories. Her heart nearly burst with pride when he explained that he'd given a house to Melanie and Jace. He wasn't a man who boasted about what he did. He told her because there were no more barriers between them. No more secrets.

"Did you hear any more from Lucy about her ranch? I made the call. Don't know if it did much good. I figure we should send David out there to see what's going on. He's good with the business side of ranching."

"You'd do that?" Sarah had asked in awe.

He'd kissed her and said, "I would do anything for you or those you care about."

And she believed him because, as frustrating as he sometimes was, Tony was a man who didn't say a word more than he meant.

Breshall Haas is sure going to be busy, because book three is already coming alive for me. My two broken characters will finally bring each other as much comfort as they do passion. She smiled as she remembered how Tony had looked tied to the bed at the cabin, as willing to be taken as she ever was. She sank deeper beneath the warm water and watched the book play out in her imagination, like a movie.

Being taken.

It keeps getting better and better.

Wrapped only in a towel, Sarah walked back into the bedroom and saw Tony happily reading her notebook. He put it down on his lap and said, "That will always remind me of the day we met."

Sarah looked down and laughed. "Let's not tell anyone that story, deal?"

He smiled and held up her notebook, revealing the evidence of his excitement standing erect beneath the sheet. "I see you have been busy. I like your new story, but I have a few questions."

Sarah sat and turned to face him, knowing that when she lifted her leg onto the bed she'd give him an intimate view. He sucked in a breath, his attention no longer focused on her writing. "What did you want to know?"

He met her eyes, desire sizzling the air between them. "What?"

Sarah ran a hand down the sheet, caressing one of his thighs through the smooth cotton. "You said you had questions."

He reached behind her head and pulled her closer, murmuring against her lips. "It doesn't matter."

The temptation to sink into his arms warred with the need to know what he thought about her writing. She put a hand on his shoulder and said, "I want your feedback. My writing isn't a hobby to me—it's a part of me. What do you think?"

He shifted and pulled her down beside him in the bed and tucked her into his side. "First, why does he have to be a billionaire? Are millions not sexy enough?"

Sarah ran her hand across the light hair of his chest. "Don't be jealous. He's not real."

Tony kissed her lightly on her forehead. "He'd better not be, because he and I share some similar techniques." Despite his obvious hard-on, he reopened her notebook and pointed to a scene she had written. "I think I could do this better than you described it, though. I had some ideas while I read it."

"You did?" Sarah asked, allowing her towel to fall to one side. She moved the sheet aside and took him in her hand, caressing him while she spoke. "I don't mind trying that again. For research purposes, of course."

"Of course," he said huskily, half closing his eyes with pleasure. He flipped to another part of the notebook and said, "And I'm not sure this particular move is even humanly possible."

Sarah moved her hand lower, cupping his balls gently. "Only one way to find out." Then she took the notebook and turned to a scene near the end. "What did you think of this part?"

He reread a line, then rolled over so they were face-to-face on the bed. His thumb circled and teased one of her nipples until it was hard and begging for his mouth. “I thought it lacked sufficient detail, but that’s something we can fix together.”

Suddenly more serious, Tony said, “I never meant to make you feel like what you described in the second book. I wasn’t ready for what you were offering me. But I’m ready now.”

Looking into his loving green eyes, Sarah thought about how much they had both changed. They’d each been lost in their own way, and together had found a way back. Nothing would change the past. Even love couldn’t do that, but they no longer had to face it alone.

There are things we can fix and things we can’t. I guess life is about figuring out which is which, and dealing with both the best you can.

And if you’re lucky, you find someone who loves you, scars and all.

Tony rolled on top of her, seeming to sense the serious direction of her thoughts. He kissed her cheek softly and said, “Let’s take it slow and gentle this time.”

Sarah dropped her notebook on the floor beside the bed.

My cowboy . . .

Gentle or rough.

When it’s right, they’re both good.

Author’s Note

Paso Finos are a wonderful, smoothly gaited breed and are not necessarily well represented by my depiction of them. I own a Paso Fino and I adore him. He’s a backyard horse that has been my best friend for longer than I’ve been married. If you’re interested in the elegance and gait of the breed, read about them online. If you prefer to think of the breed in terms of the quirky personality of one woman’s equine friend, that’s my Scooter.

Also, use discretion if attempting to re-create any of the spicier scenes in this book. The author is not responsible for those of you who feel inspired and then fall from a tree. And please, drive responsibly.

Acknowledgments

I am so grateful to everyone who was part of the process of creating first *Gentling the Cowboy* and then the republished version, *Taken, Not Spurred.* Thank you to:

My very patient beta readers—Karen Lawson, Heather Bell, Marion Archer, Yeu Khun, Kathy Dubois, Janet Hitchcock—who read multiple versions of the same chapters until I felt they were right. Thank you Karen and Janet for giving me the "Fuck-It List."

My editors: Karen Lawson, Janet Hitchcock, Nina Pearlman, JoVon Sotak, and Robin Cruise.

Melanie Hanna, for helping me organize the business side of publishing.

Melody Anne, for putting me in the back of *Seduced* in her Surrender series. She went from being an author I promote with to a real friend. Thank you, Mel, for all you do! I hope we continue on this wild ride together for a long, long time.

Bunny Giordano and Lucy Wright, for lending me their fun names for characters.

My Roadies, whose continued kindness and support often bring out my sloppily grateful and sometimes tearful side.

And finally, to my readers: Two years ago, when my teaching job was once again cut because of budget issues, I was afraid. Since then, publishing my romances has not only given me more time with my children, but it has also given me a more stable means to support my family. I cannot thank you enough.

As always, thank you to my husband, Tony, who listens to each story so many times, he dreams about the characters. I love you, hon.

And my family who supports me in this adventure and is the reason I do what do every day. Love you!

About the Author

Ruth Cardello was born the youngest of eleven children in a small city in northern Rhode Island. She lived in Boston, Paris, Orlando, and New York before coming full circle and moving back to Rhode Island, where she lives with her husband and three children. Before turning her attention to writing, Ruth was an educator for twenty years, eleven of which she spent as a kindergarten teacher. She is the author of seven previous novels including *Bedding the Billionaire*, which was a *New York Times* and *USA Today* bestseller. *Taken, Not Spurred* is the debut book in the Lone Star Burn series. To receive notification when a new book is available, sign up for Ruth's mailing list at RuthCardello.com or follow her on Facebook, www.facebook.com/ruthcardello.

Printed in Great Britain
by Amazon